THE
PACT

D0109572

JENNIFER STURMAN

THE
PACT

**RED
DRESS
INK**
™

First edition December 2004

THE PACT

A Red Dress Ink novel

ISBN 0-373-25079-7

www.RedDressInk.com

Printed in U.S.A.

ACKNOWLEDGMENTS

This book would never have been written without Michele Jaffe, who had the great misfortune to read every draft and provided invaluable encouragement and input.

Laura Langlie, my agent, guided me through this process with a sure hand, unflagging confidence and good humor. She even pretended to take my theory of jinxing seriously.

I owe a tremendous debt of gratitude to Farrin Jacobs, Margaret Marbury and the entire team at Red Dress Ink for (however clichéd it may sound) making a dream come true.

My college roommates—Anne Coolidge, Holly Edmonds, Heather Jackson and Gretchen Peters—kindly allowed me to steal bits and pieces of themselves and our past (liberally seasoned with artistic license, of course!). Rulonna Neilson, *ad hoc* image consultant, shepherded me through the jungle that is Bloomingdale's cosmetics department and captured the moment for posterity. Meg Cabot offered the wise perspective of an industry veteran and more champagne than was probably good for either of us.

My mother, Judith Sturman, my sister-in-law, Lindsay Jewett Sturman, author Gini Hartzmark and friends Stefanie Reich Offit and Karen Bisgeier Zucker graciously served as early readers, critics and sounding boards. Finally, my father, Joseph Sturman, and my brothers, Ted and Dan Sturman, managed neither to laugh at nor tease me about the excellent use to which I was putting my MBA.

Thank you all.

This book is dedicated, with love and gratitude,
to my parents.

I met Chris at the beginning of my junior year. He was tall and handsome, with thick dark hair and green eyes fringed with the sort of lashes that only boys seem to get but that girls covet. He sat next to me one September afternoon in Modern Art and Abstraction. I dropped my pen, he picked it up, our eyes met, and I fell head over heels in love with a sociopath.

Of course, it took nearly six months for me to realize that he was, in fact, a sociopath. He was a senior and a bit of a mystery to my circle of friends. He'd transferred to Harvard from a small liberal arts college out west, and he had an air about him that was part Mark Darcy and part James Bond. He swept me off my feet, and I was more than willing to be swept.

The first time I realized something was off was the night he figured out how to call in to my answering machine and play back the messages. I was at the library working on a paper, but he was convinced that I was cheating on him. A few months and a number of similar incidents later, I was out of love and desperate to be rid of him.

He wasn't easy to break up with, but after several tedious conversations that began with "We've got to talk" and ended with him still thinking I was his girlfriend, he finally gave up. Soon I heard that he was dating a sophomore, who no doubt was just as enchanted by his attentions as I'd originally been.

The night my breakup with Chris became official, my four roommates and I rose to the occasion with a Girls' Night Out, a ritual that we'd perfected since its inception freshman year. We would start with blender drinks in our common room in Lowell House and then embark on a pub crawl in Harvard Square, inevitably ending up at Shay's, our favorite wine bar on JFK Street.

By the time we arrived at Shay's that fateful evening it was after midnight. The tables were crowded with a mix of undergrads and some business school students from across the river, easily identifiable by their conservative dress and bottles of imported beer. We found seats on the front terrace and ordered the usual—a bottle of cheap red wine to be shared by everyone except Jane, who ordered a Black and Tan. As we waited for our drinks, I began lamenting my poor judgment for the umpteenth time that evening. "How could I have been so stupid?" I moaned. I was a little worse for wear after five hours of fairly enthusiastic drinking.

Hilary, never one to mince words, had a ready reply. "I don't know. Was he that great in bed?"

Luisa exhaled a stream of cigarette smoke with impatience. "Have a little sympathy, Hil. Rachel was in love. Her first love. Everyone acts like an idiot the first time."

Hilary snorted her reply but held her tongue while the waiter unloaded our drinks. Emma looked around the table expectantly. She was wearing a sleeveless Indian print dress and woven leather sandals, her mass of dark blond hair hanging loose down her back.

Jane took a sip of her Black and Tan and gave me a good-natured smile. "We all knew that you would come to your senses sooner or later. It happened to be later than we would have liked, but the important thing is that it happened."

"But why didn't I listen to you?" I asked. "You all tried to tell me what a nightmare he was—God only knows how many times—and I just didn't want to hear it."

"You were doing what you wanted to do," said Jane.

"Even though what you wanted to do was completely fucked up. I mean, it was clear the guy was bad news from day one." Hilary poured wine into her glass and passed the bottle to Luisa. "He was so full of himself."

"He was not bad news from day one," Jane protested. "He did a lot of things right at first. Remember all of the flowers? And when he took Rachel to Walden Pond? You have to give him at least a few points for that."

"He's a man," said Luisa, stubbing out her cigarette and preparing to light another. "It's a waste of time to dissect what he did right and what he did wrong." She pointed the end of the unlit cigarette at me and locked her dark-eyed gaze on mine. "The most important thing is to learn to enjoy men but also to take care of yourself. Next time you'll know better."

"But what if I don't know better?" I asked. "What if the next one is equally awful but in a different way, so that I don't recognize that he's awful?"

"Maybe next time you'll listen to us," said Jane.

"That's right," agreed Hilary. "You'll remember what a fool you made of yourself with Chris, and you'll listen."

"You know, Hil, you haven't always had the greatest judgment yourself. Remember Tommy Fitzgerald? And what about that guy from the Owl Club? What was his name again? The one with the—?"

"You're one to talk, Jane. Remember freshman year when you and Sean were taking a 'break' and you started going out with that asshole from the crew team?"

"Okay, enough," said Luisa. "We've all made mistakes—there's no need to catalog them."

"Luisa's right. None of us has a very good record on assessing the men in our lives. And when push comes to shove, the rest of us always figure it out before the one who's actually in the relationship." Emma was so quiet that when she did speak people listened closely. We were all silent for a moment, considering her words.

"Well, the point is that if any of you come to me and tell me my boyfriend's an asshole, I promise I'll listen," said Jane. This was easy for her to say, given that Sean was as close to the ideal boyfriend as a mere mortal could be. Still, her voice held a challenge in it for the rest of us. She looked around the table.

"Me, too," said Emma, thoughtfully. "In fact, I'd even make a pact on that."

"Well, I'd probably already know the guy was an asshole, but I'd listen to you," said Hilary. "You can count me in."

"No argument here, especially if it means that I never have to go through a relationship like this again," I said.

"Luisa? What about you?" asked Emma.

She gave a slight shrug. "We've made so many pacts that it's hard to keep them all straight. Remember the one about giving up caffeine? That lasted about five minutes. Why should this one be any different? What happens if we all promise to listen to each other but then we don't? Then what?"

"Then the rest of us take matters into our own hands," replied Hilary. "Obviously. We waste the guy."

That made everybody laugh. "Come on, Luisa, don't be such a skeptic," said Jane. "This one's serious."

"Fine, fine." She caved in to our pleading with another shrug of her shoulders. "I'm in."

"Good. Then it's unanimous. We're making a pact," said Emma.

"A pact," agreed Jane.

"Let's toast!" urged Hilary.

We laughed and clinked our glasses together—all except Jane, who hated when people clinked. In unison, we drank.

None of us would have guessed where this pact would lead.

CHAPTER 1

Perhaps the only thing worse than getting drunk by accident is not being able to get drunk on purpose. I'd switched from champagne to vodka tonics during the second course, but I still felt as clearheaded as the valedictorian at an AA graduation. And somehow calling for tequila shots seemed unseemly in these staid country club surroundings. Instead, I asked the waiter for another vodka tonic, meeting his raised eyebrows with an innocent smile and a request to go easy on the tonic.

The Fates were conspiring against me this evening, I all too soberly reflected. Here I was at my best friend's rehearsal dinner, and rather than overflowing with joy I wanted to put my head down on the crisp linen tablecloth and weep. And not because of the bridesmaid's dress I was scheduled to wear the following evening at half past six. (Although I was still curious as to how Emma, who I sincerely believed had only honorable intentions towards us all, had managed to find a style and color that didn't flatter even one of her four bridesmaids.)

No, the dress and the prospect of wearing it were just fanning the flames of my distress. And while I dreaded the toast I would shortly have to make, it was merely fuel for the fire.

The horror, I thought. The horror.

If I turned my head to the right and counted over three seats, I could see the reason for my silent anguish in the flesh, smugly resplendent in a custom-made charcoal pinstriped suit and vivid Hermés tie, his black hair slicked neatly back from a widow's peak.

Richard.

He was talking to a client who'd stopped by the table to say hello. He suddenly looked my way, as if he could feel the weight of my eyes upon him. He met my gaze with a smarmy wink and returned to his conversation.

I didn't know then that a smarmy wink from Richard should have been the least of my worries compared to everything else the weekend held in store. I stifled a shudder and took a big gulp of my fresh drink, trying to ignore how much it tasted like insect repellent and fighting off yet another pang of anxiety. The clock was ticking, moving inexorably toward disaster; the ceremony that would bind Emma to Richard was to take place in less than twenty-four hours.

I sent a desperate glance around the table for moral support, a reassuring word of some sort. The seat directly to my right was empty, reserved for the best man, whose flight from the West Coast had been delayed. Not that I expected any friend of Richard's to be remotely comforting in this situation. Emma, sitting next to Richard, had turned in her seat to greet one of the many well-wishers who'd come by to speak to her. She'd been so busy with the stream of visitors that she'd barely touched the food on her plate, and the shy smile on her face was starting to look more than a little forced.

To my left sat Matthew, the sort of guy you could always count on to help you out of a difficult spot. Tonight, however, he'd be the least appropriate person to turn to. He hated Richard as much, if not more, than any of us. With good reason. Matthew was the one Emma should be marrying. Unfortunately, this was glaringly obvious to everyone except Emma. I felt indignant on Matthew's behalf but more than a bit frustrated by his seemingly calm acceptance of the situation. If only he'd made Emma realize how right they were for each other, had taken action years ago, then everything would be different. But the patience and sensitivity that made him such a good doctor seemed to have rendered him tragically unassertive in his personal affairs. And if he was upset tonight he was hiding it well, slicing into his apple tart with surgical precision and chatting good-naturedly with Jane, who sat on his other side.

A cousin of Emma's sat between Jane and Hilary, and Hilary was trying her best to flirt with him, although his attempts at risqué banter were painfully bland. Still, Hilary felt it was important to practice even on the most unpromising of males. The flush that had stained his cheeks from the first glimpse she'd offered him of her cleavage had yet to subside. I almost felt sorry for him.

Hilary and her cleavage were flanked by Jane's husband, Sean, who was flanked in turn by Luisa. From the stoic set of Sean's usually relaxed features, I assumed that he had chivalrously assured Luisa that her cigarette wouldn't bother him at all. They were swathed in a blue halo of Gauloises-scented smoke. A colleague of Richard's who was serving as a groomsman the next day occupied the remaining seat at the table. I'd spoken to him during the cocktail hour and ascertained that he was entirely harmless but equally dull. He was listening to Sean and Luisa with a glazed look.

Everyone was deep in conversation with somebody else. Except, of course, me. Alas. I belatedly remembered that I'd promised myself the last time I went dateless to a wedding weekend that I would never do it again. There was nothing more depressing, nothing that could make me feel more like a total freak of nature, than to be hopelessly alone at an event that celebrated coupledom, however mismatched this particular couple was. It was fine for Hilary—she was fiercely protective of her single independence; it would never occur to her to wallow in self-pity just because she didn't have a boyfriend by her side. Luisa had Isobel, her partner of nearly three years, waiting for her when she returned to South America. All she had to worry about was fighting off her parents' pressure to marry and procreate. Jane and Sean had celebrated their tenth anniversary in June, just another in what would certainly be a long line of anniversaries commemorating their happy pairing. And I could hardly take comfort in the knowledge that while Emma had Richard, she was embarking on the biggest mistake of her life.

I sighed and flipped through my notes one more time, praying for a sudden natural disaster that could save me from making the toast. An earthquake was more than I could hope for in this part of the country, but perhaps I could bribe a waiter to pull the fire alarm? Not my waiter, of course. He made it clear from the way he set down my most recent drink that he wasn't doing me any more favors tonight, no matter how sweetly I smiled up at him. If it weren't so noisy I would have sworn he clucked his tongue as he moved on to the next table.

Resigned, I turned my attention back to the careful outline I'd made. I wasn't afraid of public speaking, not by a long shot. In my line of work, the ability to comfortably address large groups was almost a prerequisite. My colleagues in Mergers and Acquisitions at Winslow, Brown, as well as the board members of assorted clients, hostile dissenters at shareholder meetings—even full auditoriums of Harvard Business School students, eager to learn more about how to gain entrée to a top-tier investment banking firm—I'd stood before them all and delivered talks ranging from detailed slide presentations to improvised monologues. I was skilled at laying out the facts about a merger or joint venture in a professional and persuasive manner and in beating back questions that were designed to embarrass with logic, composure, and eloquence. Yet none of that was enough to prepare me for toasting the imminent merger of my best friend with Satan.

I was pushing away a mental image of the shrieking mouth in Munch's *The Scream* when Emma's mother caught my eye from her seat at the next table and discreetly tapped her watch. It was customary, I knew, for the maid of honor to give the first toast at the rehearsal dinner, and Lily Furlong was a stickler for tradition. There was no escaping it—the time had come.

I sighed again and drained the last of my vodka tonic for one final drop of liquid courage. Slowly, I scraped my chair back and stood, champagne glass in hand. My knife rapping against its crystal made a sharp, pinging noise that echoed in the cavernous room, and the hum of voices from the tables around me faded into an expectant hush.

Richard had spared no expense this evening, I noted, although I wouldn't be surprised if he was planning to write the entire affair off as a business expenditure. This rehearsal dinner was by no means a small gathering for the family and wedding party. Rather, Richard had been sure to invite everybody who was anybody among both his friends and those of the Furlongs, which was likely a far more fruitful hunting ground. None of Richard's family was present, although I secretly wondered if he even had one. It was entirely possible that Richard had crawled out from under a rock somewhere, already fully formed. Meanwhile, half the Social Register was in attendance, not to mention the leading lights of the New York arts and literary scene, seated at round tables covered with starched white linens and graced with extravagant floral arrangements. Perhaps the even greater surprise was that so many of them had made the long drive up to this remote corner of the Adirondacks, committing themselves to a weekend at one of the handful of motels and overly cutesy bed-and-breakfasts the area had to offer, not to mention battling rush-hour traffic on a Friday afternoon in August to make it here in time for cocktails and dinner. This was surely more of a tribute to their great esteem for the Furlongs and Emma than any warmth of feeling for a swine like Richard Mallory.

I cleared my throat once more, deliberately stalling to make sure that any natural disaster had ample time to strike. But none was forthcoming. I plastered a brave smile on my face, took a deep breath, and reluctantly launched into my toast.

"I'm Rachel Benjamin, and I have the honor of serving as Emma's maid of honor tomorrow afternoon." This simple declaration was met by friendly applause.

"I first met Emma our freshman year at Harvard. Actually, we met the very first day. We were assigned to the same dorm room, and we were each eager to establish ourselves as the most considerate roommate. Neither of us wanted to confess whether we preferred the top or bottom bunk, the left side of the closet or the right side of the closet, the desk by the window or the desk by the door, for fear that we would offend the other." An appreciative chuckle bubbled up from the audience. It was an easy crowd, I sensed, despite the impressive pedigrees scattered throughout the large dining room of the country club.

"We resorted to that most scientific of methods, one that you would expect to be used at only the most elite institutions of higher learning, to figure out who should take which bunk, which side of the closet, and which desk.

"I'm referring, of course, to the sophisticated discipline

known colloquially as Rock, Paper, Scissors." Much merriment from the audience at this. I briefly debated ditching my cushy corporate career on Wall Street and my steady, sizable paycheck to take my act on the road.

"I don't mean to embarrass Emma in front of you all—she did her best. But she was no match for me. I handily beat her, two out of three. And, trying to endear myself to the woman with whom I'd be sharing those less-than-spacious quarters, I tried to choose the options that she seemed to want least.

"She'd mentioned that she was a painter—I assumed that she'd want to be able to gaze out the window, so I took the desk by the door. I also chose the left side of the closet, the side farthest from the mirror and the bathroom.

"And then came the most important decision of all—should I take the top or bottom bunk?

"My noble intentions warred with my most base desires. As a small child, I begged for a bunk bed. Nothing seemed more glamorous than to sleep high above the floor in a top bunk. Tantrums, hunger strikes—even being nice to my brothers—none of my efforts could melt my parents' stony resistance. My pleas fell on deaf ears, and I had to make do with a beruffled canopy until well into my teens." Hilary emitted a mock moan of sympathy. I paused to glare at her before continuing.

"Here I was with this tempting opportunity—away from home for the first time, the world my oyster, and the top bunk beckoning me upward. I was torn, but I made the right choice, the selfless choice, and opted for the bottom bunk— I gave the top bunk to Emma. In fact, I insisted that she have it, despite her protests. And her protests were quite vehement. But I could see through her words, and I held firm to my generous choice.

"For the entire year, Emma climbed up to the top bunk

while I tried to suppress the envy that threatened to overwhelm me. When she offered to switch midyear, I swallowed my impulses and told her that wouldn't be necessary. After all, there would be other dorm rooms in the coming years. But the next year we moved into a large suite with Luisa and Hilary and Jane—we all had single beds. Ditto the next two years. My one opportunity for a top bunk—selflessly sacrificed to the cause of friendship.

"The summer after we graduated from college, Emma and I traveled to France. On a sunny June day, we found ourselves at the Eiffel Tower. There was a long line of tourists, but I wanted to see the view from the top. Emma waited patiently next to me for nearly two hours before our turn came. We squished into the elevator with our fellow sightseers and waited until the doors opened onto the top deck of the monument. I rushed to the railing, excited to see Paris spread out below us. But after a few minutes, I realized that Emma wasn't beside me.

"Instead, she was standing with her back against the wall, as far from the railing as she could be, her eyes screwed shut and her complexion a decidedly unbecoming shade of green.

"It was only then that she admitted to me that she was terrified of heights. 'But what about freshman year?' I asked. 'You loved having the top bunk.'

"'No,' she confessed. 'It's just that I thought you wanted the bottom bunk.'" The room erupted in laughter. They couldn't understand how Emma's absurd need to please had manifested itself in so many other, less humorous ways. I waited for the laughter to subside before I went on.

"I tell this story for a couple of reasons. First, I wanted to make it clear that trying to beat me at Rock, Paper, Scissors is a waste of time. I always, always win." More laughter. I took a deep breath and steeled myself for the mushy part.

"Second, and more importantly, I wanted to give all of you

a sense of what sort of person Emma is. The list of glowing adjectives could go on forever, starting with giving, loyal, and trusting. But I worry that the story doesn't do justice to all of the other traits that make her so special—her quiet insight, her subtle wit, her incredible talent.

"I feel privileged to have Emma for a friend. I think I speak for all of her bridesmaids when I say that we are honored that she wants us to stand up with her tomorrow, and that we hope that she has some small inkling of how much we want her to be happy. I trust that Richard realizes how very fortunate he is to have Emma in his life." I hesitated, wondering if my last sentence had sounded sincere. Richard was far too arrogant ever to understand how lucky he was to be sitting at the same table as Emma tonight, let alone marrying her.

Raising my glass, I scanned the assembled guests. "Please join me in drinking a toast to Emma."

"To Emma," the crowd joined in. I sat down amidst a cascade of clinking glasses.

Embarrassed, I looked over at her. A silent tear rolled down her face. "Thank you," she mouthed.

"Of course," I mouthed back. What else could I do?

CHAPTER 2

"Well done," a voice said, low and intimate and positioned mere inches from my right ear. It was a warm, deep voice, and it sent a distinctly pleasant tremor down my spine.

Startled, I turned to establish its owner.

The seat next to me, the one that had been empty all through dinner, was now filled by the most beautiful man I'd ever seen.

He wasn't beautiful in the obvious sense—the male model, movie star sense. In fact, by traditional measures, he was fairly nondescript. Thick, sand-colored hair, a regular-size nose, normal-size eyes topped by straight eyebrows that were golden at the edges, as if he spent a lot of time in the sun. He was altogether not my type—as a general rule, I preferred men who were dark, brooding and aloof. Still, I found myself wondering what our children would look like. My cheeks flushed in that lovely way that makes my freckles stand out as if I've been spattered with mud.

"I'm Peter Forrest," he said with a quiet smile, displaying even, white teeth. "Richard's best man."

My heart slid like a lead weight from the fluttering position it had assumed in my throat down to the depths of my stomach. The glowing mental photograph I'd constructed of our two (perhaps three) perfect children morphed from color to black-and-white and then faded into shadow. Surely a close friend of Richard's was, by definition, an evil troll, even if every molecule in my body begged to differ. I should have known that any handsome unattached stranger must have a tragic flaw.

"My flight was late," he continued, oblivious to the fact that his previous words had destroyed any potential for our future together. "But I got here just in time for your toast. I'm glad I don't have to give mine until tomorrow. You're a tough act to follow." As if flattery could mitigate his damning association with Richard.

"I'm Rachel," I said, hoping that my voice didn't betray the speed with which I'd just internally staged and discarded courtship, marriage and procreation. "Emma's maid of honor. We're friends from college." I gave myself a swift mental kick in the shin—after all, I'd just spent several minutes explaining precisely that to the entire room. Then I gave myself another mental kick in the shin for caring about the impression I was making on one of Richard's cronies. "But I guess you know that. And how do you know Richard?" I asked, trying to mask the despair I felt. If only his answer could in some way absolve him of the intimacy implied in being Richard's best man.

"Oh, I've known Richard since birth, practically. We grew up together in San Francisco, went to the same school and everything. At least until Richard came east for boarding school." I'd known Richard was from San Francisco, but I never gave it much thought. Yet when Peter said San Francisco, my mind instantly conjured up images of Peter on a sailboat, Peter skiing on an Alpine trail, Peter hiking up a mountain, and Peter doing all of those other healthy things for which the Bay Area is famous. As quickly as these images flashed before my eyes, I struggled to replace them with ones that more accurately would reflect the ways in which any friend of Richard's must pass his leisure time—Scotch drinking, cigar smoking, shooting small defenseless animals, and amusing his like-minded pals with misogynistic limericks. All my mental maneuverings, however, met with little success.

"San Francisco," I said, trying my best to act like a normal person making conversation with her dinner partner. "It must be hard for you to see much of each other when you're so far away." I was grasping at straws, I knew, but somewhere inside me burned a small flame of hope that hadn't yet been extinguished by the facts at hand.

He hesitated a moment before answering, contemplating the bubbles in his glass of champagne, as if he were trying to word his response with care. Then he turned his gaze back to me. His eyes were the color of rich, dark chocolate. "It is hard. In fact, I've only seen him a couple of times since we started college. His mother moved away from San Francisco years ago, and I don't think he's been back to the West Coast since then except for maybe a couple of quick business trips."

My brain sucked up that fact with the power of an industrial-strength magnet and allowed my heart to register a flicker of pleasure. After all, you can forgive anyone for his childhood friends; it's just the friends people choose when they're old enough to know better that you can hold against them. Still, I couldn't help but wonder why Richard would ask someone he was barely in touch with to be his best man.

As if reading my thoughts, Peter leaned toward me and

confided, "I have to admit, I was a bit surprised when Richard called and asked me to be in the wedding. It must have taken some doing for him just to track down my phone number. But it's hard to say no to someone you've known all your life." My heart gave another flutter when he said this; loyalty, even to someone as vile as Richard, was a noble trait, however undeserving its object might be. But Peter's words still didn't explain why Richard had asked him in the first place. Was Richard that bereft of close friends? It was entirely possible, I guessed; I was all too aware that to know Richard well was to despise him.

Richard's tedious colleague stood to give the next toast, and Peter turned his head to listen. This provided me with an excellent opportunity to observe his profile, the strong set of his jaw, and the handful of prematurely gray hairs at his temple. I pretended to listen to the toast, laughing at the appropriate moments, but mostly I was busy looking at Peter's left hand, loosely gripping his champagne glass, and thinking about how nice his left earlobe was. I caught myself unconsciously leaning toward it, the better to give it a gentle nibble. "Behave yourself," I admonished my wayward id.

The toasts went on, as they usually do, interminably. It turned out that I'd had no need to fear the audience's level of sobriety. A number of drunken but earnest souls, some of whom barely knew either the bride or the groom, stood to bless Richard and Emma's union. Finally, the last well-meaning speaker had slurred his way through a wandering speech and sunk back into his seat. I saw Emma's mother give the bandleader a discreet but urgent hand signal. Her sense of etiquette was extraordinarily well developed, and the endless toasting and clinking of glasses was probably like a form of torture to her. She hated public displays of emotion and frivolous sentimentality more than anyone I'd ever met; if I found the toasts tiresome, she probably found them excruciating.

Peter turned toward me as the band began to play. "Care to dance?" he asked.

"I'd love to," I answered, quickly, before my brain could thoroughly analyze the situation and pass down a judgment that would forbid physical contact of any sort. He helped me up from my chair and took my hand in his. His palm was pleasantly warm and dry. From the corner of my eye, I saw Jane and Luisa exchange a bemused look.

Peter led me onto the dance floor and swung me smoothly into a fox-trot. I silently thanked my parents for those nights as a child when my mother had played our old battered piano while my father twirled me around the living room, my bare feet resting atop his polished shoes as he taught me the elements of ballroom dance that he'd learned long ago in Moscow.

I was so appreciative of how well Peter led and so busy refereeing the battle raging between disparate internal constituents that I almost forgot to pay attention to anything he was saying.

"—how talented she is," I heard him say. "I mean, I'd heard her name, but I've never really followed the art scene. And somehow I never pictured Richard with an artist. I was in New York on business a few months ago, and I stopped into the gallery to see her show. I had no idea—I mean, I didn't know what to expect, really, but I was incredibly impressed. I would have been interested in buying a couple of pieces if everything hadn't already been sold. Although, I doubt I would have been able to afford anything. The prices all seemed to have an extra zero or two on them." He was talking about Emma's most recent exhibition, I realized, which had opened at the prestigious Gagosian Gallery in May and met with unqualified critical praise.

"Everything was spoken for by the end of the opening," I told him proudly. "And the reviews were great, too. As soon as I can get a day off, I'm going to have to dredge up all of my old notebooks and letters to see if Emma doodled in any of the margins. I could make a killing on eBay and retire. I'm sure she wouldn't mind." He laughed.

"What do you do now that you don't get days off and you want to retire so badly?"

"Ugh," I replied. "Do you really want to know?" For some reason, finding out about my profession was usually enough to send most men running. Not, I reminded myself, that I should care what any friend of Richard's thought of me or my chosen career.

"Of course. It can't be any worse than hawking your best friend's personal memorabilia on the Web."

"I'm an investment banker," I confessed. "Mergers and Acquisitions at Winslow, Brown." I cocked my head and waited for him to gasp with horror and run, shrieking, from the dance floor.

Instead, he chuckled. "You say that like you're a bounty hunter or a paid assassin."

"Not too far off," I said. "Even worse, it's so 1987."

"Hardly. I'm sure it's very high-powered. All of that glamorous wheeling and dealing." There was a teasing edge to his voice.

I laughed. "I guess it depends on how you define *glamorous.*" I'd spent far more sleepless nights crunching numbers and cranking out client presentations for smug bald men than I cared to remember. My life at Winslow, Brown bore about as much resemblance to Gordon Gekko's in *Wall Street* as my legs did to Cindy Crawford's. But at least the rules for a successful career in investment banking were clear, and I knew how to follow them. My hours were long and grueling, and I frequently despised my colleagues and my clients, but my bonus checks were large and if I continued to play the game, I might be in a position to retire well before my fortieth birthday with several million in the bank, financially secure and independent at last. I changed the subject. "What about you? What do you do?"

"Me? Equally embarrassing. Very 1999."

"What? Tell me," I demanded.

"I run an Internet start-up."

"How is that embarrassing? Now that really does sound glamorous. And hip. I bet you never have to wear a suit. And you probably get to take your dog to work."

"Right," he said. "I spend most of my time sucking up to venture capitalists and worrying about how I'm going to make the payroll."

"Still, it must be exciting," I told him, even though the very idea of so much risk and uncertainty was enough to make my blood pressure rise.

"It doesn't seem so exciting when you can't sleep because you don't know where your next round of financing is going to come from," he replied, but his easy tone suggested that he didn't really lose much sleep.

"Maybe I could help," I started to offer, when a sharp elbow jostled me and a spike heel stamped down on my foot. Icy liquid splashed down my dress and a glass shattered on the floor, but I was blinded by pain and hardly noticed.

"Oh, dear," I heard someone drawl in a faintly slurred lockjaw. "Now look what I've done. Darling, are you all right?" The black curtain of physical anguish that had swept before my eyes faded to jagged purple and white lines, through which I could make out one of Emma's aged great-aunts gazing at me with tipsy alarm and wearing a dress that had probably been the height of chic when she'd purchased it from Monsieur Balmain's house of couture back in the late 1950s. Its pattern clashed in an unfortunate way with the vibrating stripes that clouded my vision. She couldn't have weighed more than ninety pounds, even if you factored in the heft of her bee-hived hair, but I still felt as if a Mack truck had run over my foot.

"I'm fine," I managed to gasp out. "Really." You old bat, I added silently.

"Oh, but your frock, darling. I'm so sorry."

"Nothing a little seltzer water won't fix," I said as politely as I could under the circumstances. She was still apologizing as Peter took me by the elbow and steered me across the room and through a swinging door into the kitchen. The room was busy with staff cleaning up the remains of the elaborate meal, but a harried waitress pointed us to a side pantry in answer to Peter's inquiry about seltzer.

This was just great, I thought to myself as Peter guided me across the crowded kitchen. Only a moment ago I'd been managing to dance and have a conversation with an attractive man simultaneously. Now I had a huge splotch all over the front of my dress and had provided him with a choice demonstration of just what a clumsy oaf I was.

Peter led us through another swinging door into the pantry, a small room lined with counters and cabinets. "Alone at last," he said with a smile that acknowledged the cheesiness of his words. "But that looked like it hurt." His eyes were filled with concern.

"Which part?" I asked, trying to put up a valiant front. "The puncture wound to my foot or the destruction of a perfectly good Armani? Do you think I should get a tetanus shot? Matthew probably has his doctor's bag around here somewhere."

Peter put his arms around my waist and set me on one of the counters. This simple gesture was almost enough to make me forget the pain I was in. He knelt to examine my foot, while I studied the top of his head. I gripped the edge of the counter tightly to prevent myself from running my hands through his hair, which was full and sun-streaked, with a couple of adorable cowlicks shooting off in unlikely directions. "Okay, there's no blood. And I don't think anything's broken." He rose to his feet and looked at my dress. "I wish that I could say the same thing about the Armani."

I quickly inspected the Scotch-and-soda-colored stain spreading across the creamy silk. "It's not looking good, is it?"

"Well, if the seltzer doesn't work, maybe we could just get a bottle of whisky and dye the entire thing?"

"I'm sure Giorgio would applaud your creativity," I answered gamely.

Peter began rummaging through the cabinets. "Peanut butter, Ritz crackers, Miracle Whip—wow, we are deep in WASP country, aren't we?" He held up the jar for me to see, an eyebrow arched with amusement. "Here we go." He replaced the mayonnaise and lifted out a plastic bottle of club soda. "It's not imported, but it will probably work, won't it?"

He found a clean dishrag and doused it liberally with the bubbling water. I knew it was too much to hope for that he'd swab me down himself; still, I was disappointed when he handed me the towel. I began dabbing gingerly at the stain, more shocked by the unexpected impact this man was having on my usually tightly guarded emotions than the damage to my dress.

Peter was standing gallantly by, proffering more seltzer and tactical advice, when I heard tense words pouring in from the porch adjacent to the pantry. I froze, surprised, when I realized that one of the speakers was Emma. She was so soft-spoken—it was rare to hear her voice raised, much less laced with the bitterness that now infused her tone.

"You have no right," she was saying. "God knows, you seem to hold the world record in screwing up, so why should I listen to you? It's the only way to fix everything, and you know that."

"Emma, honey. You don't have to do this. It's not worth

it. We'll call it off, we'll figure something out." When I looked out the window over the sink, I could see Jacob Furlong's hawklike profile illuminated by a single porch light. Only the top of his daughter's head was visible.

She let out a laugh that sounded tinged with hysteria. "There is no choice. You know Mother wouldn't be able to deal. She's shaky enough as is."

"Your mother—" began Jacob, then stopped. He sighed. "Look, Emma, it's time for us all to live our own lives."

"Like you ever stopped?" she retorted. "Don't you think it's a little too late to start playing concerned father?"

Jacob looked like he'd been slapped. His craggy features seemed suddenly old and weary. He passed a hand slowly across his brow.

I looked at Peter and he looked at me. Silently, he helped me down from the counter, and we tiptoed back into the kitchen.

At least, Peter tiptoed.

I limped.

CHAPTER 3

The dining room was emptying out, and only a few swinging diehards remained on the dance floor. Judging by the unenthusiastic way the band was plodding through an old Sinatra tune, they seemed ready to call it a night. I spied Richard near the wood-paneled door that led out to the foyer, bidding the departing guests farewell. His double-breasted suit still looked as crisply pressed as if he'd just left the tailor, and a silk handkerchief peeked neatly from his breast pocket. I've never understood American men who insisted on dressing like Eurotrash.

A moment later, Emma joined him, her lips tightly set in a strained smile. I guessed that she'd walked around the outside of the club and reentered through the front. Richard slung his arm across her thin shoulders in a proprietary manner that made me want to slug him. It was all I could do not to rush to her side, pull her free from his slimy grasp, drag her into a corner and find out what was really going on. I couldn't recognize my best friend in the woman I'd overheard arguing with her father just a few minutes before, and I was even more concerned and confused now than I'd been all through dinner.

But she and Richard were surrounded; the odds of getting a word with her in private were slim. I would have to wait until the party was over.

Peter and I headed back to our table, picking our way through the maze of abandoned tables and scattered chairs. The gentle pressure of his hand on the small of my back ignited a minor fire that radiated from the base of my spine up my vertebrae, around my neck and up to my cheeks, which felt distinctly flushed. At least the pleasant warmth managed almost completely to eclipse the pain in my foot, if not the uncomfortable thoughts in my head.

Thankfully, the bland cousin and Richard's dreary colleague had disappeared, leaving only my friends, who seemed ready for the evening to be over. They had pulled their chairs away from the table and into a small circle. Jane had kicked off her shoes and was resting her feet in Sean's lap. He rubbed her toes with the practiced expertise and serene composure of a happily married man. Matthew was ribbing Hilary about something or other while Luisa looked on, her eyelids drooping with the late hour. She'd arrived just that morning on an overnight flight from South America.

As we approached, they looked the two of us over with uniformly bemused expressions. My rather long and distinguished trail of romantic disasters was common fodder for group conversations, and I could tell they were looking forward to having some new material with which to enjoy themselves at my expense.

Peter made his introductions while I sank into an empty chair. If he noticed the way that Jane elbowed Matthew or how Hilary raised one inquisitive eyebrow he didn't show it. He bore up well under Luisa's coolly assessing gaze and acted like he didn't see the exaggerated wink Sean gave me or the finger I flipped back at him.

Jane and Luisa bent forward to examine the stain on my dress. "It doesn't look good, Rach." Jane's voice was somber. When it came to weighty matters of what could and could not be removed from fabric, Jane was an expert. I gazed down at the brown splotches despondently. The soda water treatment may have lent some romantic intrigue to the evening, but it hadn't done much to undo the damage wrought by Emma's great-aunt.

"However," said Luisa in a stage whisper, "something else looks quite good." She shot me a knowing glance. I tried to muster up a haughty look, but instead the flush in my cheeks deepened even further.

"Well, I think the time has come," Matthew announced. "If we don't get out of here soon they'll be kicking us out. Peter, you're staying at the Furlongs' house, aren't you? Do you need a ride there?"

"That would be great," said Peter. A lock of hair had fallen across his forehead, making him look even more adorably boyish than he had before. "I took a taxi straight here from the station so I don't have a car. Let me just go get my bag—I left it in the cloakroom."

"I'll go with you," Matthew volunteered, putting a hand on Peter's unsuspecting shoulder and guiding him toward the exit. Sean gently removed Jane's feet from his lap and rose from his seat to follow them.

"We'll see you all back at the house," he called over his shoulder with a barely disguised grin. This was more of a commandment than a suggestion. I watched their blue-blazered backs head toward the door, with Peter caught innocently in the middle, and inwardly groaned. The two of them could never resist the chance to play big brother, even though I had two of my own who were required by blood to play the role and did so exceedingly well. Peter would be thoroughly interrogated by the time they got back to the house, at which point Matthew and Sean would let me know in no uncertain terms if they found him a suitable candidate for me.

I sighed and turned my head to meet the unabashedly curious looks of my old roommates.

"Well?" asked Hilary.

"Well what?" I retorted with, I hoped, dignity. She stretched out one long bronzed leg and kicked me. Fortunately, she'd removed her high-heeled sandals. I tried to stare her down, but after a couple of seconds gazing at her jade-green eyes I began to giggle.

"He's cute," said Jane. "I mean, I know old married women aren't supposed to notice these things, but he really is very cute. And you certainly seem to think so. I haven't seen you blush like this in years. He seems nice and normal, too." In direct contrast to the sort of guy I usually went for, she was no doubt thinking but was too kind to say. She ran a hand through her bobbed brown hair, which gleamed in the dim light. Her arms were tanned against the simple blue sheath she wore.

"Quite handsome," agreed Luisa, her faint South American accent elongating her words. She pulled a cigarette from a silver case and lit it with an engraved lighter before returning the case to an embroidered black evening bag. She inhaled luxuriously, exhaling a stream of smoke from her full lips. For what must have been the millionth time I wondered how she managed to keep her lipstick on for an entire evening.

"But why is he friends with Richard?" demanded Hilary. "I mean, do we know if he's worthy? Can he possibly be worthy?" Ah. The question on all of our minds. Trust Hilary to be the first to pose it aloud.

"Oh, do be quiet, Hilary," said Luisa. "Rachel's a grown-up. She can take care of herself." These were disingenuous words from the woman who'd taken it upon herself to cancel a date she deemed "inappropriate" for me our senior year.

"I'm sure the Inquisition will have that all figured out in no time," I said, referring to Matthew and Sean. I paused then continued in a more serious tone. "I have to admit, I have the same concern. I mean, Peter seems smart and nice, and he's a really good dancer and he smells incredible, and he's got the most wonderful eyes and he has a great sense of humor—and did I mention how good he smells? But he's a friend of Richard's." The way I said Richard's name could leave no doubt as to how I felt about him. "Peter said that the two of them grew up together and that they haven't really been in touch for years. And he seemed pretty surprised that Richard wanted him to be his best man. That's a good sign, but is it enough to outweigh being friends with Richard in the first place?" I looked around for affirmation. I'd learned long ago that, when it came to men, my judgment left much to be desired and it was wise to seek a second opinion.

"Speak of the devil," muttered Hilary. I followed her gaze and saw Richard nearing the table with Emma trailing alongside. She looked exhausted; even her long, golden hair seemed to droop with fatigue.

"Girls, how are you?" asked Richard in that fake hearty way I hated so much, acting as if we were all the best of friends. Girls, indeed. Normally I wouldn't get too worked up about politically incorrect terminology, but coming from Richard this was particularly irksome. I bit my tongue to keep from pointing out that we'd just attended our ten-year college reunion.

"We're just fine, Dick," answered Hilary, giving him a big smile. He didn't even flinch.

"Emma," I called. "Come sit with us. We haven't gotten to spend a minute with you all night."

"I'd love to," she said, her quiet voice hoarse from all of the talking she'd had to do that evening. "But I have to get back to the house. My mother's completely stressed out about tomorrow and all of the logistics, and she wants to go through the master plan one more time. If she's calm enough, maybe we can all have a nightcap by the pool?" Richard didn't wait for us to respond before he started shunting her toward the door. "I'll see you at the house," she called, casting a wistful look over her shoulder.

"God, I hate that man," said Hilary, not waiting for them to be out of earshot. She angrily brushed a strand of platinum hair back from her face.

"Of course you do," said Luisa. "He's appalling."

"That's one word for it," I said.

"What is Emma thinking?" asked Jane.

"We could sit here all night without answering that," said Hilary, sounding uncharacteristically dejected. She stood up abruptly, smoothing her short skirt over her thighs. "Let's go."

The club's valet was nowhere to be seen and the parking lot was nearly deserted as we made our way out to the car I'd borrowed from a colleague for the weekend. It was a huge black Suburban that made me feel as if I were driving a tank on the way up from New York.

"Does anybody else feel like driving?" I asked. "I probably shouldn't."

"Why—too much to drink or too dazzled by love?"

"Shut up, Hil."

Jane took the keys and we piled into the car, lapsing into silence as she swung onto the narrow country road that led from the club to the Furlongs' house. An air of sadness settled over us; doubtless, each of us was thinking about Emma and Richard and the ceremony that would take place the next day. On top of that, I still had the exchange I'd overheard between Emma and her father spinning in my head.

★ ★ ★

If anyone had asked us to take bets years ago as to which one of us was most likely to make a disastrous matrimonial mistake, the odds would have been on me as the winner, hands down. Yet here we were, on the eve of Emma's wedding, and I desperately wished that I could find even one thing I liked about the bridegroom, or at least a sign that maybe things would work out for the best.

Unfortunately, when it came to Richard, there just wasn't much to like. Even I had to admit he was handsome, although that fluke of biology was completely offset by the disproportionate level of interest he took in his clothes. He was also clever and knowledgeable, able to hold his own on topics ranging from high finance to obscure Scandinavian writers.

When Emma first showed up with Richard on her arm, I tried to give him the benefit of the doubt. After all, I never knew for sure what exactly had happened between him and Luisa all those years ago. But during the months that Emma and Richard dated and then the months during which they'd been engaged, I hadn't discovered even one mildly redeeming quality.

That Richard had fouled a deal I was involved in soon after he and Emma started dating was just the tip of the iceberg. I'd been representing a major publishing house in the acquisition of a boutique literary press. Richard, an agent for a number of well-known writers, had quietly lured away the boutique firm's bestselling author, a loss that reduced the value of the acquisition tremendously. My client was too far down the acquisition path to retreat without losing face in the industry; the letters of intent had already been signed. The acquisition went through, although the price my client paid was widely criticized by Wall Street. The company's stock price had languished since.

The client blamed the mishap on Winslow, Brown, and

the Winslow, Brown partner who'd insisted on taking the lead on the deal, enjoying all the hobnobbing it entailed with the literary world, did his best to deflect the blame onto me once things went sour. This was an easy task in the firm's testosterone-heavy environment, where a woman's competence was always in question. I calculated that Richard's coup had added at least six months and probably a year to the already onerous path to partnership at my white-shoe firm.

To a certain extent, the sequence of events was business as usual. As "expert" advisors, we should have negotiated contingencies into the original agreement that protected our client in the event that a significant change in the target company's author list occurred. For that oversight we could only blame ourselves. You could also argue that Richard was only doing his job—the author he'd stolen away signed a much more lucrative deal with another publishing house.

What bothered me was that Richard knew that I was involved in the deal, or I assumed he did, because I'd found him in my study during a cocktail party at my apartment, leafing casually through my notes on the preliminary negotiations. He didn't even have the grace to look flustered at being caught, but just glibly explained that he was looking for a piece of paper to write down a phone number. I wordlessly pointed to the blank legal pad that sat front and center on my desk, returned the file to the drawer in which it had been stowed, watched while Richard pretended to jot something down, and escorted him out of the room.

While this was enough to earn Richard a place of honor on my blacklist, it was far more than a professional grudge that fueled my dislike. Quite simply, I was convinced that his interest in Emma had everything to do with gold digging and social climbing and nothing to do with love and respect.

Emma was one of the most compassionate, well-intentioned people I knew. However, growing up in the shadow of two exceedingly good-looking, glamorous parents hadn't done much for her self-esteem. She'd had a few boyfriends, but even she had seemed to recognize that they tended to be more interested in the vast wealth she'd inherited from her mother's blue-blooded family, the fame of her artist father or even in her nascent reputation as an artist in her own right than in her as a person. Overall, she was woefully inexperienced with men and doubtful that anyone would ever love her for the right reasons, no matter how frequently I listed her many virtues in an effort to bolster her confidence.

Yet all her insecurities seemed to melt away under the sheer force of Richard's initial onslaught. In the early days of their relationship he romanced her aggressively. He deluged her with flowers and chocolates, intimate dinners, weekends in the country and extravagant gifts, and Emma was overwhelmed. For several months she was glowingly happy, and I was eager to believe that he was on the up and up, at least as far as Emma was concerned. I even tried to be nice to him when I saw him, which wasn't easy.

Even before they were engaged, however, he rapidly downshifted into taking her for granted. He'd cancel arrangements with her at the last minute or arrive late without an apology, let alone an excuse. There were no more flowers or chocolates, although he did seem to take a fastidious interest in the gifts they registered for at Tiffany's. Instead of intimate dinners, or weekends in the country, Richard turned his attention to the types of events covered by the society pages, displaying Emma on his arm like a trophy. It was around then that I started to avoid making plans to see them together and would instead arrange to have lunch or dinner with Emma alone. But when I did see Emma, she seemed despondent, and the radiant excitement she'd once shown when she spoke of him had dulled.

I'd tentatively tried to broach the subject with her a few

months after they announced their engagement. We'd met for a late dinner at a quiet restaurant near her loft, and after I'd had a glass of wine I worked up the courage to ask her if everything was all right between Richard and her. Up until that point our conversation had skipped easily from a movie that we'd both seen to a discussion of my work and then of her work. Emma had her first gallery show when she was only twenty-one, and although there were more than a few disgruntled followers of the New York art scene who complained that Emma's father had smoothed her way, few could dispute her artistic talent. Whereas her father's work was still entirely abstract, Emma focused on landscapes and portraits that inspired comparisons to Edward Hopper and John Singer Sargent. The first show as well as the ones that followed in the ensuing years met with great critical acclaim. Now, however, she seemed worried. "I think I have the artist's equivalent of writer's block," she confided. "I can't get anything done."

It was then that I asked her about Richard, thinking that the question would seem like a natural part of the discussion. I had hoped that she would open up a bit and allow me the opportunity to voice my concerns. Instead, it seemed as if an invisible wall suddenly went up around her. "Oh, Richard's just fine," she answered quickly, and then she abruptly changed the subject.

The rest of our conversation that night was stilted, and I went home wondering if I should have forced the issue but hesitant lest I should alienate her. Her response had felt like a warning to me, a clear sign that she did not want to talk about her relationship with Richard. And, except for the occasional glancing reference, we didn't talk about him in the months that followed. It was awkward maintaining a friendship when there was such a large and obvious topic that we danced around without discussing.

This wasn't the first time that I'd been upset by how Emma let herself be treated like a doormat by a boyfriend. But this time was serious; it was marriage.

I hoped she knew what she was doing. I sure didn't.

CHAPTER 4

It was easy to lose one's way on the twisting roads that led to the Furlongs' house. Streetlights and signposts were kept to a bare minimum, and the trees effectively blocked out the sky. I suspected the families who had houses in the area preferred it that way—the last thing they wanted was to point out their tranquil country refuge to strangers.

Yuppies from Manhattan and Boston had already descended upon old-money enclaves in the Hamptons and Cape Cod. From Water Mill to Osterville, and even on Martha's Vineyard and Nantucket, they were busily buying up modest summer cottages for exorbitant prices, tearing them down and replacing them with sprawling mansions. Their slick German luxury sedans and Land Rovers clogged the country roads and vied for parking spaces with the battered Buicks and Lincolns favored by WASP holdouts.

By comparison, the Furlongs' corner of the Adirondacks had remained pristine. The general store in town continued to do a healthy trade in Wonder bread and domestic beer. If

you were looking for goat cheese, Chilean sea bass, or imported mineral water, you were definitely in the wrong place.

It was so dark that Jane nearly missed the turn for the Furlongs' house. The stone pillars on either side of the gate were
almost completely hidden by bramble, and ivy draped over
a faded sign that read Quail Lake. Luisa dug the slip of paper
on which she'd written the gate code out of her purse, and
Jane rolled down her window and punched the numbers into
the keypad. The wrought iron panels slid soundlessly apart
and then closed shut behind us.

The house itself was nearly a mile from the road, and we
were quiet as Jane carefully steered along the narrow drive.
I listened to our wheels crunching on the loose gravel. The
thick woods on either side contributed to a sense of isola-
tion that had always felt peaceful when I'd visited before. The
crisp northern air with its scent of pine brought to mind unbidden memories of long-ago evenings as a child at summer
camp, an unfortunate experiment initiated by my parents in
the vain hope of instilling in me a love of nature.

We rounded the last turn and the house came into view.
From this angle it looked deceptively modest. Every time I
came here I wondered how Mrs. Furlong managed to main-
tain the wooden shingles in exactly the same state of shab-
biness, not quite dilapidated but dangerously close. In this
case, however, looks were completely deceiving. There were
five bedrooms in the house, along with a number of rooms
for sitting and lounging, all luxuriously appointed in a manner that was so discreetly expensive that only the most finely
trained eyes could appreciate the value of the well-worn
rugs, the graceful lines of the Early American antique furnishings, and the sheer scale of investment required to main-
tain such a lavish household in this simple but elegant
comfort.

Light spilled from an upstairs window onto the wide circle before the house. Jane parked the truck next to the line of cars that had accumulated in the clearing along the edge of the drive. I recognized Mrs. Furlong's aged Mercedes convertible, Mr. Furlong's even older Volvo, Richard's spanking new BMW, and Matthew's battered Saab. Only family members and family equivalents were staying at the house tonight.

The front door was unlatched—the gate at the drive and the high fence around the property made locks unnecessary—and we passed through it single file just in time to catch Lily Furlong ascending the stairs to the second floor. Hearing us come in, she paused and turned to greet us, stifling a ladylike yawn in a delicate fist.

"Oh, there you are, girls," she said, giving us all a warm smile. "We were getting worried that you'd gotten lost. The roads up here can be so confusing. Did you all have a nice time at the dinner? And, Rachel, what a lovely toast you gave! It was very charming, dear. I know Emma was touched by it."

"I'm glad you liked it," I said. Somehow, even when I knew I was saying the right thing, Mrs. Furlong always made me feel gauche.

"Well, I was just about to turn in. We have such a big day ahead of us tomorrow. I think the boys are all sitting out by the pool having a nightcap if you want to join them. The seamstress is coming early in the morning to put some final touches on Emma's dress, and the poor child was exhausted, so I sent her to bed." I was sad to hear this; I was impatient for some time alone with Emma before she became Mrs. Richard Mallory. I toyed with the idea of following Mrs. Furlong upstairs and waking Emma up but resolved instead that I would sit her down for a long talk in the morning, seamstress notwithstanding. Besides, I doubted if Mrs. Furlong would appreciate my interfering with Emma's mandated beauty sleep.

Lily smiled tiredly in our direction. "You all know which rooms you're staying in, don't you?" We nodded our acquiescence. "Good, good. Well, don't stay up too much longer," she called over her shoulder. "I don't want any of you ladies dozing off tomorrow during the ceremony. Everything must be perfect for Emma's big day."

We bid her good-night, and I led the way toward the back of the house. I'd spent so many summer vacations as a guest here that I knew nobody would begrudge us taking a bottle of champagne from the kitchen refrigerator and borrowing four plastic tumblers from a cupboard.

We'd decided in the car that some private time was in order, so we let ourselves out the kitchen door and tiptoed down the path that led to the lake. I could hear the low rumble of male voices from around the corner of the house, but we continued toward the dock. One by one we removed our shoes and padded out along the planks that stretched over the water.

We lowered ourselves down to sit side by side at the end of the dock, dangling our legs over the edge. The icy water was soothing, and I waggled my toes with pleasure; my feet had had a rough evening, between the three-inch heels I'd worn and the damage Emma's great-aunt had inflicted. A promising lump was beginning to rise on my instep. I peeled the foil off the top of the champagne bottle and gently worked the cork free. It came loose with a subdued but satisfying pop, and I poured some of the sparkling wine into each of our glasses and passed them down the row.

"Should we toast?" I asked when everyone had a drink in hand.

"Toast what?" asked Hilary. "The wedding?" She made no effort to disguise the sulky tone in her voice.

"No, I'm definitely not in the mood for that," said Jane. Things were bleak indeed if even Jane couldn't find a way to put a positive spin on the situation.

Luisa didn't say anything, but I heard the familiar sounds of her cigarette case opening and the swoosh of her lighter. I wondered idly how many cigarettes she'd smoked that day. Her cigarette case seemed, magically, to be always full of imported Gauloises.

"God," said Hilary, taking a big gulp of her drink. "I can't believe Emma's actually going through with this. If only there were some way to talk her out of it."

Jane had stretched out on her back to observe the night sky, but now she struggled back up into a sitting position and turned to face us. "You know, I've tried to talk to Emma about Richard and the wedding and everything. More than once. I thought that coming from me, since I've already been married for such a long time and everything, it might have some weight. But she shuts down as soon as you try to talk to her about him. She just gets really tense and says that everything's fine and then changes the subject."

"It's true, Hil. I've tried to talk to her, too," I said. "And it's pretty much a guaranteed way to end a conversation of any depth with Emma. I don't understand it at all. I mean, it seems so obvious that she's not really happy with him. She's clearly not eating enough or sleeping well, and she can't get any work done. But she also seems determined to go through with this." The argument she'd had with her father had made that all too clear.

"I know all that," answered Hilary, exasperated. "The last time I was in New York I kept her up half the night haranguing her about all the rumors I'd heard about Dicky when we both lived in Los Angeles, after college. All of the sleazy business deals and random affairs. He was notorious when he was there, he really was. And Emma didn't bother to deny any of it, or to defend him. In fact, she didn't even get upset. I sort of thought it would piss her off, my saying all of those things. But she just nodded her head and didn't say anything except that she'd be fine and not to worry about it. It was like talking to a wall."

Luisa exhaled an impatient stream of smoke. "Look, Hilary, I've spoken to Emma about Richard as well. When she came to me about the prenuptial agreement—"

"What? Emma signed a prenup? Why? She's the one with all of the money!" Hilary was incredulous. So was I. This was the first I'd heard of a prenuptial agreement.

"*Mierda*. I thought you all knew. Forget I mentioned it."

"The cat's out of the bag on this one, Luisa. You might as well tell us the whole thing now," said Jane.

"Did Emma's parents make them sign one? To protect her in some way from Richard?" I asked. That would have been a relief.

"No, no. Nothing like that. It was all Richard's idea. Apparently he insisted on it."

"Richard's idea?" I repeated. "I don't get it." Emma's family could buy and sell Richard a hundred times over. I doubted that they had any interest whatsoever in his assets, whatever they might be.

"But," protested Hilary, "isn't the point of a prenup to make sure that the person with the money gets to keep it in case of a divorce?"

"Usually," said Luisa, lighting another cigarette.

"Well, what does the prenup say?" I asked.

"I don't know—I never read it. As far as I could tell, it was already a done deal when Emma came to me. Richard and his lawyers had prepared it, but Emma needed to review it with independent counsel before she signed it, and she wanted me to help her find someone. I had to send her to another firm, of course. We focus on international commerce, not New York State law, let alone domestic affairs."

"Why didn't she go to her family attorney?" I asked. I couldn't imagine that people as wealthy as the Furlongs didn't have an entire battalion of lawyers at a discreet midtown firm, watching out for their interests and billing for every six minutes of service.

"She did. But for whatever reason they suggested that she get someone else to represent her. It seems hard to believe, but perhaps their firm doesn't have a department that handles marital law." Luisa sounded skeptical. Or, I thought, reading into what she'd left unsaid, they couldn't advise Emma, in good faith, to sign it.

"I don't get it. Why would Richard insist on a prenup? I mean, if Emma's the one with all the…" Jane's voice trailed off. She was too well brought up to remark explicitly on Emma's extraordinary wealth.

"Ugh. God only knows what goes on in Richard's slimy little mind. He probably had some slimy reason of his own," said Hilary.

"Maybe he was trying to prove that he didn't have any slimy reasons," Jane ventured. She insisted on looking for the good in everyone, even when there was none to be found.

"Oh, Richard's all about slime and slimy reasons," said Hilary. "I don't trust his motives one bit. I bet he can't wait to get his hands on Emma's money."

"From what I've heard, he already has," I said. "There are rumors in New York that the Furlongs are the silent partners backing Richard's new agency. They're only rumors, but where there's smoke there tends to be fire in situations like these. I don't know where else he could possibly have gotten the money. The offices are gorgeous, and the launch party he had must have cost a fortune."

"You're kidding," said Jane in disbelief.

"I wish," I replied.

"What a skunk," said Hilary. "You'd think he could at least wait until after the wedding to start raiding Emma's bank account."

"The money's certainly attractive to him, but I think he's even more excited about all of the other advantages that come with being part of the Furlong family," said Luisa.

"What do you mean?" Jane asked.

Hilary snorted. "Come on, Jane. Money can buy some things, but not everything. Talk about a name that opens doors! Emma's father is literally world-famous and has all of these incredible art world connections. And Emma's mother is related to half of American history, what with all of the Winthrops and Mathers and Jeffersons in her family tree."

"And let's not forget the Astors and Rockefellers and Du-Ponts," I added.

"Plus all of the things that money can't really buy," Hilary continued. "All the Social Register bullshit and seats on philanthropic boards and photos in *W* and *Vogue*. Oh, and did I mention club memberships? Dicky's probably drooling over the prospect of his own locker at the Racquet Club."

"Okay, okay, I get the point," said Jane. "But if this is all so clear to us, why isn't it clear to Emma? What is she thinking?"

In the moonlight I saw Luisa arch one thin dark brow. "I wish I knew. It's as if she's sleepwalking through the entire thing."

"Maybe there's something to Richard that we can't see," Jane said.

"Like what?" Hilary challenged. "He loves animals? He's kind to his mother?"

"I don't think even that's true," said Luisa dryly.

"Emma's not stupid," Jane answered. "And while her taste in men has always—" she struggled to put it delicately "—left something to be desired, she's always figured it out in the end. There must be something good in him." She was clearly hoping that if she said it enough times she would start to believe it.

"Well, whatever it is, he's managed to keep it pretty well hidden," said Hilary.

"That's for sure," said Luisa.

"Here's what else I don't get," said Hilary. "Even if Emma's been suckered by Richard, I can't imagine her parents falling for him. They're much too savvy. And Emma's so close to them—if they had any objections, she would have taken them seriously. But they—well, especially Mrs. Furlong—seem completely gung ho about this wedding. It sounds like it's going to be a real three-ring circus, what with the hundreds of guests and two bands and champagne flowing out of fountains."

I wondered if I should say anything about the exchange I'd overheard earlier between Emma and her father. It was bad enough that I was guilty of eavesdropping. Surely I shouldn't compound the sin by gossiping about things I hadn't been meant to hear. "Maybe her mother's doing the entire parental reverse psychology thing," I replied while I was internally debating the merits of full disclosure. "You know, where they don't want to tell you exactly what they think because they're afraid that that will make you do exactly what they don't want you to do? Or that if they tell you what they think and you go ahead anyway, the situation gets really awkward?"

"Is that how they handled these things when you were growing up in Ohio?" asked Hilary. My midwestern childhood had provided almost as much amusement to my friends as my romantic history, particularly after they discovered that *Leave It to Beaver* was set in my hometown. In fact, Ward Cleaver had once boasted to his sons about having been the best kite flyer in all of Shaker Heights in his youth. That my parents, with their thick Russian accents and bookish ways, bore not even the faintest resemblance to the archetypically all-American white-bread Ward and June Cleaver didn't seem to matter.

"No need to be snotty," I said, but even I recognized that my reverse parental psychology hypothesis was fairly lame. I decided to go for full disclosure. "Besides, regardless of what Emma's mother thinks, I'm pretty sure her father's not too happy about Richard." I briefly told them about the argument I'd overheard. I felt slightly guilty, as if I'd betrayed a confidence, but I was so worried about Emma. Perhaps I was hoping that somebody could explain what I'd heard in a way that would make everything all right. I was out of luck, however; my friends found this information just as disturbing as I had.

"What could possibly make Emma talk to her father like that?" asked Jane, shocked.

"I don't know. They've always had such a good relationship. I don't think I've ever heard her raise her voice to him before."

"He was really telling her to call it off?" Luisa asked.

"He was practically begging her to," I confirmed.

"Unbelievable," said Hilary.

"I know."

"It must feel awful to be about to get married and to have so many people expressing their concern to you," reflected Jane. "Marriage is scary enough when you're confident you're doing the right thing and so is everyone around you."

"Yes, but you were doing the right thing when you married Sean," Hilary pointed out.

"I really wish I could feel as good about this as I felt when you two were getting married," I added wistfully.

"I wish *I* could feel as good about this as I did when we were getting married. Still, we should be supportive of Emma. She must have some good reason. Maybe she really loves Richard. And whatever her reason, we're Emma's best friends. We should try to give him the benefit of the doubt." Jane's voice, however, betrayed her lack of conviction. She'd never been a good liar; even the simple white lie was beyond her.

"What doubt?" asked Hilary. "There is no doubt. Richard is a complete and utter snake."

"You're absolutely right," Luisa agreed. "But it still doesn't explain why Emma's going through with this."

"She's making a major mistake," said Hilary.

"She really is," I agreed.

"He is a disaster," said Luisa.

Jane sighed. Her optimism was tapped out. "He sure is."

We lapsed into an unhappy silence, sipping the chilled wine. The light from a half moon glossed over the gentle ripples on the water's surface, and clouds moved slowly across the black sky. I breathed in the clean air, taking in the quiet brilliance of the night. In Manhattan it was probably well over eighty degrees, and so humid that the sounds of traffic and sirens would seem muted by the oppressive heat. Still, even with the heat and humidity, I would rather have been there than in this beautiful spot, dreading the day to come.

Hilary was the first to break the silence. Her voice was calmer now, and she spoke casually, as if she were picking up on a discussion that we'd started a few minutes ago but hadn't finished.

"So. Is this a pact we're going to keep?"

CHAPTER 5

I woke up early the next morning and couldn't fall back to sleep. This was highly irregular—I was famous in certain circles for my ability to sleep deeply and at great length, no doubt as a result of my usual work-induced state of sleep deprivation. Perhaps on some level I already knew what had happened and my curiosity to know yet more nudged me awake.

My mouth was dry and my head fuzzy from too many drinks the previous evening. All that champagne, and then the vodka tonics, and then even more champagne, had seemed like such a good idea at the time. But now I had a pounding headache, and every muscle in my body ached, and I had only myself to blame.

I was sharing Emma's room, but she was still sleeping in the other twin bed, and, eager as I was to talk to her, it seemed criminal to disturb her peaceful slumber. Careful not to wake her, I slipped out from under the down-filled comforter, exchanged my nightie for a pair of cutoffs and a cotton sweater, grabbed a few Advil from my bag, and tiptoed down the stairs in flip-flops to search for something to wash the pain relievers down. The house was quiet, and the hands of the kitchen clock told me it was only half past six, a time of day that I hadn't seen on a weekend in at least two years.

I reached into the refrigerator, took the pitcher that the Furlongs' housekeeper kept filled with freshly squeezed orange juice, and poured myself a tall glass. I swallowed the pills down with a generous slug. Then I stepped through the kitchen door and onto the porch that wrapped around the house. Between the Advil, the juice, and the fresh air, I hoped I would shortly feel brand-new.

I strolled past the long oak table and wicker chairs where the Furlongs ate their meals during the summer and paused at the railing. Sipping my juice, I took in the panorama before me. While money couldn't buy everything, it could most definitely purchase beauty and access to beautiful places. The view from the porch was breathtaking. Beyond the mirrored surface of the lake, the distant hills were thick with pine, and while the sky was still hazy, the early morning fog was beginning to recede, yielding to an intense, cloudless blue. In the foreground, the lush green of the lawn and gardens led down to the water's edge. The tapestry was marred only by the billowing white tent that had been erected to one side, an ominous reminder of the ceremony that was to take place that afternoon.

It was gorgeous weather for a wedding. Richard had probably insisted on it when he made his pact with the Devil. I sighed, dreading the day ahead.

From the corner of my eye I could see the glint of the pool, which Emma's mother had installed around the other side of the house the previous summer to better accommodate some of her more squeamish friends from the city. Emma and her father had argued with her about this for years, saying it was absurd to put in a pool when the cool expanse of lake stretched only a hundred yards away, but Lily had ultimately won out. Not everyone, she'd protested, was comfortable swimming with the water snakes and other slippery creatures that made the lake their home. And what Emma's mother wanted, she inevitably got. So the pool had gone in beside the house, along with a pool house that contained changing rooms, a sauna and two guest rooms, each of which undoubtedly could have swallowed my New York apartment in one gulp.

I continued along the porch to get a better look at the additions. We'd arrived just in time for the wedding rehearsal the previous day, and after that we had to rush to change for dinner. This was my first chance to check out the pool and the pool house in the clear light of day.

Maybe it was the lurking possibility of wildlife that caused my heart to skip a beat when I glimpsed a dark shape floating on the water's surface. I don't know what I thought it could have been—a bear or some sort of mountain lion, perhaps?—but living in Manhattan had rendered me both alert to danger and skittish about animals that weren't on a leash. I reminded myself that the porch stood several feet from the ground and gingerly made my way around the corner and toward the pool for a better look.

I noted with relief that the shape was neither furry nor moving before I registered that it was Richard. One of the custom-made shirts that usually hung just so from his lean frame was plastered to his torso, and his wet black hair gleamed in the sun. His face was in the water, but I knew it was him and I knew he was dead. It seemed somehow unjust that he should go just like Gatsby, when he had none of Gatsby's charm or surprising innocence. That was my first thought. My second thought was muffled by my own deafening shriek.

Matthew came running out of the pool house in boxer

shorts and a faded T-shirt, toothbrush in hand. "Rachel—what is it? Are you—" He stopped short when he caught sight of the body. Before I could respond, he dropped his toothbrush and dove into the water, flipping Richard over with the practiced moves of a lifeguard. I watched, paralyzed, as Matthew hoisted the body up out of the water and checked for a pulse. "Call 911!" Matthew yelled to me, already beginning CPR.

"I just did," I heard a calm voice say behind me. "They're on their way. I gave them the gate code, so they'll be able to get in." I turned, startled. Luisa was standing in the open French doors that led to the downstairs sitting room. Her curvy figure was wrapped in a silk kimono, and her dark hair hung nearly to her waist, freed from its usual thick knot. She pulled her silver cigarette case and lighter from a pocket. Her expression was almost bemused, and she dropped her voice, speaking as if to herself. "It looks like it's too late, though, doesn't it?"

The click of her lighter melted my paralysis, and I ran down the steps to the pool. I crouched next to Matthew, listening to him counting under his breath as he pumped Richard's chest. "Come on, you bastard, breathe already," he muttered.

I watched him for what felt like hours but was probably only a minute or two. Finally, he sat back on his heels and shook his head. "He's dead," he told me. He glanced at the back of his hands, lightly freckled and sparsely covered with light-brown hair, as if in disgust at their inefficacy. He seemed unaware of the water streaming from his drenched clothing to puddle at his feet.

I looked at the body stretched on the flagstones before us. In death Richard looked a lot like he had looked in life—just paler and wetter. His icy blue eyes stared unblinking at the sky, and his thin lips were bloodless and tinged with purple. I shivered as Matthew leaned over and gently smoothed his eyelids shut.

I heard footsteps and voices as other members of the household appeared, awakened by the uproar. Hilary stepped onto the porch dressed in a leopard-print negligee. She rubbed sleepily at her eyes, visibly grumpy at the disturbance. There was some distance between us, but from where I was I could have sworn she brightened considerably when she got a good look at the scene before her. "What have we here?" she asked in a tone that sounded more excited than distraught. She leaned over the wooden railing to get a closer look. Luisa grabbed her elbow and admonished her in a low voice.

Hilary was followed by Jane and Sean. I knew that happy couples frequently tended to start dressing alike, but surely their matching striped pajamas were a little much, even if they hadn't deliberately intended to match? They joined Hilary at the railing and made a quick assessment of what had happened. "Dead?" Sean asked, his arm grasping Jane around her waist. I nodded.

Emma's mother was right behind Jane and Sean, her petite form swathed in a simple terry bathrobe that she wore with the same unstudied elegance as the Chanel suits she favored in the city and the designer sportswear she wore in the country. Absent her usual subtle makeup and with her dark-gold hair hanging loose about her shoulders, Mrs. Furlong looked like an eerily faded version of Emma. "What—?" she started to ask. Then she took in Richard's body and let out a shriek that made mine seem distinctly amateur.

Emma ran out after her mother, a long T-shirt hanging halfway to her knees. She looked no older than she had freshman year. "Mother—what's wrong?" she cried, her voice trailing off as she followed her mother's gaze. "Oh. Oh. Is he…is he…?" A wave of white washed the color from her face.

Matthew looked up at her wordlessly, his expression blank. Hilary and Mrs. Furlong caught her as she crumpled to the floor.

I wasn't sure when, exactly, Emma's father arrived, but I remembered that he was panting, having run from his studio in the old stables. He stopped short at the edge of the pool area where the grass gave way to flagstone. I'd just noted his presence when I heard cars pulling up the drive toward the house. Their sirens echoed in the quiet morning air, the sound ricocheting from hill to hill.

I had a strange sense of déjà vu, as if I had woken up in an Agatha Christie novel. The only missing pieces were the vicar and Miss Marple.

CHAPTER 6

The first question to ask was whether Richard had committed suicide. But I knew the chances of that were all but nil.

Richard had treated the world, and everyone and everything in it, like his oyster. He was far too self-important to even play with the idea of putting an end to himself. And even if he had, he would never have arranged to die by drowning. He had been a varsity swimmer in college, before practices and meets began putting too much of a damper on his playboy aspirations. There was no way he would ever do anything that would call into doubt his erstwhile athleticism. Much less expose his handmade English shoes to chlorine. No, Richard would write a long and vindictive suicide note before blowing his brains out in such a way as to keep his handsome face intact while splattering enough blood and guts and gore to make cleaning up after him a royal pain in the ass.

I couldn't have been the only one thinking such thoughts as the paramedics went through the appropriate motions over Richard's body. The local police officers who'd arrived shortly after the ambulance had immediately roped off the pool area with bright-yellow tape. They now spoke in low voices off to the side, trying to look as if possible foul play was a staple of life in this remote corner of the Adirondacks. Sean had picked up Emma after she fainted and carried her inside, escorted by Mrs. Furlong and Jane and followed by Luisa and Hilary.

Matthew had disappeared into the pool house, but he quickly reemerged in a dry T-shirt and shorts and came to perch beside me on the steps leading up to the porch. We watched Mr. Furlong talking to the paramedics, his lined face inscrutable.

"What do you think happened?" Matthew asked me in a low voice.

"I don't know," I answered. "If he were anyone else, I would guess that he had too much to drink or something and fell in. But Richard could always hold his liquor. Maybe he slipped, and hit his head, and then fell in?" I was angling for death by accident, and I was eager for Matthew to validate my hopes with solid medical evidence.

Matthew was quiet for a moment, as if carefully choosing his words. "I don't think he drowned, Rach. I think he was dead before he hit the water."

"What do you mean? How do you know?"

"I don't know, at least not for sure, but I was doing CPR on him, pumping his chest. If Richard were breathing when he went underwater, he would have water in his lungs. If he had water in his lungs, it's almost impossible that some of it wouldn't have come up. But none did."

I considered this. A police photographer had arrived to record the scene for posterity and, I would assume, for evidence of a crime. She asked Mr. Furlong and the paramedics to back away from the body.

"There's something else," added Matthew. "His pupils were dilated."

"What does that mean?"

He sighed. "I see a lot of ODs—overdose cases—at the clinic. And their eyes look a lot like Richard's did."

"He OD'd?"

"Possibly."

"But Richard didn't use drugs." In fact, I remembered him holding forth in a nauseatingly self-righteous way on the topic, complete with several ideas about how the war against drugs should be fought. That most of his suggestions would violate the civil rights guaranteed by a number of constitutional amendments hadn't seemed to bother him.

"I'm not necessarily talking about heroin or cocaine."

"Even pills. He didn't even like to take aspirin when he had a headache—he thought it was for wimps."

Matthew shrugged. "This is all speculation, Rach. I don't know anything for sure."

I ran my hands through my disheveled hair. Had Richard been drugged, poisoned in some way, without his knowledge? Did someone kill him, perhaps slipping something into his drink, and then push him into the water in an attempt to mask the crime?

And while part of me wanted to know the answers to these questions, part of me was scared to find out.

I'd thought that nothing could be worse than Emma marrying Richard, but maybe I'd been wrong. If Richard had been killed, it meant that someone here—one of this close-knit circle of family and friends—was a murderer. And that was an idea I didn't like one bit.

I closed my eyes and took a deep breath, trying not to think about Emma's pained exchange with her father the previous evening, or Luisa's rapid appearance on the scene this morning and surprising composure, or Hilary's ill-contained excitement, almost bordering on glee. And then, of course, there was Matthew.

I opened my eyes and looked over at him. He was silently watching the paramedics and police, his expression neutral. I'd realized long ago, however, that Matthew wore his plain, unassuming face like a mask. This wasn't the first time I'd wondered what he was thinking.

Matthew was Emma's boy-next-door in just about every sense of the word. His mother and Mrs. Furlong had been friends since birth, practically, classmates at both Miss Porter's and Wellesley. He'd grown up in a discreetly luxurious apartment a few blocks up Park Avenue from the discreetly luxurious apartment in which Emma's family lived. The Furlongs had been regular guests at the Weirs' summerhouse in the Hamptons, and the Weirs, including Matthew and his elder sister, Nina, had visited the Furlongs' Adirondack camp for a few weekends each year. The two families had vacationed together, whether on the beaches of Saint Bart's or on the slopes of Alta. They had celebrated holidays together, as well—Thanksgiving in the country and Christmas on Park Avenue. Nina and Matthew were in college when their parents were killed in a car crash, and in the years that followed the Furlongs had become their surrogate family.

Matthew's family tree was even more lushly hung with cash than Emma's, if such a thing were possible. Regardless, he was one of the most down-to-earth people I knew. I had first met him when Emma and I were freshmen, sharing a double room in Strauss Hall. He was then in his second year at Harvard Medical School. He came by during Freshman Week, per the orders of Emma's parents, to take Emma out to dinner and make sure that she was adapting smoothly to college life. He arrived bearing an armful of flowers to brighten our drab dorm room and a tin of brownies to mitigate Emma's well-documented chocolate cravings.

He was funny-looking, tall and gangly with shaggy brown hair, a beaky nose and bright-blue eyes. Even if his features had been more regular, he wouldn't have been my type— even then I preferred them dark and neurotic. Still, he had a quiet strength of character, and he seemed so genuinely nice and trustworthy that he put one instantly at ease. He was clearly smitten with Emma, who treated him exactly like one would treat a big brother, with a mixture of affection and annoyance. Matthew was a fixture in our lives all through our college years, during which he finished medical school and his internship and began his residency at Mass. General.

Matthew played the big brother role flawlessly, not only to Emma but also to her friends. He rescued us from the endless succession of tasteless cafeteria meals with dinners at unusual restaurants in far-flung corners of Boston. My parents had done their best, like most immigrants, to embrace American culture. So with the exception of the occasional meal of borscht or blinis, I'd grown up on the relatively bland food that they felt was typically American. It was Matthew who taught me to enjoy the rich spices of Indian curries, the intricate blend of flavors in Vietnamese dishes, and the stinging pungency of wasabi. While we stuffed ourselves, he listened to our anguished stories about unwritable papers and unbearable crushes, providing kindness, advice and affirmation along with sustenance. When Emma and I joined Luisa, Jane and Hilary in our sophomore year in Lowell House, he adopted them as easily as he'd adopted me.

Matthew had a life of his own, and he even had the occasional girlfriend. But it was clear to everyone that he and Emma were meant to be together—at least, it was clear to everyone but Emma. The rest of us debated endlessly about when Emma would finally figure it out. Even when Richard and Emma had announced their engagement, on some level I was always confident that eventually it would be Matthew and Emma who would one day make their wedding vows to each other.

Now it looked like that once again was a possibility.

The paramedics had bundled up Richard's body in a zippered black bag and taken it away, but a host of technicians had joined the police photographer. A couple were busily dusting for fingerprints on the pool furniture and using hand vacuums to collect any shreds of evidence that might lie on the flagstones. The others had disappeared into the pool house, where I assumed they were exploring the guest room Richard had occupied. Mr. Furlong was talking to the policemen on the far side of the pool. The original two had been joined by another two who I guessed were detectives since they didn't wear uniforms. I could tell from his posture that Mr. Furlong was angry, and I could also tell from their postures that the policemen were intimidated. Mr. Furlong was not a force to be toyed with. His every gesture radiated strength, even when it was as simple as running a paint-stained hand through his bristly gray hair.

With an exasperated shrug he turned from them and made his way toward where Matthew and I were sitting. "What's going on?" Matthew asked him. "What do the police think happened?"

Mr. Furlong gave Matthew a tired smile, but his eyes were cold as he spoke. "Our local law enforcement experts are intent on blowing up what was clearly an accident into a major event." The way he said *experts* made the word sound like an obscenity, and his voice still bore a faint twinge from his Louisiana upbringing. "This is probably the most exciting thing that's happened up here in a long time. They don't get many opportunities to use all of their fancy equipment, and they want to make the most of it."

"They don't think it was an accident?" I asked.

Mr. Furlong responded to my question with a bitter laugh. "They find the circumstances *suspicious* and feel that they need to look into the situation more closely. I explained to them that my daughter just lost her fiancé and it would be appropriate of them to demonstrate at least a bit of courtesy, but they're insisting on talking to everyone present. They also ask that nobody leave the premises until given permission to do so. As if we don't have enough to worry about with hundreds of guests arriving this afternoon for a wedding that's not going to happen."

"Is there anything we can do?" asked Matthew.

Mr. Furlong flashed him a grateful look and responded quickly, as if he'd already thought everything through. "Could you make sure that the police do whatever it is they have to as quietly and quickly as possible? Put them somewhere in the house and make sure they talk to whomever it is they need to talk to and don't harass anyone. You could probably use the downstairs library."

"Sure," Matthew agreed.

But Mr. Furlong had already turned away from us. "I'll be in my studio if anyone needs me," he called over his shoulder. I was taken aback. Was he really just going to abandon the situation and return to work?

"Unbelievable," said Matthew, his voice barely audible, giving words to my own reaction. Then he pulled himself up from the steps and, with a parting pat on my shoulder, ambled over to the policemen.

CHAPTER 7

Unbelievable, indeed.

The Furlongs, so I'd always been led to believe, were the consummate happy family. But I was having difficulty reconciling this long-held conviction with Mr. Furlong's nonchalant delegation of responsibilities, not to mention the cryptic and heated exchange I'd overhead between him and Emma the previous night. Surely he should be carefully supervising the activities of the police or rushing upstairs to check in on his daughter, and perhaps even his wife, rather than deserting to his studio? He didn't seem to fully appreciate the gravity of what was happening. If someone in the household had killed Richard, it would be better for one of us to figure it out before the police did so that the situation could be managed properly. Not that I had any idea what would constitute proper management in such unusual circumstances, but I could cross that bridge when I got there. Years of training in sorting out data and figures had made the orderly arrangement of information almost a religion to me, and one thing I had learned was that you had to have your fact base in place before you could make any good decisions.

I rose to my feet and headed through the French doors to the living room. At this time of day, it was bathed with early morning light, which spilled over the glossy butter-yellow walls and comfortable furniture, all upholstered in variations on the theme of chintz. This was the room where Emma and I had spent most of our evenings when I'd visited before, sprawled on sofas reading or playing Scrabble around the coffee table with her parents or Matthew.

I was confident that Jane, with her usual unflappable calm and organizational prowess, would have the situation well in hand upstairs, so I paused to gather my thoughts. My eyes settled on the collection of silver-framed photographs on top of the gleaming Steinway, including a black-and-white picture of the Furlongs on their wedding day. Lily was radiant in a satin dress that accentuated the graceful lines of her collarbone, and Jacob was resplendent in a morning suit. He had the dark good looks of a young Sean Connery, and they set off Lily's delicate fairness beautifully.

Over the years, I'd learned a lot about Emma's family, not only from Emma herself but from magazines like *Vanity Fair* and *Vogue,* where you could often find articles about Emma's grandmother, Arianna Schuyler, who had rivaled Jackie Onassis as an icon of style and elegance, or about Lily and Jacob, who had been one of the most prominent couples in New York for decades. I knew that Lily's parents had quite a different husband in mind for their youngest daughter, somebody who shared their own blue-blooded and Ivy-draped backgrounds.

Instead, Jacob Furlong was the son of a dirt-poor Louisiana farmer. He broke upon the New York art scene in the mid-1960s with a splash that was as much about his bold paintings as it was about the notoriety he quickly gained as a man about town. His picture was just as likely to appear on Page Six of the *New York Post,* which breathlessly chronicled his exploits with companions like Andy Warhol and Edie Sedgwick, as it was to appear next to a favorable review in the *New York Times* or *ArtWorld.*

But the press he received in his early years in New York was nothing compared to the scoopfest that began when he started squiring Lily Schuyler around town. The Schuylers epitomized old-guard society, and Lily shattered convention in her unusual choice of a beau. It was hard to imagine where the two of them even crossed paths, but somehow they did. And after a whirlwind courtship, they announced their engagement. The Schuylers were stunned by the willfulness and determination with which Lily met their objections. Never before had she strayed from the path they'd set out for her, nor were they prepared for the onslaught of charm combined with tenacity that Jacob used to overcome their misgivings. Lily withdrew from Wellesley after her freshman year, and she married Jacob in June of 1970 in front of five hundred guests at Saint James Episcopal on Fifth Avenue.

If you were going only on the photographs before me, the elder Schuylers' fears were unwarranted. The pictures documented the happy life of a golden couple, complemented by their golden-haired daughter and a wide circle of friends. There were photos of the Furlong family with socialites and artists, corporate titans and noted intellectuals, all set against the background of the world's most expensive and exotic locales.

Without warning, I felt a pang of sympathy for Richard. While I was beginning to suspect that the golden surface masked complex depths, if you saw only the surface it would be easy to think that it was an accurate representation of life with the Furlongs. What little I knew about Richard's childhood suggested that it had been a far cry from this Elysian existence. I could only imagine the appeal that the Furlongs would have held for him, perhaps not only for the ambitious and avaricious reasons my friends and I had discussed just a few hours before while we sat on the dock, but as part of a far more human desire to be a member of a real family.

It was odd to think of Richard having such a basic need for familial warmth and security. The most unlikely emotion he'd ever stirred in me was empathy, even when I met him more than a dozen years ago at Harvard. Then, he was a senior and already the ultimate in dashing sophistication. He presented such a seamlessly polished face to the world that it was hard to imagine any sort of emotional neediness. Emma had always been a soft touch—sophomore year she'd brought home the meanest stray cat in existence, who promptly shredded the upholstery on the sofa in our common room and gave lie to the assumption that any cat can be litter trained. She only agreed to give him up when she'd placed him with a family in Cambridge. Perhaps emotional neediness was the quality that drew Emma to Richard, the trait that kept her with him long after he stopped making her happy. Richard was the human equivalent of the mean stray cat, albeit better groomed.

But somehow I knew that wasn't the answer, the secret to her motivations. I wondered what the real answer was, and if it had been connected in any way to the end Richard had met.

That was an unsettling idea.

I heard the slap of tennis shoes descending the front stairs, and the sound dragged me back to the present with a guilty jolt. I hadn't meant to spend so much time on a psychological retrospective of Richard Mallory. Sean entered the room at a brisk pace, and his burly, familiar form was a welcome distraction. He'd changed out of his pajamas into a pair of khakis and a faded polo shirt. His simple presence was reassuring, not only because of the sheer bulk of it but because his character was so solid and dependable. If a WASP could be a mensch, then Sean won that title hands down.

Jane was lucky enough to meet Sean early our freshman year, when he was a junior. They were both on the sailing team, which was a haven for hard-core outdoorsy-variety New Englanders. Sean was one of the cocaptains of the Varsity team, and Jane, a former medalist in sailing at the Junior Olympics, was the rare freshman to bypass JV altogether to take a place in the first boat. The two of them were well matched, with the clean bone structure, long healthy limbs, and sun-streaked hair that were the most common by-products of generations of WASP in-breeding. They also shared the same easygoing, down-to-earth way of navigating the world. They dated almost continuously throughout college, and their wedding on the Cape the summer after we graduated felt inevitable, from the blond-haired flower girl to the white tent that shielded the guests from the cool winds blowing off the Atlantic. It was hard to believe that they had been married for more than ten years, especially when the rest of us had so steadfastly maintained our single states. At least, all of us except Emma.

"Hey, there, Rach," he said, his trademark grin diminished in deference to the morning's events. He crossed the room to join me by the piano and put a large comforting hand on my shoulder. "How are you doing? You got quite a wake-up this morning, didn't you?"

It had been so hectic that it hadn't occurred to me that I was, in fact, a bit shell-shocked at having awakened to discover a body, but I decided not to think too carefully about that. There would be plenty of time to process it all later; figuring out how Richard had died would have to take precedence for the time being. "I'm okay," I said. "A little freaked out, but I'll get over it. More importantly, how's Emma?"

"I'm not sure. Jesus. I've never seen anybody faint dead away like that. I took her upstairs and then Mrs. Furlong shooed me off. Jane and Luisa and Hil are up there, too, so she's in capable hands. I thought I'd come back down to see if I could help out with anything."

"Matthew's out by the pool dealing with the police," I offered. "I'm sure he'd appreciate a little moral support."

"Right," said Sean. "I'll go see what I can do." He started toward the door.

It occurred to me then that he might be able to shed some light on things. "Hey, Sean," I called out, "wait a second."

"What is it? Is everything all right?" he asked, pausing and turning back to face me. The sun pouring in through the open doorway silhouetted him, and his bulk cast a long shadow across the floor.

"I was wondering—you had a nightcap with Richard last night, didn't you? Out by the pool?"

"Yep. All the guys did. Just a quick drink and a little male bonding before we went to bed."

"Did everything seem…normal?" *Normal* seemed like a lame word choice, but Sean would know what I meant. I was hoping for easy enlightenment, something that could explain—without implicating anyone I knew or cared about—how Richard had ended up floating facedown and lifeless in the pool.

"Did everything seem normal?" he repeated thoughtfully, his hand on the door's brass handle. "Yeah, as far as I could tell. Nothing strange happened that I noticed. Nothing out of the ordinary. That's what's so weird about this whole thing. I mean, Richard seemed like his same old self." Sean was too nice to say what Richard's same old self was like. He'd known Richard longer than any of us—they had both lived in Eliot House while at Harvard, an enclave that prided itself on its reputation for preppy elitism. "Lowest GPA, highest starting salary," bragged the house T-shirt one year, only partly tongue-in-cheek. They also belonged to the same finals club, one of a handful of exclusive fraternities housed in discreet redbrick buildings around campus. Neither Eliot House nor the club really suited Sean, but he was reluctant to be the first Hallard in five generations to stray from tradition. Both of these venues gave Sean ample opportunity to get to know Richard, and I knew from comments that Jane had let drop that his opinion of Richard was no higher than my own.

Sean continued, "It's so bizarre to think that there we were, just a few hours ago, talking about how the Yankees are doing this season and other nonsense, and the next thing you know…" His voice trailed off. "It doesn't make any sense."

"No," I agreed. "It doesn't."

"I keep wondering what could have happened. There must be a good explanation, but for the life of me, I have no idea what it is. I thought for a moment that maybe he committed suicide, but Richard was as far from suicidal as…" He didn't finish his sentence, unable to find the appropriate simile.

"Was he really drunk?" I asked, trying to mask the hopeful tone in my voice. It felt awkward and inappropriate to probe like this, but I desperately wanted to believe that it had, in fact, been possible that Richard could have had so much to drink that he could have fallen into the pool and been too far gone to save himself. Matthew's assessment and Richard's well-documented ability to hold his liquor notwithstanding, I was definitely rooting for accidental drowning as the cause of death. If suicide was out of the question, the only other alternative was less than appealing.

Sean considered this for a moment and then gave a decisive shake of his head. "Well, he seemed to have had a good bit to drink, but we all had. And he's always been able to drink even the most serious drinkers under the table. I think the rest of us were far worse for wear than he was. I was practically ready to pass out by the time I went in to bed." He flashed me a self-deprecating smile. "Quiet married life hasn't done much for my level of alcohol tolerance. I only have a hazy memory of Jane coming in, although, according to her, I really distinguished myself on the snoring front last night."

I had to laugh. Sean's snoring was legendary, capable of raising roofs and setting windowpanes to shaking in their frames. Then I thought about what he'd said. If Sean had gone to bed before Jane, he must have come in before 2:00 a.m., which was when I'd arrived in the bedroom I was sharing with Emma, also a little worse for wear from several hours of steady drinking, after my friends and I had decided to call it a night. Almost unconsciously, I started putting together a mental chronology of the early morning's events.

"Did the other guys go to bed when you did?" I asked.

"No," Sean said with another shake of his head. "I was the first to go. Jane and I were going to take advantage of being up in the country to take a long run before all of the wedding action began." Some people, myself included, exercised for normal reasons like wanting to look cute in one's clothes. Jane and Sean, however, actually thought exercise was fun. I'd always prided myself on being able to stay friends with people who enjoyed marathons but didn't find them sufficiently challenging.

"Still," Sean went on, "everybody was getting tired. I don't think they lasted that much longer." Especially not Richard, I couldn't help but think with morbid humor.

"So, let me get this straight," I summarized, "you all were drinking by the pool while we were out on the dock, you then came in before two, we all came in around two, and you're not quite sure when the rest of the guys went to bed but you think it was pretty soon after that." That meant that whatever happened took place sometime between two and six, which was a big window for foul play.

He gave me a quizzical look and then grinned again, more fully this time. "What's going on, here, Rach? You thinking of tossing in your banking gig to become a private investigator?"

I gave him a sheepish smile. "I don't know. Do you think I'd be any good?"

"Good or not, I don't think it pays enough to keep you in the style you'd like. You might want to stick with Wall Street."

"Thanks for the tip," I said.

"Any time. Now, assuming you have no more questions, Madame Detective, I'm going to go make myself useful."

"That's Mademoiselle, to you. And you're dismissed." He gave me a mock salute and I waved him out the door.

CHAPTER 8

I found my friends upstairs in Mrs. Furlong's sitting room, where the air seemed infused with palpable relief. Or perhaps I was just projecting my own emotions. Mrs. Furlong was bent over her desk, sorting though piles of papers, while everyone else looked on expectantly, still dressed as they'd been when we'd discovered Richard's body.

"Hi," I said to announce my presence.

Mrs. Furlong looked up at me, a pair of silver-rimmed reading glasses perched on her nose. Her usual air of gracious composure appeared to be firmly back in place, as if the woman who'd emitted the bloodcurdling shriek at the pool had been someone entirely different. I wondered if she'd learned how to deal with situations like this one in finishing school along with French and needlepoint.

"Hello, Rachel, dear," she said. "The girls and I realized that it's going to be a scramble to cancel all of the arrangements for this afternoon. I'm trying to get everything together so that we can get on the phone and start calling the various tradespeople and the guests. It's nearly eight, and I think it would be all right to start making calls around eight-thirty or so."

"Where's Emma?" I asked. "How is she doing?"

"This is such a shock for her, poor thing," said Mrs. Furlong. "We gave her a sedative and put her to bed in my room. It seemed like the best thing to do."

"I just checked on her again and she's asleep," added Jane. "It's probably better this way than making her deal with everything right away."

"Wow," I said, at a loss for any but the most banal words. "I can't imagine what she must be feeling right now."

Hilary rolled her eyes. She was standing behind Mrs. Furlong and safely out of her line of sight. Fortunately, she omitted the snort that usually accompanied this familiar expression of impatient disgust.

"What did the police say?" asked Luisa, flashing Hilary a warning glance.

"Nothing much. They're still looking around by the pool. But they're going to want to talk to everyone. Matthew's helping to arrange everything."

"Where's Jacob?" Mrs. Furlong's voice took on a sharp edge, and behind her glasses her eyes seemed unusually bright.

"Um, I think he went back to his studio."

"You're kidding." Her tone was flat, but her expression had hardened.

"Uh, no," I answered.

She swore under her breath and her hands gripped the edge of her desk, their knuckles white. "I can't believe it. I just can't believe it. That bastard. We have a body in the backyard and all he can do is…" She didn't finish her sentence, and her words met our embarrassed silence. I had the slightly guilty sense of seeing something I shouldn't have seen. Never before had Mrs. Furlong deviated in any way from her usual flawless decorum in my presence, but this morning, in the space of a few short hours, I'd seen more emotions, including shock and fury, than I'd seen in all of the years I'd known her.

She recovered herself after a moment, embarrassed as well. She slowly straightened up, removed her glasses, and carefully put them back in a leather case.

She handed a neat pile of folders to Jane. "All of the information is here, Jane," she said, her voice back to normal. "The caterers, the florists, the band, the minister, the guests—all of the details and contact information should be in these files. You all should just try to reach whomever you can. You can use the phone in Jacob's study down the hall and the one in the third-floor den. You know where it is, don't you? Perhaps you could all split up and—what is it that you business people say, Rachel? Parallel process, right? We had a new phone system put in a few months ago—it's all very high-tech. There are three lines, but we should probably keep one free for the police. So two of you can use the land lines. And if any of you have your cell phones, sometimes you can get them to work up here. The reception's not great, but it will do in a pinch."

We promised her we'd take care of everything and she thanked us politely for our help. Then she smoothed a hand over her hair and pulled her white terry robe around her a bit more tightly. "Now, if you'll excuse me, I should check on Emma and get dressed."

"Of course," said Jane. We all moved toward the door.

In the hallway we agreed to go back to our rooms to change clothes and then to meet in Mr. Furlong's study to divvy up the call lists. I hurried to Emma's room and took a quick shower. Between my hangover, the smell of Luisa's cigarette smoke in my hair and the scene this morning, I felt more than a little grimy. I lingered a few extra minutes under the stream of water, lathering my hair with a liberal dose of Emma's favorite shampoo and rinsing with her favorite conditioner. I reluctantly shut off the water and wrapped myself in a towel, then searched my suitcase for something appropriate to wear.

I had packed for a wedding weekend, not for finding a groom's body, undoing the logistics for a wedding and being questioned by the police. Somehow, the strappy sundress I'd intended for the bridesmaids' lunch seemed a little inappropriate given the change of events, but I put it on since my only other alternatives were the shorts I'd been wearing, an ancient pair of Levi's 501s, or a seafoam-green bridesmaid's dress. I ran a comb through my wet hair and pulled it into a hasty knot. Then I slipped on some sandals and was almost out the door before I remembered the rumpled beds—if we were quarantined, it was unlikely that any of the household help would be allowed in to make beds or care for any other domestic details, and I knew enough about being a houseguest to realize that leaving the beds unmade would be a faux pas. I did a haphazard job of smoothing the duvets and plumping the pillows before heading toward Mr. Furlong's study, clean if not fortified.

I thought for sure that I'd be the last person to get there, but I beat Jane and Luisa. Only Hilary was in the room, her nose pressed against the glass of the bay window that overlooked the pool. Where Mrs. Furlong's sitting room was a perfect example of delicate femininity translated into décor—all light colors and smooth surfaces, serene watercolors and cozy sofas—Mr. Furlong's study was, in contrast, archetypically masculine, from the wood-paneled walls to the worn leather furniture. It even smelled of pipe smoke. An original Furlong dominated one wall, its bold sweeping strokes and use of color marking the painting as unquestionably his. It could easily have fetched a price in the high six figures if Mr. Furlong was willing to part with it. A much earlier work hung on an adjacent wall, an abstract so different in style that it could have been painted by a different hand. I wondered if Mr. Furlong hung them together to remind himself of the dramatic evolution of his work over the path of his career.

"What's going on, Hil?" I asked.

"You smell like Emma," she said absently.

"Her shampoo."

"Makes sense," she answered, distracted by the scene below. "Come here and check this out. It's just like the movies down there." From her tone, you would have guessed that Richard's death had been orchestrated purely for her viewing pleasure.

I crossed the room to join her by the window. The technicians were still at work, and Matthew and Sean stood near the pool house talking to the detectives. "Who's that guy?" Hilary asked.

"Which one?"

"The hot one, obviously. With the dark hair. Standing next to Matthew." I followed her finger with my gaze. The man she pointed out was the detective who seemed to be in charge. He wore a gray suit that looked like it had seen better days, and the way he wore it suggested that he didn't usually wear suits. He must have been well over six feet since he had a few inches on Matthew. He had close-cropped curly black hair and blue eyes that pierced even from this distance.

"I don't know, Hil. He's one of the detectives, but I don't know his name. You'll get to meet him—they want to interview all of us."

"Goody," she said, making no effort to hide how much she was looking forward to being interrogated by the police. Part of me was relieved.

"Goody what?" asked Luisa, who'd materialized at my side.

"Hilary's just figuring out which cop she wants to hit on," I explained.

"Charming," said Luisa dryly.

"Isn't it?" I responded.

"Shut up. You're both just jealous 'cause I've staked first dibs." I didn't point out that given Luisa's sexual orientation, she was unlikely to be jealous. "Where's Jane already?"

"Right here," said Jane, as she entered the room. She carried a tray with mugs and a carafe.

"Is that what I'm hoping it is?" asked Hilary.

"If you're hoping for coffee then it is indeed what you're hoping for."

"Caffeine," cried Hilary, and swooped down on the tray.

"You're a mind reader. Bless you, Jane," said Luisa, gratefully accepting a mug.

"Don't worry, Rach—I didn't forget about you." Jane handed me a can of Diet Coke.

"You're a goddess. Thank you." I preferred my caffeine cold and carbonated, particularly in the morning. I popped the can open and took a satisfying swig. "Breakfast of champions."

"That's disgusting," said Hilary. "How can you drink that stuff so early in the day?" I shrugged and took another gulp.

"What's going on down there?" asked Jane. She peered out the window.

"Standard crime scene stuff," I answered. "Matthew's the designated liaison."

"He must be psyched," said Hilary. She had a unique gift for happily blurting out things that were both obvious and unspeakable.

"Behave yourself," admonished Luisa.

I giggled. I couldn't help myself. Even in these circumstances, it was nice to have all of my closest friends in one place instead of spread across the globe, and I basked in the easy familiarity of the usual joking banter, however black the current comedy might be. None of us was having an easy time mustering up much remorse at having seen the last of Richard Mallory.

"Okay. We should get to work." Jane seated herself behind the desk and began sorting through the files Mrs. Furlong had given her. She held one out to Hilary. "These are the local inns and hotels where people are staying. Why don't you take care of calling them? They can alert the guests that the wedding's off. Do you have a cell phone in your room?"

Hilary nodded. "Of course I do. I'm a journalist for chrissakes," she answered impatiently. "We practically had to take an oath in journalism school not to go anywhere without a cell phone, tape recorder and notebook."

"Good. Why don't you use your phone to make these calls. I have all of the *tradespeople* in this folder, and I'll go call them from my cell phone." From her quiet smile, I knew that Jane was amused by the term Mrs. Furlong had used. As Emma had once put it, "My mother is such a snob she doesn't even realize she is one." Her view of the world did seem to have been frozen in place at some genteel point in time during the late 1950s.

"What about us?" I asked. "What should Luisa and I do?"

"There's a list of people who didn't come to the rehearsal dinner but are supposed to come to the wedding. Most of them probably are driving up today. I thought you could try to reach them all before they leave to get here. If you split up the list, you can use two lines and still leave one free for the police."

"What should we say?" I asked. "I can't imagine that the Furlongs want us to tell everyone that Richard turned up dead in their pool this morning."

"Why don't you just say there was an accident, and that everyone's fine but the wedding has been called off?"

"It seems a little disingenuous, but I guess that will work for now." It was a lot better than having to tell people that the bridegroom was dead.

"Consider it done," said Luisa.

"Good luck. Let's meet back here when we're finished." Jane handed Luisa a folder and picked up her own, balancing her coffee mug in her spare hand as she followed Hilary out the door.

Luisa turned to me. "Which part of the alphabet do you want?"

"Ugh," I said. "Neither, really." She shrugged and handed me the list of names beginning with *M* though *Z*. I leafed through it quickly. Somebody, probably Mrs. Furlong's personal assistant, had kept thorough records of the guests, noting who would only be attending the wedding and not the rehearsal dinner and thus not scheduled to arrive until the afternoon. "There's an extension up on the third floor. I'll head up there and you can use the phone in here."

"Okay." Luisa had already seated herself behind the desk in the big leather chair Jane had vacated and was lighting a cigarette as she studied her half of the list.

I left her to her calls and headed up to the den on the third floor, which could more appropriately be called the attic.

This was the only room in the house with a television, a medium that Emma's parents scorned. The TV itself looked like something from the midseventies, and the VCR that sat under it dated from shortly thereafter. The furnishings were comfortable and old, clearly discards from one of Mrs. Furlong's renovations of their New York apartment, and bookshelves filled with well-thumbed paperbacks and videotapes lined the walls.

I sank into a chair by the phone, which was indeed high-tech. It looked anachronistic in this setting. There was a button for each line, as well as an intercom system that allowed the user to call any other extension in the house. I picked up the receiver and pressed the one unlit button on the panel to get an outside line.

It was only a quarter past eight, so out of habit and guilt, the first call I placed was to check my voice mail at work. It was rare for me to go more than a couple of waking hours without checking messages; Winslow, Brown employees had elevated voice mail to an art form, and I frequently sent and received more than a hundred messages in any twenty-four-hour period. It was well understood that we were expected to check voice mail several times a day, even on weekends or when on vacation. The size of a banker's voice mailbox was directly correlated with his or her status in the Winslow, Brown hierarchy. Of course, judging by their behavior, most of the men in my department seemed to feel that it was more directly correlated to a certain part of the male anatomy. When I'd been promoted to vice president, the capacity of my box had been doubled, from forty-five minutes to ninety minutes, but I still needed more than all of my hands and feet to count the number of times it had been entirely filled with messages.

I punched in my extension number and password and awaited with mild dread the friendly automated voice that would tell me how many new messages I had. It had been at least twelve hours since the last time I'd checked in, which was more than enough time for all hell to break loose on any of the deals I had underway.

"You have sixteen new messages," the voice announced with jubilation. I winced and steeled myself to start going through them. Most were unimportant—department-wide announcements, the daily capital markets wrap-up and messages from my assistant about meetings that had to be rearranged the following week. Only one really concerned me, a message from Stan Winslow marked Urgent.

The knowledge that Stan had programmed his voice mail so that all of his messages were marked Urgent wasn't enough to stave off the feeling of impending doom. A call from Stan on a weekend was never good news. Stan headed up Mergers and Acquisitions. Whether this was due to his deal-making prowess or to his last name, which was indeed related to that on our firm letterhead, was not much in doubt. Stan was part of a dying breed of old-school investment bankers, a generation that had come of age when the profession was still very much controlled by men who had prepped together at various prestigious boarding schools, joined the same exclusive clubs and fraternities at their Ivy League colleges, and got by on their connections and skills on the golf course.

I felt the tension spread up my spine and into my shoulders. Stan had finally embraced diversity as a cause, probably at the urging of his third wife, who fancied herself a feminist, albeit of the sort who disdained activism as "unattractive." Stan was now making an aggressive attempt to establish himself as a mentor to the diverse elements in the department—namely, me—the only woman. I was sure he would have preferred that I were black, but my skin was so pale as to be nearly translucent, particularly during the long winter months when it took on a lovely bluish tinge. His idea of mentoring was to involve me in every deal that came over his transom.

I couldn't complain—success in our line of work was based almost entirely on the revenue we generated, which was based in turn on the number and size of deals we could bring in and close. Still, most Stan-originated projects derived from people of Stan's ilk—while other bankers carved out specialties in telecom or energy deals, I seemed to be building a franchise in serving the Old Boy Network.

His message was incoherent, at best. I guessed it had been sent after a martini-saturated conversation at the Knickerbocker Club. "Rachel, old gal—Stan here. Something interesting has come up. A friend of mine is mounting a takeover of some sort. He wants our help, and I told him you were just the man—er, harrumph, the gal, I mean, the person for him. I'll be out in East Hampton this weekend. Give me a call and I'll fill you in. We want to hit the ground running on this one." He slurred the number of his country house, and I jotted it down on the back of the guest list.

Great, I thought to myself. I already had more on my plate than I could handle, but saying no to Stan was not a possibility—not, at least, if I wanted to be elected partner one day, preferably sooner rather than later. I deleted the message and hung up the phone with a sigh.

I'd carried my soda up the stairs with me, and I took another large gulp. I wondered if it should worry me that so many of the duties I'd had to perform of late seemed to require either alcoholic or caffeinated fortification.

I checked my watch. It was twenty past eight. Reluctantly, I picked up the phone again and dialed Stan's number in East Hampton.

"Hello?" I recognized the voice on the other end as belonging to Wife Number Three, whose given name was Susan but was referred to by much of the department (at least outside of Stan's presence) as "Cupcake."

"Hi, Susan," I said. "It's Rachel Benjamin. I'm so sorry to bother you at home, but Stan asked me to call him ASAP. I hope it's not too early."

"Oh, hello, Rachel. He's been expecting your call. I'll get him for you." The spouses of investment bankers were quick to learn that their lives could and would be invaded at any time by work. Most, however, found it a small price to pay for the hefty year-end bonus checks and the lavish lifestyle the checks afforded. I heard Susan calling out Stan's name, her voice echoing in the cavernous rooms of their oversize beach house.

Stan picked up a moment later, his voice all collegial jo-viality. "Rachel—how goes it? You were off to a wedding this weekend, weren't you?" I was surprised he'd remembered, but knowing my weekend plans didn't seem to have deterred him from disturbing them.

"Yes," I replied, unwilling to go into the details. "I'm up in the Adirondacks. What's up?"

"I was having drinks last night with an old friend of mine, Smitty Hamilton. Great guy, Smitty. A real demon on the golf course—can sink a putt from fifty feet blindfolded. When we were over in Scotland playing Saint Andrews, why Smitty put us all to shame…." Stan's voice wandered off as he reminisced about golf games past. I waited, glad that he couldn't see my impatient expression over the phone.

He cleared his throat and collected his thoughts. "Well, Smitty runs Hamilton Tech, as you may know. And, there's an acquisition they want to do. Something techie—silicon chips or X-rays or amoebae or some such thing. I figured I'd let you handle the details. The target doesn't want to sell, but the company's so strapped for cash I don't think they'll have a choice. They're about to default on a bank loan they have outstanding. This should be a piece of cake."

"Great," I said, trying to sound enthusiastic. "Sounds exciting."

"Anyhow, we're meeting with Smitty first thing on Monday. I wanted to send you some of the materials he gave me so that you can get up to speed. I left them with Office Services in New York—if you call them with your fax number they'll make sure that you get everything." Winslow, Brown had round-the-clock staff that made copies, typed up documents and took care of faxes and other clerical details seven days a week.

"I'll call in and make sure I get everything," I said. The last thing I wanted to do was to start preparing for a new business meeting, but it looked like I wouldn't have much say in the matter.

"Sounds good. See you Monday."

"Right. Thanks, Stan."

"No problem, old gal. And Rachel—?"

"Yes?"

"Don't screw up."

CHAPTER 9

"Old gal, this, you drunken preppie," I muttered after I hung up the phone, favoring it with an obscene gesture.

I heard a good-natured laugh. "Something wrong?"

I shrieked for the second time that morning, bolting up from my chair and dropping my can of Diet Coke. Luckily, I'd drained it during my conversation with Stan. My heart was beating alarmingly fast, and I struggled to compose myself.

Somehow Peter had managed to enter the room unnoticed. I had no idea how long he'd been standing behind me, but there he was, barefoot in a T-shirt and pajama bottoms, his hair sweetly mussed from sleep. I noted with surprise that the events of the morning had managed to wipe any thoughts of him from my mind, even though seeing him now made me recall with a blush the vivid role he'd played in my dreams the previous night.

He looked abashed. "I'm sorry. I didn't mean to startle you."

I blushed even deeper. "No, I'm sorry. I didn't mean to spaz out. I'm just a bit jumpy." I knelt to retrieve the can.

Peter bent down at the same time, and our hands met as we both reached for it. His touch was warm, and he extended his free arm to help me up. I gripped it, noting with appreciation how nicely muscled it was. He placed the can on the table next to the phone, and I smoothed my dress down over my thighs. "Where—where did you come from?" I stammered.

"I'm staying in the guest room up here." He gestured to an open door on the opposite side of the den. I'd forgotten that there was yet another bedroom on this floor; in a house of this size it was easy to lose track. Through the door I could see a rumpled bed, barely visible in the thin light that managed to pass through the drawn curtains. "I completely overslept," he continued. "Still on California time, I guess."

"You must be a world-class sleeper," I observed. It hadn't exactly been quiet around here this morning, what with the assorted screaming and sirens.

"Like a rock. If only it were a marketable skill. I take a sleeping pill and use earplugs when I travel, which probably helped." He grinned, and my heart did a small flip. "So, what's going on that has you so riled up at a poor defenseless phone? Or is it just the abstract concept of drunken preppies that disturbs you?"

"Oh, no, um," I struggled for words. "It's just been sort of a difficult morning so far, and I'm a little grumpy."

"I wish I hadn't overslept. Have I messed up on any important prewedding responsibilities?"

I gulped. His question implied that he was entirely in the dark on the events of the past several hours. I had no desire to tell him about the death of his oldest friend, but it looked like I wasn't going to have much of a choice. "Um, well, actually. Oh, dear. Gee." I realized that I sounded like a complete idiot, but I had no idea as to how to proceed.

He moved closer and smiled engagingly. "Come on, you

can tell me. Have I totally neglected my best man duties? Was there something I was supposed to be doing? Distracting Richard? Picking up rings? Escorting early arrivals to their seats? Some other critical obligation?" His breath had a nice, minty toothpaste smell to it.

"Why don't you sit down," I suggested, sinking back into my chair. He remained on his feet, concern washing the smile from his face.

"What is it? What's wrong?"

"I don't really know how to tell you this," I began. "It's about Richard."

"Let me guess. Has he gotten cold feet?"

"To put it mildly," I answered, then cursed my reflexive flippancy. "Oh, bugs. That was the wrong thing to say. You see, it's just that there's been an accident."

The expression on his face downgraded to outright alarm. "What happened? Is he all right?"

"Well, no. In fact, he's dead."

"Dead?"

I nodded. He lowered himself slowly onto the sofa next to my chair.

"Dead?" he asked again.

"Yes." We were both silent for a few minutes. I noted that his face was even more handsome when he was stunned than when he was bemused. I heard my grandmother's voice in my ear wondering if he was Jewish. With a name like Forrest, it seemed unlikely, but perhaps that was an Ellis Island translation of something of which my grandmother would approve. I moved to sit next to him, wanting to put my hand on his shoulder but too chicken to do so.

"What happened?" he asked.

"Nobody's sure, yet. He, um, he was floating in the pool this morning. I found him there." The tableau I'd encountered earlier flashed before my eyes, and I stifled a shudder.

"The pool? He drowned? That's impossible. He's—he was—I mean, the guy's the strongest swimmer I know. Knew. He was an all-state champion in middle school."

"As I said, nobody's quite sure. The police are here checking into it."

"I can't believe it." He ran his hands through his hair. "We were hanging out, talking, just a few hours ago. I just can't believe it," he repeated. He jumped up and began pacing the room.

My curiosity, which had a tendency to rear at inappropriate moments, was piqued. I wondered if Peter had been the last person to see Richard alive. "What time did you go to bed?"

"What?" he asked, distractedly pausing in midpace.

"What time was it when you came in?"

"Hmm," he said, thinking. "I guess it was a little after three. Yes, in fact I know that's what time it was because I checked my watch when I came in. We'd stayed up for a while after Matthew and Sean turned in—Richard and I hadn't seen each other in so long, we had a lot of catching up to do."

"Did he go to bed also? When you left to come inside?"

"What?" He'd resumed his pacing, obviously trying to digest the news. His brown eyes had a faraway look.

"When you finished talking. Did he go to bed, too, when you did?"

"Uh, no. He said he had a rendezvous. I assumed with Emma. You know, one last prenuptial tryst of some sort." He hesitated, gathering his thoughts. "Yes, it was definitely with Emma. He didn't actually say so, he was being sort of coy about it, but I looked out the window before I drew the blinds and saw her out there with him."

We were both quiet, thinking. I, too, was a deep sleeper, but I was surprised that Emma had managed to sneak out of our room and back in without waking me. She'd been soundly asleep when I crept into bed a little past two. And the news that she'd been with Richard before he died made me more than a little bit anxious.

Peter crossed back and forth several more times before he finally spoke. "Has anybody told his mother?"

"Not yet," I said. "I don't even know if anybody knows how to get in touch with her." The words were barely out of my mouth when my gaze landed on the folder I'd brought up with me. *M* through *Z*. Just my luck. I opened it up, reluctantly, hoping against hope that I wouldn't find the information in there. The last thing I wanted was to tell Richard's mother, however awful she might be, that her only son was dead.

But sure enough, there was her contact information, exactly where it should be, at the head of the long list of last names beginning with *M*. Lydia Mallory Shannon di Malvisano, an address in Campo San Polo in Venice, and a phone number that began with the Italian country code.

"Well, there's one question answered. I guess I should call her." I stared at the carefully printed number and tried not to groan. This was hardly a task I would have volunteered to undertake.

"No, you shouldn't have to do that," Peter protested. "It's bad enough that you had to find him like that, you shouldn't have to be the one to tell his mother. At least she knows me, or did, at one point. I'll call her."

"I can do it. Really. It's okay." I tried my best to sound as if this were a task I could take in stride.

"No. Absolutely not. You've had enough trauma for one morning. Besides, it would probably be best if she hears it from someone familiar. And I know a little Italian, which might come in handy. Here." He reached out for the piece of paper with Lydia's information, and I relinquished it, unable not to appreciate the slight tingle I felt when his hand touched mine.

"Thank you." I made a mental note of how chivalrous it was of him to take on this burden.

"Sure," he said. "I have my cell phone in my room. I can make the call from there." He paused and looked at me. "Are you all right?" he asked. "It must have been quite a shock for you to find him like that."

I nodded, feeling guilty. I couldn't very well tell him that after shock my next emotion had been relief.

"Well, then," he said. "I'll go call her now." I watched him walk slowly across the room and back through the open door. He shut it gently behind him.

Seeing Peter so clearly distraught aroused my moribund sense of shame. We'd all been so casual and easy, divvying up tasks and joking about the detectives. It was harder to be so cavalier when I considered that Richard had actually meant something to someone. At least, he seemed to have meant something to Peter, his oldest friend. I heard the muffled sound of his voice from behind the closed door.

I wondered how Richard's mother would react. She was now married to her fourth husband, a minor Italian count with a decaying palazzo in Venice. Emma had told me in shocked confidence that she had declined to make the trip overseas for the wedding, sending instead a set of Italian ceramic dishes along with a short note wishing the couple well. Emma was stunned by this maternal disinterest. What sort of mother would skip the wedding of her only child? I wondered if she would skip his funeral, too.

With a sigh, I returned to my folder and tried to concentrate on the remaining list of names rather than how absurdly appealing Peter was, even in these unfortunate circumstances. There were careful notes indicating which guest would be arriving when. It was easy to figure out who might still not have arrived in town. All in all, there were only a dozen people whom I needed to try to track down, mostly with phone numbers in New York and Connecticut, but between checking voice mail, talking to Stan, and then talking to Peter, I was behind schedule. I would have to hurry if I was going to reach any of them.

I picked up the phone, ready to dial the first number. Mistakenly, however, I'd selected a line already in use. I opened my mouth to apologize to whomever was speaking, but shut it immediately when I realized that I didn't recognize the voice.

"—the scene around here. Maybe this is just how rich folks behave, but there's not a lot of wailing or chest beating or hair tearing going on. These people seem to be more pissed off about the inconvenience than anything else. Doesn't seem like anybody's going to miss this guy too much." The man speaking had a deep, resonant voice that was colored by a faint Boston accent, more Kennedy-esque than Dorchester. I guessed that it was the detective Hilary had her eye on.

"Interesting. Now, you're sure it wasn't an accident? If we bother these people without a good reason they'll probably have their lawyers all over us in no time."

"Well, we won't know anything for sure until the medical examiner has his say, but I would be pretty surprised if that were the case. The paramedics said that all of the physical signs indicate an overdose, rather than a drowning. There're no external injuries of any sort, so it doesn't look like he bumped his head and fell in or anything. My guess is that he was poisoned and then somebody shoved him in the pool to make it look like an accidental drowning."

"Someone who knows next to nothing about forensics," pointed out the other voice. "How else could he expect to pass it off as a drowning?"

"Maybe rich people don't watch any crime shows or read

police procedurals," said the detective dryly. "Anyhow, the medical examiner's on his way and promised to have his initial findings by tomorrow morning. The nice thing about working up here is that there's not a lot of competition for resources—this body definitely takes precedence over a couple of senior citizens dying in their beds. We can rush through a lot of the lab work. And we should be able to get a subpoena for phone records and anything else we need pretty quickly. The judge will be ecstatic to have something to do."

"And you think it has to be someone at the house?"

"Absolutely. This place is like Fort Knox. The security's out of control. You practically have to pass a retinal scan to get through the front gate."

I replaced the receiver as quietly as I could. So Matthew had been right. Richard had been dead before he hit the water. And the police thought somebody here had killed him. The plot was thickening, and I was growing increasingly nervous that someone I cared about would be trapped in its sludge.

The sound of the shower running from the bathroom adjacent to Peter's bedroom shook me out of my reverie, and I dutifully punched an unlit button on the phone to get a line that wasn't being used, newly eager to get my phone calls out of the way so I could get back downstairs and find out what was really going on before the situation spun further out of control.

Mostly I only reached people's answering machines, and I left polite but generic messages explaining that the wedding had been canceled and apologizing for the late notice. I did speak to a couple of people directly, and I hurriedly explained that there'd been an accident and that I couldn't provide further information at this point, except that the wedding would not take place.

Glad to have that out of the way, I picked up my empty soda can and the folder. I could still hear the sound of the water running through the closed door to Peter's room. Clearly, he, too, had felt the need for a long, hot shower after absorbing the news. If I were Hilary, I probably would have offered to help him scrub his back.

Instead, I went back downstairs. I ran into Matthew talking to Mrs. Furlong on the second-floor landing.

"How's Emma?" he was asking her.

"She's asleep, poor dear. We gave her a pretty hefty sedative. It's probably the best thing for her, right now."

"What exactly did you give her?" he asked in his professional voice. "Not to lecture or anything, but you really shouldn't be administering medication that wasn't prescribed. I've got my medical bag with me. If she'd needed anything, I could have given it to her."

"Oh, Mattie," Mrs. Furlong said, brushing away his concern with a smile. "It's always hard to believe that you're all grown-up, let alone that you've graduated medical school. But you have nothing to worry about. We were very careful. There were some painkillers left over from what Jacob was prescribed after the knee surgery he had last year. I only gave her half of one, and it knocked her right out."

"I should probably go look in on her," said Matthew.

"Oh, let her sleep for a little while, darling," she urged him, placing a restraining hand on his arm. "Don't disturb her yet. It's going to be such a terrible day for her once she does wake up. There's no need to rush it." They both turned when they heard me approach.

"How are you doing, Rachel?" Mrs. Furlong asked. "Have you managed to make all of your calls?"

I nodded. "I was just going to check in with everyone else to see if I could help them finish. I'm sorry to ask you this, but would it be all right if my office faxed some papers to Mr. Furlong's fax machine?"

She made a sympathetic noise. "Do those people never let you rest? Please feel free to have them send whatever they need. The fax machine is in Jacob's study."

"Thanks," I said.

"Now, Matthew, the police will probably want to talk to Jacob and me first. He's in his studio?" Her voice didn't betray that she'd referred to her husband as a bastard barely an hour before.

Matthew shifted uncomfortably. "Um, I think so."

"Well, he'll have to come up to the house. Will you call him?"

"Sure," he agreed. He gave me a reassuring look as I passed and then followed Mrs. Furlong down the stairs to the first floor.

I found Mr. Furlong's study empty except for Luisa, who was on the phone having a conversation with a wedding guest that sounded as awkward as the conversations I'd just concluded with the few people I'd reached in person.

She glanced up when I came in, and her harried look told me that she was enjoying the task even less than I had, although she seemed to be handling it with infinitely more grace. She wasn't rushing people hurriedly off the phone. "—an accident," she was saying. "Yes, I'm afraid that's all I can say at this point. Yes, Emma's fine, everyone's fine. I'm sure they'll be in touch with you soon. I'll give them your regards, of course."

Whoever was on the other end continued to talk, and Luisa was too polite to do anything but make courteous replies. Remembering my conversation with Stan, I turned my attention to the fax machine that sat on a small table in the corner. Its digital screen displayed its direct number, which

I hastily scribbled on a piece of paper. Then I picked up the receiver attached to the machine and called Office Services at Winslow, Brown.

Office Services—or OS, as it was commonly referred to—occupied a full floor of Winslow, Brown's Wall Street building and housed all the equipment and personnel that enable an investment bank to crank out documents twenty-four hours a day, seven days a week. I often thought that if God were an environmentalist, all investment bankers were doomed to hell. I'd already gone through forests worth of paper in my relatively short career.

A corps of aspiring artists, musicians, actors and writers manned the fleet of copiers and word processors that comprised the OS infrastructure. These creative souls were by far the most interesting group you'd find anywhere within the walls of the firm. Winslow, Brown offered them decent pay, flexible hours, and superb benefits, allowing them to pay their rent and put food on the table while they struggled to make it big.

Cora, the weekend supervisor, answered the phone, and I greeted her warmly. She had played the role of savior several times during my banking career, managing to turn battered piles of handwritten papers into sleek, colorful, neatly bound presentations in record time. She was a middle-aged, nondescript woman who had published several mysteries set in medieval Germany. I'd read a couple of them and been impressed. Alas, the market for her work was small, and Cora needed Winslow, Brown to make ends meet.

Cora and I spoke for several minutes—the way I saw it, nothing but good could come out of being friendly with the OS staff. And Cora knew all about my relationships in the publishing world and was always eager to learn useful news or gossip. Eventually I brought the conversation around to Stan. She had the papers he had sent for me and promised to fax them through shortly. We commiserated a bit about our fearless leader (apparently, the original documents she'd received bore evidence of being used as a coaster), and she urged me to call if I needed anything else.

I thanked her and hung up the phone just as Luisa finished her conversation. The expression on her face was pure exasperation.

"That was a talkative one," I commented.

"If you only knew. I thought she'd never shut up. Fortunately, she was the last on my list. This is beginning to qualify as one of the worst mornings I've ever had." She reached for the carafe of coffee and topped off her mug.

"If it makes you feel any better, I just got to tell Peter what happened. He's one of the few people here who seemed genuinely upset by the news. But he still volunteered to call Richard's mother, thankfully. I think that would have put me right over the edge."

"Gracious. How did he manage to sleep through all the noise before?"

"Earplugs and a sleeping pill," I explained.

She raised an eyebrow. "Impressive. It was quite a commotion."

"I guess he travels frequently. I know lots of people who use earplugs when they travel."

"And is Peter as handsome when he's upset as he was last night?" She had a mischievous glint in her eye.

"Of course. Not that I noticed." We both laughed. I settled into one of the big leather club chairs opposite the desk, and Luisa lit a cigarette.

"Well, perhaps this isn't the most auspicious weekend for romance, but surely it will be a good test of his mettle," she observed.

"And mettle is so attractive," I agreed.

She smiled, and we fell into a companionable silence. I

watched as the smoke from her cigarette spiraled lazily upwards, pierced by shafts of light streaming in through the windows. She was her usual elegant self, dressed in a black linen sheath and black sandals. I only had to look at linen before it started to crumple, but the material looked crisp and cool on her. A bright streak of prematurely white hair ran from one temple back to the knot at her nape. It would have aged anyone else, but on Luisa it just added to her allure.

Without thinking, I asked the question I'd wanted to ask for years.

"What really happened that night?"

She sighed. Somebody else would probably have pretended not to know what I was talking about, would have feigned incomprehension. But Luisa understood immediately.

"He raped me," she said. "But you must have figured that out." She inhaled deeply on her cigarette.

CHAPTER 10

Images from the night in question flashed before my eyes. It was freshman year, and we were at a Valentine's Day party, an annual event hosted by the Hasty Pudding Club. Its theme was Leather and Lace—partygoers were supposed to dress in one or the other—and it had a reputation as an unusually wild event, with hundreds of the Type A overachievers who made up much of the Harvard student body drinking to excess and shedding their inhibitions both on one night.

I'd had my eye on a sophomore from my English survey course, attracted by his brooding good looks and the exquisite doodles he drew in the margins of his *Norton Anthology of English Literature* (I sat behind him in class whenever I could). I ran into him early in the evening, he asked me to dance above the thrashing chords of the latest New Order single, and one dance melted seamlessly into another. From the limited conversation we could have over the heart-throbbing pulse of the music, I was thrilled to learn that he seemed to have all of the various neuroses that I found appealing.

We stopped for a drink between dances, and I was waiting patiently for him to return from the bar when I caught sight of Luisa across the room, standing by the window and smoking a cigarette. Richard sidled up to her and handed her a drink, which she accepted. I saw them again a few minutes later, still by the window, deep in conversation. I didn't think much of it at the time.

Luisa didn't tell anyone but her closest friends that she was gay until well after college, and during her years at Harvard she was pursued by scores of men. While Harvard had its fair share of beauties and heiresses and even some beautiful heiresses, Luisa had an air of mystery and sensuality that distinguished her from the hordes of field hockey players and lockjawed debutantes. Luisa's family, the Caselanzas, practically owned a small Latin American country, and Luisa had the sort of self-assurance that only comes with great wealth and beauty. While most freshman girls rushed about Harvard Yard in jeans and turtleneck sweaters, Luisa's wardrobe was a study in understated sophistication. Her sweaters were of the finest cashmere or silk and her trousers and slim skirts fit her subtle curves in a way that only expert tailors could achieve. Her long black hair was invariably pulled back into a plain knot or ponytail, except for the occasional formal event when she allowed it to cascade magnificently down her back. Her eyes were large and dark in a fine-boned face, and her lips were full.

Luisa had been the first of my friends to meet Richard, which wasn't surprising. She lived with Jane freshman year, across the hall from Emma and me and upstairs from Hilary in Strauss Hall. We were all a bit scared of her at first, although she quickly won us over with her sly sense of humor. Still, we couldn't help but be in awe of the men who lined up at her door. Her suitors included the president of the Porcellian (the oldest, most exclusive, and most secretive of the finals clubs), the president of the Lampoon (widely rumored to be homosexual but apparently willing to make an exception in Luisa's case), the most eligible Kennedy cousin in Boston, and the son of an exiled Middle Eastern potentate. Luisa allowed each of them to take her to dinner precisely once before politely rejecting further invitations. In all but the most unusual cases, the rejections seemed to make her suitors more determined, judging by the flowers that arrived daily.

One of Luisa's most aggressive pursuers was Richard. On a crisp fall day, I came upon the two of them standing in front of our entryway when I returned from class. Next to Luisa, I always felt scrawny and gauche and as worldly as a four-year-old. Luisa greeted me and introduced me to Richard, and I stopped to talk to them both. She seemed relieved that I'd shown up, whereas Richard was visibly annoyed at the interruption. After a few minutes of awkward three-way conversation I excused myself. Luisa made her excuses as well.

"So, I'll see you on Wednesday? In class?" Richard asked Luisa.

"Hmm," replied Luisa noncommittally, allowing the door to swing shut behind us. "Creepy," she muttered as we climbed up the three flights to our rooms on the fourth floor.

"Him?"

"Yes. Very creepy."

"I thought he seemed nice. Cute." At seventeen, my skills of perception were all but nonexistent. Not that they were so finely tuned at thirty.

Luisa paused on the landing between the second and third floors and turned to face me. Her brow furrowed as she chose her words. "There's something sort of off about him. He seems great, you know, good-looking and friendly and all that, but there's something there that bothers me. I don't know what it is—I can't put my finger on it. He followed me out of class and started talking to me and then he ended up walking me back here. I got this sense that he's been watching me for a while."

"Of course he has, Luisa. Every man on campus has been watching you," I said as we continued our trudge up the stairs.

"That's not what I mean, Rachel. I can't explain it. It's what—about a five-minute walk, not even, from Sever Hall to here—and he must have mentioned three or four things that nobody could know about me unless he'd been...observing me. Stupid things—he knows I'm left-handed—but it's like he's keeping a file on me somewhere. And he seemed to know automatically that I lived in Strauss." She gave an involuntary shudder.

I don't remember how I responded. I probably said something reassuring—but I also thought to myself that I wished I had Luisa's problems—exciting upperclassmen didn't seem to be noticing me at all.

Luisa never did accept any of Richard's invitations for a date, and she maintained a polite but chilly distance from him when she saw him. But we began running into him a lot, mostly because Sean began inviting us to parties at his and Richard's club. We had many a debate as to whether or not we should grace this club or any other with our presence in light of their unabashed refusal to consider women as members and their general odor of snobbery. But, as Hilary frequently pointed out, a free drink was a free drink, and besides, how better to dismantle the establishment than from within? We felt conflicted but we went when Sean invited us, and we usually enjoyed ourselves.

The odds of running into Richard during one of these evenings out were high. Especially since Richard was all but stalking Luisa, to her disgust. He appeared around every corner—whether at the library or in class or running errands in Harvard Square—at least that's how it seemed to Luisa, who confessed her annoyance and vague fear to me in a rare moment of intimacy. To say rare was not an exaggeration—Luisa was the most self-contained person I'd ever known. Maybe part of the reason the men flocked to her door was the lure of unplumbed depths in her eyes.

It was thus curious to see Richard and Luisa talking together that night at the Pudding, but I was too busy pursuing my own romantic objectives to pay much attention. At some point, they must have left, because I didn't see them again that evening.

My new friend and I were at the party until 2:00 a.m., and then we went on to a late-night gathering in Adams House. We ended up at the Tasty in the wee hours of the morning. The Tasty was a small and downtrodden diner, a Harvard Square landmark that has recently been converted to a Gap or Starbucks or a similar outlet of a generic chain. He ate a hot dog and I sipped hot chocolate as the sky began to lighten. Exhausted, and with the unfortunate knowledge that I had a paper to complete the next day, I eventually let him escort me across Mass. Ave. back to Strauss before giving him a chaste kiss at the door and sending him on his way. I was searching my coat pockets for my keys when Luisa came barreling out of the entryway.

"Oh!" she cried. We were both startled.

"Luisa? Where are you going?" She was wearing a long dark coat and had a leather satchel slung over her shoulder

"To see my sister," she said, visibly flustered. Luisa's sister was several years older than us and lived in New York with her husband, a banker who headed up the Caselanzas' New York operations.

"At five in the morning?"

"There's a train that leaves South Station at five forty-five."

"But—when did you decide to go?" I studied her in the murky light. Her face looked gray, and there were dark circles under her eyes, which were bloodshot. She looked as if she'd been crying, I realized, shocked. I'd never seen Luisa cry. "Luisa—what's wrong? Are you all right?" I reached out to touch her elbow.

"I'm fine," she told me, but her voice caught on her words.

"No, you're not. What happened?"

"Nothing. Nothing at all. I've got to go, or I'll miss my train. I'll call from New York." With that she hurried out of the small quadrangle bordered by Strauss, Matthews, and Mass. Hall, her long dark hair streaming out behind her.

She did call later that day, with a story about her sister being upset and wanting Luisa to come down and help to take care of her niece and nephew for a few days. I didn't believe her— if her sister had asked her to come she would have told me when I ran into her. Not to mention the fact that her sister had a veritable army of nannies and governesses to tend to her children. My suspicions were heightened when Jane mentioned that she and Sean had walked back to Eliot House with Richard and Luisa after leaving the Pudding and that the two of them seemed to be getting along surprisingly well. The couples parted at the entryway, with Richard saying that he and Luisa were going to stop by another party. Jane admitted somewhat sheepishly that her memories were a bit hazy, having had more than enough to drink.

I sat in the library that afternoon trying to work on my paper, but conflicting images of Luisa and Richard standing by the window at the Pudding and of Luisa flying out the door of Strauss in the predawn light kept running through my head. I tried to replace these images with thoughts of my own encounter with the brooding sophomore, or, at the very least, with some insights into the role played by colonial economics in the Salem Witch Trials, but I kept coming back to Luisa.

She returned midweek, cheerful and composed. I tried again to ask what had happened, but she made it clear that she had no desire to discuss the events of that evening. The only change I noticed was that she carefully avoided situations where Richard might be present—begging off Sean's parties and studying in her room rather than the library.

Whatever happened, Richard, for his part, seemed magically to disappear afterward. I would see him every so often, across a crowded lecture hall or a smoke-filled party. I heard that he'd gone to work at a talent agency in Los Angeles after he graduated. I'd almost forgotten about him when he suddenly rematerialized at my twenty-ninth birthday party, his arm confidently slipped through Emma's.

"I think he put something in my drink," Luisa continued.

"Why did you never say anything?"

She shrugged in a way that only Europeans and Latinos can pull off. "What difference would it have made? It happened, it was done with. There was no erasing it. And I didn't want everyone probing into my business. That would have been truly unbearable."

I felt chilled to the bone, despite the summer sun that lit the room.

"Come on, Rachel, don't look so stunned."

"I'm not," I blurted. "Well, I guess I am. It's just that—given what's happened…it wouldn't look good. Does anybody else know? Does anybody else know what he did?"

"No. How could they? I never told anyone, and I can't imagine that he did. Of course, when Emma and he became engaged, I thought about trying to tell her, but she seemed so set on her course. I ultimately decided that it would be a waste of time, at best." She stubbed out one cigarette and lit another.

"Luisa," I pressed on. She didn't seem to understand the

gravity of the situation. "You can't tell anyone else. Please don't tell anyone else. It really wouldn't look good," I repeated.

"Why, because it gives me a reason to hate Richard's guts and explains why I would rather have seen him dead than married to Emma?"

"There's that," I said, laughing despite myself, although even I could hear the slightly hysterical edge to my laughter. I told her what I'd overheard on the phone—the detective's belief that Richard had been poisoned in some way and then shoved in the pool in an attempt to cover up the murder.

She sipped her coffee, absorbing the information. "Well, nobody will be shocked by that. Of course he was murdered."

"But if the police think so, too—they have no choice but to figure out who did it." What I didn't say but left unspoken was that I couldn't see any benefit in handing them Luisa's motive.

"Well, I have no desire to tell them. Whoever did kill him certainly has my blessings. That said, I don't see any reason to point the finger at myself." She paused and then added in a thoughtful tone, "Wouldn't it be a sort of poetic justice, though, if they found out that somebody had put something in his drink?" She smiled and lit yet another cigarette, forgetting about the one she already had burning in the ashtray. This uncharacteristic absentmindedness was the only indication she gave that she was even the least bit disconcerted.

I didn't reply. I was contemplating poetic justice and the many different forms it could take.

"Buck up, darling," she said to me, narrowing her eyes through the smoke. "It looks like we're in for quite an interesting weekend."

CHAPTER 11

Interesting was one way to describe how the weekend was shaping up. A number of other adjectives came to mind, but I was momentarily speechless.

Luisa was silent, too. She turned in her chair and stared out the window. Then, after a few minutes she shrugged again and turned back to me, as if she'd made up her mind about something.

"Listen, Rachel," she said. "While we're in true confessions mode, there's something else you should know—"

But Matthew's shaggy brown head appeared around the door before she could tell me. "Hey, there. What are you two doing?"

"Just hanging out," I answered, in as casual a tone as I could manage. Internally I was still reeling. "We finished all of the phone calls the Furlongs wanted us to make. What about you?"

"Well, I settled the detectives in the library, and then, after they talked to Lily and Jacob, I had my first official police interrogation ever." He leaned against the door frame and put his hands in his pockets.

"And was it everything you could hope for?" I asked.

"Not at all. In fact, it was sort of disappointing. No bright lights shining in my eyes or threats of brutality. They didn't even read me my rights." He, too, was doing his best to sound lighthearted.

"How exciting for you, nonetheless," said Luisa. "But surely this can't be your first police interrogation? You've never had to face down a malpractice suit or anything?" She gave him a teasing glance. She seemed to be recovering from our conversation far more quickly than I.

"No, thank you, I haven't. The nice thing about working with the poor is that they tend not to be litigious. But I assure you, if I ever do find myself in such a situation, I will call on the finest Harvard-trained lawyer I know. Would you be willing to do the honors? Pro bono, of course."

"Of course," Luisa agreed amiably.

"Speaking of doing the honors, are either of you willing to volunteer for a police interview? They asked me to bring down the next person I found."

"Ugh," I said.

"Good Lord," said Luisa. "Could you pretend you haven't seen us?"

"Don't everyone volunteer at once," said Matthew. Luisa and I looked at each other.

"Rock, Paper, Scissors?" I suggested.

"I don't think so," she replied.

"It was worth a shot."

"Indeed."

"Seriously, I need to send someone down there," interjected Matthew. "They want to talk to each of us, sooner or later."

"I think I'll choose later," said Luisa.

I threw up my hands. "I'll go. I might as well get it out of the way." Luisa didn't protest. I pulled myself to my feet, telling myself that it would be best to get the interview over with but still daunted by the actual process. Not to mention that my mind was a hotbed of confusion, what with all the various puzzle pieces I kept unearthing, none of which seemed to fit together in a logical way.

"The library?" I asked.

"The library," Matthew confirmed.

"Okay. If I'm not back in an hour, call my lawyer. Oh, bugs. I don't have one."

"Sure you do," said Luisa. "Although, I know how ridiculously well-compensated you banker-types are, so I wouldn't count on the pro bono treatment."

"Good to know," I answered. I left them in the study and walked slowly down the stairs to the ground floor, taking my time while I tried to take stock of the various things I knew and sort of wished I didn't: Emma arguing with her father and then sneaking out to meet Richard in the middle of the night, Luisa admitting that Richard had raped her, Hilary dredging up long-ago pacts, Matthew silently harboring his love for Emma. My hands were trembling, I realized, and that had nothing to do with either my hangover or caffeine. I paused in the foyer to take a few deep breaths and to smooth my hair in the mirror that hung on the wall across from the library. Satisfied that I at least appeared composed, even if I felt like a quivering mess, I squared my shoulders and turned toward the closed door. I lingered for a moment to see if I could hear anything, but the heavy wood was far too thick to let words escape. Finally I screwed up my courage and knocked, my knuckles sounding a dull thud on the sturdy surface.

"Come in," a voice answered. I felt as if a strange, leaden weight had taken up residence deep in my gut as I pushed the door open. The library was paneled in dark walnut, much like Mr. Furlong's study. Shelves along two walls held rows of books that looked as if they'd actually been read at some point, and an aged Oriental rug stretched across the polished floorboards. The handsome detective was standing by the stone fireplace, flanked by a colleague who appeared to have only recently graduated from high school. They both turned toward me as I entered.

"I'm Detective O'Donnell," said the handsome one. Hilary had been right—he was hot. And I recognized his voice immediately from the phone conversation I'd listened in on. I pegged his age at mid to late thirties, a few years older than us, but not so much older that it would present a problem. He was a dead ringer for a young Pierce Brosnan, but with a crooked nose that looked as if it had been broken more than once and lent him a dangerous air. He towered over me, but Hilary stood five feet and eleven inches in bare feet, so I doubted that his height would pose any obstacle for her. I shook his hand and reminded myself that it was important to concentrate on matters beyond matchmaking.

"Rachel Benjamin," I introduced myself.

"And I'm Officer Paterson," said the other man. Actually, boy would be a more accurate description. His voice was squeaky, and he was nearly a head shorter than O'Donnell, with wiry red hair, freckles and a prominent Adam's apple. I shook his hand as well.

"Why don't you have a seat, Ms. Benjamin," said O'Donnell.

"Thank you." I gingerly perched on the edge of a sofa. Thus far, this felt more like a tea party than a murder investigation. I half expected one of them to offer me some cucumber sandwiches or a scone with clotted cream. Unbidden, my stomach emitted an audible rumble which neither of them acknowledged.

Instead, they took two chairs facing me across a coffee table. Behind them, an old grandfather clock wheezed into action, letting us know that it was now 10:00 a.m. We looked awkwardly at one another, waiting for the peals to subside. Time was inching along slowly today.

"Ms. Benjamin, do you have any objections to this conversation being recorded?" asked Paterson. He gestured toward a small tape recorder on the coffee table.

"That's fine. And please, call me Rachel." I smiled at him, and a deep scarlet flush spread from his collar up to his face. I felt a stab of pity; if I was having this effect on him, he'd have a meltdown when it was time to interview Hilary. I almost felt as if I should warn him.

Paterson pressed the Record button. "Testing, testing, one two three…" he said. Once he was confident that the machine was working, he stated today's date and our names. I had the sense that he'd read every single Hardy Boys book and had perhaps taken them a bit too seriously. O'Donnell cast a dubious look in his direction and cleared his throat. He took out a small notebook and flipped it open.

"Ms. Benjamin," began O'Donnell. "The purpose of this interview is to get your description of the chain of events of the last twenty-four hours, in an attempt to gather further information about the death of Richard Mallory. Could you please state your name, address, age and occupation for the record?"

"Sure. I'm Rachel Benjamin. My address is 179 East Seventy-Ninth Street, New York, New York. I'm thirty years old, and I'm a vice president in Investment Banking at Winslow, Brown in Manhattan." Paterson looked impressed. I wondered if I should explain to him that Winslow, Brown alone had several hundred vice presidents, and that there were enough on Wall Street to fill Madison Square Garden, should they ever allow themselves to be pulled away from their downtown deal making to be carted en masse up to midtown. And that didn't even take into account the hundreds who had been laid off in the economic downturn.

"And what was your relation to the deceased?" asked O'Donnell.

"Well, I didn't have one, really. I'm a friend of Emma's. We were roommates in college. I was supposed to be her maid of honor today."

"And could you tell us how long you knew the deceased?" It was creepy to hear Richard referred to in such a cold, technical way.

"I first met Richard in college—about a dozen years ago. He was a senior when we were freshman. I didn't know him well, and I believe he worked out in California after graduation. I think he moved back to New York a few years ago, but I didn't see him again until he and Emma started dating. Which was about eighteen months ago." My answers sounded rehearsed to my own ears, and I hoped that they didn't sound the same way to O'Donnell and Paterson.

"And did you spend a lot of time with him during that period?"

"No, not really. I mean, I work pretty long hours, and I think he does—did—too. Mostly just the occasional party or dinner."

"I see." Saw what, I wondered? That I avoided Richard like the plague and went out of my way to see Emma only when Richard wasn't around? "Could you tell us about the last twenty-four hours or so? When you arrived here, what you did, etcetera?"

"Sure. I drove up from New York yesterday afternoon with Luisa and Hilary. Luisa Caselanza and Hilary Banks. They're also friends of Emma's—we were roommates in college, along with Jane Hallard, who's here as well. The four of us were all supposed to be bridesmaids today. Anyhow, we got to the house around four-thirty. We hoped to arrive earlier, but we hit some weekend traffic and then got a bit lost." I didn't add that nobody in the car was capable of reading a map; that's the sort of thing people never let you forget if you happen also to have a Harvard degree.

"The roads up here can be confusing. Especially if you've never been here. Have you? Been here before?" The way he slipped this in made me think it was more than an idle question.

"Yes, several times, in fact, over the years. But usually I came with Emma or her parents—people who knew the way."

O'Donnell jotted something down in his notebook while I continued my narrative. "Anyhow, right when we arrived we had to start the rehearsal for the wedding, out by the lake. After that, we all rushed to change for the rehearsal dinner, which was at a country club in the next town over. We were there until a little before midnight, and then we came back to the house. Emma was already in bed, but a few of us—Jane and Hilary and Luisa and me—went out to the dock for a nightcap. We stayed there talking for a while, and then came in to go to sleep. That was probably around two or so."

"So, you went to sleep around two. And did you see the deceased before then? Here at the house?"

"No," I said, glad I could answer honestly. "I guess the last time I saw him alive was at the club. He and the other guys were out talking by the pool when we came in. We could hear them, but we didn't actually go out that way, so we didn't see anything."

"Did you hear them when you came back inside?"

I thought for a second. "No, I don't think so. At least, I don't remember hearing anything. We came in the side door, by the kitchen." We'd put the glasses in the dishwasher and the empty champagne bottle in the recycling bin. I wondered if I should tell them what Peter had told me, about being up with Richard until three, and then I decided that that was not my responsibility. And I certainly wasn't going to tell them about Richard's rendezvous with Emma.

"Which room were you staying in last night?"

"Emma's room. It has twin beds. And Emma was already asleep when I came up." I hoped I sounded natural when I tacked on that last part.

"So, you went to sleep at two, and Ms. Furlong was asleep when you came in. Then what happened?"

"Well, I woke up early. A little after six." I told them about going down to the kitchen and out on the porch, and then about finding Richard's body. It felt like a decade had passed since then, not a few hours. "The rest you know, I guess." I concluded my account, hoping I was done.

My hopes were unfounded. O'Donnell had more questions.

"What did you think of Mr. Mallory?" he asked.

"What did I think of him?" The question seemed unprofessional, at best.

"Yes. Did you like him? Were you glad that he was marrying your friend?"

I hesitated, briefly debating how best to address this, weighing the different odds. It was bad enough that I'd already let Emma down, betrayed my long-ago promise to her by letting her get into this mess with Richard. To question her judgment in front of a stranger seemed like a further betrayal. Ultimately, however, I decided to go with the honesty-being-the-best-policy approach. It couldn't hurt to let O'Donnell know that lots of people harbored neither warm and fuzzy thoughts toward Richard nor any eagerness to see Emma married to him. Nor did I want O'Donnell to work up too much sympathy on behalf of the deceased. "Well, no. I wasn't particularly fond of him. Not many people were, to be blunt."

O'Donnell looked at me, his expression inscrutable. "Why not?"

"I can't speak for everybody, of course." I wondered how far I should go. "Let's just say that he wasn't the most scrupulous of men. I had some exposure to him professionally, and I found his conduct to be—" I searched for the right word "—unethical."

"Unethical," repeated O'Donnell. "What do you mean by that?"

I briefly explained how he'd screwed up my deal the previous year. "And I doubt that I'm the only person who had a similar experience with him," I concluded.

"But Emma—Ms. Furlong loved him?" O'Donnell looked at me, quizzical.

"Apparently. They were getting married, after all."

"I see." I didn't see how he could if none of Emma's closest friends could understand their engagement. He said nothing after this, perhaps thinking that his silence would encourage me to say more. I, however, had said all I was going to say voluntarily on this topic. I shifted in my seat, uncrossing and recrossing my legs.

After a few, long moments, O'Donnell stood. "Well, that will be all for now. Thank you for your time."

"That's it?" I asked. I don't know what else I expected, but this seemed like an abrupt ending. I was oddly disappointed but relieved at the same time.

"That's it. Unless, of course, there's anything else you'd like to tell us?" Something in his querying tone made me feel absurdly guilty.

I shook my head and rose to my feet. "No. Nothing that I can think of."

"Then we're done," he said. "Although, we've asked that all of the guests stay until we give them further notice. I assume that won't be a problem?"

"No. That's fine. I was planning on spending the weekend here for the wedding."

I was tempted to ask them what they believed had happened, but then I thought better of it. The last thing I wanted to do was to give them the impression that I had reason to think that what had happened wasn't an accident or that I'd listened in on O'Donnell's phone call. But then I worried that if I didn't ask they would wonder why I wasn't curious. So I asked.

"Do you have any sense at all of what happened to him? To Richard, I mean?" I tried to make it sound like a casual question, tossing it out as I headed for the door.

"What do you mean, what happened?"

"How he died. Do you know how he died?"

"How he died?" replied O'Donnell. Somebody needed to tell him that answering one perfectly clear question with another was an exasperating habit.

"Yes, how he died."

"I'm afraid it's difficult to say, exactly, at this point. Nothing will be clear until the medical examiner has finished his work." I shuddered. Medical examiner meant autopsy, at least according to all the mystery novels I'd purchased in airports, and I had a sudden vision of Richard being cut open. I'd never had much of a tolerance for blood and guts, and the mental image before me was horrifying.

"Ms. Benjamin? Are you all right?" Paterson was at my side.

"Oh. I'm sorry. I just got distracted for a second. I'm fine." I tried to sweep the image of Richard's innards out of my head.

"However," continued O'Donnell, "it does appear that Mr. Mallory did not die from drowning, which complicates the matter considerably. Particularly given the tight security system here."

"Oh," I said lamely.

"Would you mind bringing in someone else for us to talk to?"

"Sure. Anyone particular you had in mind?"

"No. Whomever you find first will do. The only people besides you we've already spoken to are Mr. and Mrs. Furlong and Dr. Weir." O'Donnell's tone was dismissive, and he was flipping through his notebook.

I promised them I'd send in someone else and left the room, closing the door securely behind me. My heart was beating fast, and my palms were sweating. I was surprised at my reaction. After all, I'd faced down far worse before.

CHAPTER 12

I slowly made my way back up the stairs, replaying the interview in my head. As far as I could tell, my answers to O'Donnell's questions had seemed perfectly innocuous; still, I wondered what they could read between the lines, and if they had any sense of all of the things I'd left unspoken. Perhaps I should have let them believe that we were all thrilled that Richard was going to marry Emma. It seemed entirely unfair that now that I didn't have to worry about the damage he could do as her husband, I did have to worry about the potential consequences should the police decide that somebody here was capable of murder.

At the top of the stairs I followed the sound of low voices and muffled laughter coming from Mr. Furlong's study. Matthew was gone, but Luisa was still there and Jane and Hilary had joined her. They were sitting closely together on the sofa, their three heads bent together as they talked. Luisa's sleek ebony hair and Jane's rich chestnut framed Hilary's platinum blond. The overall effect was that of a Clairol commercial, lacking only Emma's dark gold and my own deep red to make it complete. They stopped talking and looked up expectantly when I appeared in the room.

"Hey—where is everyone?" I asked. "I'm supposed to send in the next victim." I blushed as soon as the words left my mouth. Hilary let out a cackle of laughter.

"Lovely choice of words, Rachel," commented Luisa. At the same time, she gave Hilary a sharp jab in the ribs with her elbow.

"Ouch," said Hilary, not in the least bit cowed.

"Last I heard," said Jane, "Mrs. Furlong was making all of the guys try to take down the tent. She said she wanted any reminder of the wedding out of sight before Emma wakes up."

That seemed like a futile gesture, at best, but Lily had her own way of looking at things. This wouldn't be the first time Emma's mother had been struck by a sudden whim that needed immediate fulfillment. "How fun for them," I said.

"I'm sure that's exactly what Sean's thinking," Jane answered, her voice laced with dry humor. "I'm probably going to have to spend every holiday for the rest of my life with his family just to make up for his suffering this weekend." While Sean was indisputably a prince among men, he was the youngest of five. Combined, his siblings and their respective spouses had produced a total of eleven grandchildren to date. This in itself made holidays at the Hallard house an adventure akin to being trapped in a nursery school. Still worse, Sean's parents were itching for yet more descendants, and Jane spent most of their visits with her in-laws fending off questions about when they could expect additions to their brood.

"Yet another reason not to get married," said Hilary. "In-laws and their small children. Not to mention compromise. And sharing. I hate sharing." We ignored her.

"So, how were the police?" asked Jane, getting right to the point.

"You weren't down there for very long," added Luisa.

"It was pretty low-key," I responded. "They just asked me about what we did yesterday. I told them about the rehearsal dinner and then going out to the dock last night and how we came in to go to bed around two. Then they asked me a few questions about Richard—what I thought of him, stuff like that."

"What did you say?" asked Hilary.

"What could I say?" I shrugged. "I was hardly about to pretend that he was a paragon of virtue. I thought the best thing to do was to tell the truth—that I didn't know him well nor did I like him much. And that I didn't know many people who did. They did confirm that they think Richard met with foul play."

"Really?" asked Jane. She was the only one who seemed even mildly surprised. "What did they say?"

"Just that they don't think Richard drowned." I could have sworn that Hilary and Luisa exchanged a furtive look, but Hilary quickly changed the subject.

"So, what's the guy's name? And what's he like?" She had more important matters on her mind than what I'd learned from the police. Somehow she seemed to have completely missed out on the relative gravity of the situation.

"What guy?" I feigned ignorance. She put her hands on her knees and gave me a beseeching look.

"Come on, Rach. Have a heart, here. Don't hold out on me."

Under normal circumstances I would have done precisely that, but I lacked the energy on this particular morning. "His name is O'Donnell. I get the feeling that he thinks we're all snotty rich folks. But he's really, really tall."

"Yum. Maybe I should go next. How do I look?"

"Shameless," said Jane.

"Like a brazen hussy," supplied Luisa.

"Perfect," said Hilary. "That's just the effect I was going for.

Is my hair okay? Who took my lipstick? Do you think he'll be able to tell that I'm wearing thong underwear?"

"I'm surprised you're even wearing underwear," said Luisa.

I left them to Hilary's preinterrogation primping and went down the hall to check in on Emma.

I cracked open the door of her parents' room as quietly as I could. The sheer curtains were drawn, but in the dim light that seeped through I could see Emma sprawled on her stomach on the king-size bed. I gently shut the door behind me and studied her still form. She had tangled herself in the blankets while she slept, and her bare feet poked out from between the smooth sheets, their nails neatly painted a shell-colored pink. Her skin was pale, even against the flawless white of the Pratesi linens, but a bit of color stained her cheeks. In profile, her sleeping face looked more relaxed than I could remember having seen it in months. Was it the sedative or the relief of not having to go through a wedding ceremony today? After what I'd overheard the previous night, I wasn't sure.

I'd never been in this room before, and I glanced around, absorbing the details. The walls were painted a soothing sage green, offset by glossy white trim on the moldings, and a well-worn Aubusson rug covered the floor. The bedstead was carved of heavy mahogany and flanked by twin night-stands. A stack of books sat on one, accompanied by a water glass, a box of tissues and some magazines. The other night-stand was completely bare of anything except an orphaned-looking reading lamp. It appeared that Mr. Furlong had long since made sleeping in his studio more the norm than the exception. My heart went out to Lily; it increasingly appeared that the photos on the piano downstairs were misleading and life with the Furlongs was not as golden as they let on.

There were no paintings on the walls by either Emma or

her father; instead, a single seascape hung over the fireplace. I crossed the room to examine it more closely, gratified to learn that the art history course I'd taken to fill a requirement of some sort in college hadn't been a complete waste and that I'd identified it correctly as an original work by Winslow Homer. I briefly wondered if Stan Winslow was any relation to the artist then quickly discarded the idea as improbable. I tried next to calculate how many years worth of investment banking bonuses it would take to purchase an equivalent piece of art.

I sank onto the chaise longue by the window, pushing aside a threadbare flock of tapestry pillows and stretching out my legs. I was glad for a moment of peace. If it weren't for Richard and this whole fiasco, I would be safely where I belonged right now, at home in the city. I would have woken up early, gone for a long run in Central Park, and perhaps met some friends for brunch. My stomach rumbled again, as if in protest at this willful self-delusion. More likely, it reminded me, I would have woken up early, gone for a short run in Central Park, and then headed down to the office to work on the latest assortment of deals Stan had netted on the golf course or squash court.

Sighing, I pulled myself to a sitting position and turned toward the window, pulling aside one of the sheer panels to peer out. The view from this side of the house was of the lawns stretching out toward the lake and, off to the side, in the distance, the old stable that had been converted into Mr. Furlong's studio. I couldn't see Matthew, Sean or Peter, but their handiwork was readily apparent; where the tent had stood was now a neat stack of planks and stakes and a massive roll of white canvas. An expanse of matted grass marked where the dance floor had been.

Beyond the matted grass, I spied Mr. and Mrs. Furlong together under the shading branches of an ancient maple tree.

Even from where I sat it was clear that they were arguing. At least, Mrs. Furlong seemed to be delivering an earful to Mr. Furlong, accompanying her words with short, sharp gestures while he stood silently, looking stoic and grim. Each attempt he made to interject seemed only to intensify her flow of words.

Finally, he grasped his wife by the elbows, trying to contain her. She shook him off and took a step back, suddenly still. Then she lifted her hand and slapped him, hard and deliberately. I flinched, feeling the blow as if it were me that she had hit. He stood, stunned, hand to his cheek. Abruptly, she turned her back to him and strode toward the house, her head down and her flowered summer dress rippling behind her. He stared after her for several moments, then turned and headed back to his studio.

"He's leaving her, you know."

I started. Emma was behind me, watching the scene below. A small, odd smile played across her features.

"Emma? What are you doing up?"

"He's leaving her. This time it's for real."

I struggled for the appropriate thing to say but came up empty. Instead, I tried to change the subject. "Emma, shouldn't you go back to bed? Do you want me to get you another pill?"

She scowled. "No. I don't want to be numb. Everything hurts. But I want it to hurt. Otherwise how will it ever go away?"

"Em—what do you mean?" I looked at her closely. She stood next to me in the same oversize T-shirt she'd been wearing when she saw Richard's body. The tips of her pelvic bones jutted sharply through the material. When had she gotten so thin?

"Come on, Rachel. He's been cheating on her for years. Just like Richard was cheating on me. Well, not exactly just

like it. My mother really cares. I, on the other hand, didn't."
Her voice was curiously flat.

"Emma. You're upset. Are you sure you don't want another
pill?" I was easily flummoxed by visible emotion, even in my
closest friends. And I wasn't particularly eager to learn more
about the undercurrents that dwelled beneath the smooth
surface of what I'd assumed had been the elder Furlongs' perfect marriage. It was hard to let go of long-cherished myths.

"I probably do." She gave a giggle that was tinged with hysteria. "Let's see—do you want the good news or the bad news
first? The good news is that my fiancé's dead. The bad news
is that my parents are splitting up and my mother's totally losing it—again. Do you think a pill would make me feel any
better?"

"Em…"

"Do you?" she asked again.

I tried to find the right words. We'd known each other for
our entire adult lives, but I'd never seen her like this—distraught and bitter, her voice dripping sarcasm.

"Emma, I'm sure you've misunderstood something. Your
parents—why, they're one of the happiest couples I've
ever…" I didn't have it in me to complete the sentence. After
all, what I'd just witnessed gave lie to my words. I changed
tack. "What makes you think that—"

"That he's cheating on her?"

"How do you know? I mean, every relationship has its ups
and downs, but that doesn't mean it's falling apart. And
they've been married more than thirty years. You just don't
throw something like that away, that sort of shared history.
A shared life."

"I wish that were the case. But they've been fighting non-
stop. Actually, that's not true. They alternate between fighting and not speaking to each other. From the way my
mother's acting, you'd think this was his first affair."

"How do you know it's not?"

"I know. But this time is even worse than the first time she found out he was cheating on her. As if that time wasn't bad enough. She practically had a breakdown."

"What are you talking about?"

"Do you remember that little trip I took to the British Isles with my mother a couple of years ago?"

"Of course. You brought me back that gorgeous sweater from Ireland."

"I told you that my mother had sprung it on me as a surprise, a belated birthday gift, but it wasn't that way at all. It was all my idea. I had to get her away from New York for a while. She was so devastated—she was convinced that everyone in the city knew about the way he was carrying on. She felt completely betrayed. So did I."

"Emma—why didn't you ever say anything?" She'd been so good to me over the years, arriving on my doorstep after every breakup or work disappointment with a supply of white wine and chocolate, helping to nurse my woes with comforting words and always eager to whisk me off for a bout of retail therapy. She knew just about everything that had ever happened to me in excruciating detail, and she'd been invaluable in getting me through it all. While I had always recognized how intensely private she was, I hated to think that she wouldn't come to me when she needed to talk.

"I just couldn't, Rach. I wanted to, but my mother was so embarrassed about the entire thing. I felt like it would have been like another betrayal of her...of her privacy."

"Oh, Em. I wish I could have done something."

She gave a sad shrug. "There was nothing you could have done."

"Still. I'm so sorry."

"But what I can't believe, after all that, is that he would go and do it again. But this time really takes the cake. Guess who it is?" The bitter tone was back in her voice.

"Emma, I don't want to guess. I'm just worried about you." I would have gone on, but I was silenced by the look on her face.

"Have you noticed anyone missing this weekend? Perhaps a close family friend?"

"You can't mean—"

"Oh, yes, I can. It doesn't matter to him that Nina's mother was my mother's best friend."

"Are you sure?" I asked, shocked. I had noted that Nina was not around this weekend, but I hadn't given it much thought. Matthew had made a vague comment about his sister having a schedule conflict of some sort, an exciting overseas assignment. Nina worked at one of the fashion magazines in New York, which meant that she frequently was away on boondoggles to Paris and Milan. I'd simply assumed that she was at a Fashion Week or design convention or some such event.

"Positive. I've even seen them together, in the city. And I assure you, there was no mistaking the fact that they're an item. God. It's sickening." She giggled as a thought occurred to her. "Why, if he's old enough to be my father, he's also old enough to be her father." She turned away from the window and sat on the bed.

"Does Matthew know?" I asked.

"That his sister's sleeping with my father? I don't think so. Although, he's more perceptive than we sometimes give him credit for. Still waters and all that." She fiddled with a bottle of pills on the nightstand.

I was at a complete loss for words, even though now that I'd had a moment to digest some of what Emma had said, my curiosity was kicking into overdrive. The look on her face was so pained and so empty, and her words were so jarring. I felt as if I were getting the first glimpse of what was going on in her head that I'd seen for months.

"Emma?"

"Hmm?"

"What's going on? What's this all about? What was going on with you and Richard?"

She sighed. "I can't tell you that. I wish I could, but I can't. And, frankly, it's better that you don't know."

Those weren't comforting words. "We're all here for you. You understand that, don't you? We'd do anything for you."

She looked up, her blue eyes clear and strong. "That's exactly what I'm afraid of."

Somebody rapped softly on the door. "Come in," I called, both frustrated and relieved at once.

The door opened and Matthew's familiar face appeared.

"Hi," he said, his gaze settling on Emma. "How're you doing?"

"Oh, Mattie." Emma looked at him and her face crumpled. He was across the room in an instant, cradling her in his arms. Her body shook with silent sobs as he rocked her slowly, gently stroking her hair.

I discreetly took my leave.

CHAPTER 13

I closed the door behind me and leaned against it. Matthew's interruption was inconvenient because it meant that all the questions I had would remain unanswered for the time being. Not that Emma seemed ready to tell me anything. But I was also unsettled by how inevitable Emma and Matthew seemed together; their closeness, now of all times, could be interpreted as inappropriate. I was glad that the police hadn't just witnessed what I had.

I tried to shake the scene from my head and moved away from the door. On cue, my stomach gave an ominous rumble, the perfect distraction for the tempest of intrigue and raw emotion swirling around in my brain. I was glad to have something more practical—and far more easily addressed—on which to focus my attention.

As a general rule, I tried to avoid any undue extension of the interval between meals. By my calculations, I was now going on fifteen hours and I was starting to feel testy. If my needs weren't met soon, there was a danger that I would become downright cranky, and in such a state I could not be held responsible for my actions. Maybe all the other delicate souls in the house had lost their appetites in the face of unexpected death, but I could hardly be expected to waste away in silence simply to accommodate their squeamishness. A raid on the Furlong refrigerator was very much in order.

Decision made, I started off for the kitchen at a brisk pace, only to stumble into Luisa, Jane and Sean, coming from the direction of Mr. Furlong's study. They met me at the top of the stairs.

"I can't take it anymore," I announced. "I'm going to find food before malnourishment sets in. If any of you are even toying with the notion of standing in my way, you'll regret it."

"Rachel's sort of scary when she's hungry," observed Sean, his voice deadpan.

"Don't joke," warned Jane. "She may look fragile and helpless, but it's dangerous to taunt her when she hasn't been fed."

"It's dangerous to taunt her when she *has* been fed, too," added Luisa. They shared a chuckle all around. Meanwhile, my hunger pangs were gaining intensity with each passing second.

"Look, don't get me wrong, but I can't handle being ganged up on without any sustenance. You can tease me as much as you want once I've had something to eat." My voice sounded plaintive, even to me.

"Relax. We were actually heading to the kitchen ourselves—Mrs. Furlong asked us to round up some lunch for everyone," said Sean.

"Are you sure she wasn't asking you to move water from one side of the lake to the other?" I asked. "Or perhaps to uproot some trees and plant them elsewhere?"

"No, I'm pretty confident she said lunch. But please don't put any ideas in her head. I'm not used to heavy labor."

"Well, then, why are we standing around yapping when we could be eating?" I asked, peevishness getting the better of me. I led the way down the stairs.

Just as we reached the first floor, the library door cracked open. Jane put a restraining hand on my shoulder and used her other arm to prevent Sean and Luisa from moving forward. "Shh…" she whispered, putting a finger to her lips.

Hilary's voice—to be specific, the voice she reserved for only the most demanding of flirtations—carried out to the hallway. "You must see a lot of excitement in your line of work, Detective." She placed a special emphasis on the word *excitement,* rolling out the syllables as if she could taste them. I couldn't see her, but if I knew Hilary, she had placed her hand on O'Donnell's forearm as she said this.

"If only that were true, Ms. Banks, if only that were true." O'Donnell's voice was polite but formal. "Thank you again for your time," he continued. "Now, if you'll excuse us?" He was, without doubt, dismissing her.

There was a brief silence. Could it be that Hilary, our Hilary, was at a loss for words? If so, she only took a moment to recover. "Of course. It was good to meet you both." She stepped out of the room, closing the door behind her with a level of force that wasn't a slam but was definitely far from gentle. She leaned against it, hands on her hips, the unfamiliar taste of rejection twisting her red lips into a pout. I hitched my assessment of O'Donnell up a notch. Anyone who could resist all five feet and eleven inches of a determined Hilary clad in an outfit that depended heavily on spandex was a man to be respected, and potentially feared. She narrowed her jade-green eyes. "Who the hell does he think he is?" she asked, presumably to nobody in particular, since she hadn't yet seen us.

"Just a nice man trying to do his job?" offered Jane. Hilary had the grace to look at least a bit startled to see us watching her. She straightened up and grinned.

"Oh, well. I've always enjoyed a challenge. What's up?"

"Food," I answered. "We're getting food, and there's no time to waste on chitchat." I continued on to the kitchen.

Hilary fell into line behind me. "Who let Rachel's blood sugar get so low?" she asked. Then her tone brightened. "Maybe that's what his problem is. He's hungry! Well, that's easy enough to fix. I nominate myself to bring lunch to the detectives."

"Okay," Jane told her. "But just remember what happened the last time you used the 'Coffee, tea, or me?' line."

The kitchen was completely empty. Usually the Brouchards, a French-Canadian couple who played handyman-chauffeur and cook when the Furlongs were in residence, would have been there. Today, however, Mrs. Furlong had had to call and let them know that the police weren't allowing anyone to enter the house who hadn't been there the previous evening. There was also a police car stationed on the road at the end of the drive preventing anyone from entering. Otherwise, Hugues and Marie-Louise would have been here long ago. I sighed. Marie-Louise would never have let me go so long without a meal.

Still, I knew that we would find the restaurant-size Sub-Zero stuffed to the gills with all sorts of delicacies. I used the last of my rapidly fading strength to tug open the massive door and pull out the first thing my hands met—a crockery bowl overflowing with fruit. Nearly crying with relief, I set the bowl on a countertop, hoisted myself up beside it, and selected a polished red apple. It was hardly a meal, but it would do as an appetizer until somebody could whip me up something that involved more of my favorite food groups, like salt, butter and processed flour.

"Don't you worry about a thing, Rachel," said Jane. "We'll figure something out for everyone else's lunch." She stepped forward to study the refrigerator's contents.

"I won't," I assured her, my mouth full. She started removing items from the overstuffed shelves and drawers and placing them on the counter beside me—eggs, cheese, the makings for a salad, some cold cuts. She'd always been the most domestic of us all, and I was happy to let her take the lead.

"Should we do omelettes or quiche?" she mused aloud. Luisa shrugged. She'd positioned herself in a chair at the butcher-block table and lit a cigarette.

"Whatever," said Hilary. "Does anybody know where they keep the liquor?" She started opening cabinets in the pantry while Jane and Sean discussed the relative merits of different egg preparations and the opportunities presented by the ingredients at hand.

Jane handed me a bowl of ripe tomatoes, a cutting board and a sharp knife. "Slice these," she said.

"Um. Okay. Any special way?"

"For salad. Can you do that?"

I was offended. "Of course. Do you think I'm a total incompetent?"

"No, but I can't forget your mother telling me how you once broiled a batch of brownies."

"Well, how was I supposed to know that broiling is so different from baking?" I was indignant.

"I don't think you really want to have this discussion," Jane countered.

"She really broiled brownies?" asked Sean, who had found a large mixing bowl and begun cracking eggs on its rim. One-handed, he poured the whites and yolks into the bowl and discarded the shells in the garbage disposal. Show-off.

"Yep. Don't even ask about the time we put her in charge of boiling water for pasta."

"It would have been fine if you'd just let me use the microwave, the way you're supposed to," I protested. "Stoves are so archaic."

"You can't boil a gallon of water in the microwave, Rachel."

I knew that I wasn't going to win an argument about cooking methods. My lack of domestic skills was well documented. Usually I ate most of my meals in the office. On those rare occasions that I was home for dinner, I simply ordered in like any reasonable person would do.

I slid off the counter, threw the apple core into the garbage can under the sink, and turned my attention to the tomatoes. They sat innocently on the cutting board, unaware of the butchery that awaited them. I picked up the knife and began scoping out the appropriate angle at which to make the first incision.

"Bloody Mary, anyone?" Hilary had emerged from the pantry with a pitcher of drinks.

"Oh, yes, definitely," I said, glad of a reason to put the knife down. She began pouring glasses for each of us.

"Wonderful," said Jane. "If ever there's an occasion for drinking before noon, this must be it."

"It's practically noon already," I pointed out as I reached for a glass. "Besides, it must be after noon somewhere." Hilary had made the drinks just the way I liked, painfully spicy with lots of Worcestershire sauce, Tabasco and a healthy dash of horseradish.

"If we only had some music," Hilary mused, "this would be just like *The Big Chill*. Where is William Hurt when you need him?" She prattled on while the rest of us turned back to preparing lunch.

I took another swallow of my drink and then picked up the knife and gingerly halved a tomato. My mind began to wander. Everything felt so normal, from the house where I'd spent so many long, lazy weekends to the comfortable back-and-forth of familiar voices. It was hard to believe that somebody had committed a murder. In fact, it was really too much to contemplate on a practically empty stomach; my investigation would have to wait until I'd had something to eat. I tried to steer my thoughts toward Peter instead, a much more appetizing topic.

As if summoned by my train of thought, he stepped into the kitchen, freshly dressed in khakis and a sky-blue oxford cloth shirt. I tried not to seem unduly interested as he exchanged a subdued good morning with everyone. The air of casual gaiety that had filled the room abated, out of a sense of deference to Peter—we may have been a hardhearted, callous bunch, but at least we had the sensitivity to realize that Peter was upset about Richard's death, even if we weren't.

Hilary broke the awkward pause that followed the chorus of greetings. "Tomato juice?" she asked.

"Sounds good," he said, accepting a glass. Before anyone else could intervene, he took a big swig and then spluttered with surprise. He wiped his mouth with the back of his hand.

"It's spiked," Hilary added, a wicked gleam in her eye.

"Thanks for the warning," he said with a quiet grin. "Actually, it's probably just what the doctor ordered." He took another sip, this time more cautiously. The atmosphere seemed to lighten with his good-natured reply.

"Be careful," said Luisa. "If you spend enough time with us you'll end up thoroughly pickled."

"On a day like today, I think I'll take the chance." He ambled over toward where I stood at the counter. I did my best to display my total absorption with my task. The problem, however, with handiwork, is that one's skill level is immediately visible, even to the casual eye. He watched me silently for a moment, studying the havoc I'd wrought.

"You're a real wizard at the cutting board, aren't you?" he asked in a teasing voice. I wheeled around, knife in hand, but drew a complete blank when I reached for a snappy retort. "Here," he offered, extending his hand out for the knife. "Why don't you let me take a crack at it?"

"Okay," I acquiesced. "But be careful. The one I just sliced seemed particularly unruly."

"It sure looks like you beat it into submission," he observed. I followed his gaze. I'd meant to slice the tomato neatly into wedges for a salad; instead, I'd reduced it to pulpy mush.

"My God, Rachel. What have you done?" This was from Jane, who'd glanced over to inspect my labors. She reached around me, picked up the cutting board and slid the red goop I'd created into the garbage disposal with a swift, decisive movement.

"You told me to slice the tomato, and I sliced the tomato," I said indignantly. "It was a bit slippery, but I think I did a pretty good job."

"Slicing and pureeing are not one and the same."

"Who died and made you Julia Child?" I asked.

"Rachel gets a bit snitty when she feels threatened," Jane confided to Peter.

"Don't worry," said Peter. "I'll take it from here." Jane handed him the cutting board, and turned back to the concoction that she and Sean were creating on the opposite counter. Hilary and Luisa resumed their seats at the kitchen table, preparing a platter of sandwiches while they chatted quietly.

"So, do you think O'Donnell's a mustard or a mayonnaise kind of guy?" I heard Hilary ask Luisa.

"You are completely insane," Luisa answered.

"I'm thinking mustard," said Hilary. "Yes, definitely mustard."

"So, were you able to reach Richard's mother?" I asked Peter in a low voice.

He reached for a fresh tomato and halved it cleanly. "Yes. It took some doing. My Italian came in handy. The number on the list was out of date, but I finally tracked Lydia down. She and the new husband are staying at the Gritti while some renovations are being done on their palazzo."

"How did she take it?"

He shrugged and continued cutting until the tomato had been reduced to a professional-looking pile of wedges. I noticed a speck of shaving cream nestled under his right ear and fought the urge to reach over and wipe it off. "About as well as could be expected, I guess. Have you ever met her?"

"No. Never."

"Well, she's a real piece of work. What exactly do you know about his family?" Peter asked.

"Not much, really," I said. Peter briefly filled me in, sketching out a portrait of Richard's family life that was a far cry from my own relatively normal childhood. He set out the facts in a quick, polite way, clearly loath to speak ill of anyone, but I filled in his outline with some of the details I'd heard previously.

The story of Richard's mother, Lydia, read more like a Judith Krantz paperback than real life. She had been a struggling actress when she met husband number one, the octogenarian producer who launched her Hollywood career. When her roles onscreen met with a lukewarm response at the box office, Lydia recast herself in the role of society doyenne, aided by her husband's deep pockets. Regardless of her questionable origins, she quickly developed a demeanor of such haughty elegance that Grace Kelly could have taken lessons from her. With breathtaking speed, she established herself as the most powerful hostess in town, a woman whose guest lists defined who was in and who most assuredly was not in the ever changing constellation of Los Angeles society. When her husband passed away five years into their marriage at the tender age of eighty-nine, Lydia sold their Holmby Hills estate and set her sights to the north, where the more rarified social strata of San Francisco offered a fresh challenge.

She conquered this snobbish city with the finely honed

skills she'd gained in the more rough-and-tumble world of Hollywood social politics. Within a couple of years, her lavish spending on both fashionable charities and designer gowns had landed her on the boards of the symphony and the ballet, and she cochaired the annual Opera Gala. This was where she first encountered Richard's father, Edward Mallory, a trustee of the opera. Mallory was a relatively spritely seventy-two, but he was no match for Lydia's perseverance. He shortly became husband number two.

He was seventy-four when Richard was born, and perhaps the shock of a new baby in the house after so many decades of affirmed bachelorhood was too much, because he keeled over of a heart attack well before Richard's first birthday. After his death, Lydia hung around long enough to appear about town looking appropriately mournful and lovely in a series of rush-ordered black Escada suits. But once her rounds had been made and Mallory's estate settled, yielding far less than she anticipated, the grieving widow departed for points more exotic. She occupied herself spending her dwindling funds and traveling the globe until she met husband number three, a Scottish aristocrat with a drafty castle that was highly unsuitable for small children. Concerned about raising her son in such an environment, she left Richard in San Francisco in the care of assorted nannies and housekeepers until he was old enough for boarding school at Saint Luke's, his father's prestigious alma mater in Connecticut.

"He was, quite literally, raised by a medley of household help," Peter concluded.

"How sad," I said, feeling a pang of unwelcome sympathy for Richard.

Peter picked up another tomato and continued slicing until it, too, had been transformed into a neat mound. He then slid the cut tomatoes into the bowl of freshly rinsed greens Jane had left next to the cutting board. He looked up to meet my eyes. "Let's just say that, whatever faults Richard may have had, and whatever unfortunate decisions he may have made along the way, he was dealt a bad hand at the start."

I nodded. It was so much easier when issues were black-and-white. Someone should be evil or good, innocent or guilty. Thinking about the whims of fate that helped to mold Richard into the nefarious creature I'd known made it harder to so easily shrug off his death with some banal words and a couple of stiff drinks. And Peter's stoic calm drew me into the emotional undercurrents of Richard's life and his death in a way I'd managed to resist thus far.

Before I could stop myself, I reached over and wiped off the speck of shaving cream from under his ear. He caught my hand and gripped it lightly. "Thanks," he said. "I still haven't mastered the shaving thing."

CHAPTER 14

"If you two are done over there you can set the table on the porch," Jane called out to us.

"Sure," I answered, turning away quickly before Peter could notice the flush staining my cheeks. Although, by this point he probably thought the natural tone of my complexion was beet-red. I gathered place mats and napkins from a drawer in the pantry and showed Peter where the silverware was. We went out to the porch and began setting the long oak table.

We took our time about it, and I was relieved that I could at least set a table without further demonstrating my utter lack of domestic ability. In fact, Peter seemed impressed by my one kitchen-related trick—folding and twisting the cloth napkins into the shape of a fan. I promised to teach him at some point, provided he remained on his best behavior. He appeared suitably excited by the prospect.

We came back in to get glassware, and Peter boasted on my behalf about what a lovely job I'd done.

"Let me guess," said Hilary. "She wowed you with the napkin fans."

"It's a very challenging maneuver," I protested.

"She definitely gets high marks on both technical and artistic merit," said Peter, coming to my support. Chivalry was alive and well, at least where he was concerned.

"Rachel skipped all of the beginning and intermediate steps and went straight for the advanced," teased Jane. "She's a whiz at napkin folding and hors d'oeuvres assembly."

"Just don't ask her to make toast or scramble an egg," added Sean.

"Not a lot of respect for genius around here, is there?" Peter commiserated, loosely draping an arm around my shoulders.

"Did you ever read *The Fountainhead*?" I asked. "Just call me Roark."

Hilary snorted.

As if on cue, Emma's mother walked in. "What is it that you're making, Jane?" she asked in her gracious hostess voice. "It smells wonderful." The words were right, but she sounded as if she were on autopilot.

"Oh, we're just whipping together a frittata and some salad," said Jane.

Mrs. Furlong nodded absently and crossed directly to the refrigerator. She removed a bottle of white wine and then reached into a drawer for a corkscrew. Her manicured hands fumbled with the foil. Peter went to help, taking the bottle from her and deftly inserting the corkscrew and pulling out the cork. Fantasies about Peter and me touring the California wine country together, or perhaps the Rhône Valley, quickly started germinating in a corner of my mind. I took a goblet from the cabinet, and he poured the chilled liquid into it and handed it to Lily.

"Thank you, dear," she said, accepting the glass with hands

that trembled. She downed its contents quickly, and Peter topped it off for her. She strolled over to the table where Luisa and Hilary sat. "Do you mind, darling?" she asked Luisa, gesturing to her silver cigarette case.

"Of course not." Luisa proffered the open case, and Mrs. Furlong removed a cigarette with shaking fingers. Luisa lit it for her and she inhaled deeply, exhaling a stream of smoke with a practiced air.

"Just like riding a bicycle," she said. "You never forget how to do it. This is fabulous. Why did I ever give it up?" She took another deep drag.

"Because it's really bad for you," said Matthew, entering the kitchen.

"Dr. Weir to the rescue," said Hilary.

"No lectures today, please, Matthew. And please don't tell Emma. She was the one who made me quit in the first place."

"I'll overlook it this once," he agreed. "I was just going to grab some food for the detectives."

"We've made them some sandwiches," said Hilary, proudly displaying the platter. "I'll help you take them in."

"That's all right, Hil. I can handle it." He tried to take the plate of sandwiches from her hands, but she continued to hold on.

"No, you don't. If you bring in the food, how will O'Donnell know that I prepared everything especially for him? And they'll need something to drink. Do you think they'd like some Bloody Marys?"

"You take incorrigible to a whole new level, Hil," said Matthew.

"Come on, work with me here. Do you want me to die a virgin?"

"How, precisely, are you defining virgin?" I asked.

"This is not a joking matter," said Hilary, drawing herself

up to her full, imposing height. "Matthew needs to get his priorities straight."

"Never fear. Furthering your romantic pursuits is, as always, my first priority."

"You could at least say it like you mean it," she grumbled.

"I'll just grab some sodas and we can go together." He took a couple of cans of Coke from the refrigerator.

She sighed. "Okay. Sodas, then. Now, let's go."

Lunch on the porch was a strange affair. Mr. Furlong was still in his studio, and Mrs. Furlong oscillated between playing the gracious hostess and staring into space. She left her food almost completely untouched but drank liberally and helped herself to several more of Luisa's cigarettes. The rest of us did our best to keep up a stilted conversation.

I'd realized a long time ago that people's parents were individuals in their own right, with their own passions and problems and quirks of character. Still, I'd always found Emma's parents to be such glossy, larger-than-life personalities. Mr. Furlong had always played the avuncular host, assiduously remembering the details of my life that Emma shared with him and asking after my family and career, and Mrs. Furlong had always made me feel warmly welcome on my constant visits to their home, her charm so great that it made anyone in her presence feel charming by simple association. Still, their fame and wealth and style seemed to cocoon them; I'd always felt as if they operated on a different frequency than most people I knew.

Between my disturbing thoughts about the Furlongs' relationship and my even more disturbing concerns about my friends' various motives for doing away with Richard, it was hard for even a talented professional like myself to eat much. Nobody else seemed to have much of an appetite either, although everyone was probably getting a bit tipsy, between the Bloody Marys and then the additional wine we'd opened with lunch. However, Mrs. Furlong seemed to have polished off the better part of a bottle on her own. Still, she sat at the head of the table with her back ramrod straight and the hand that was not gripping her wineglass placed neatly in her lap. She'd complimented Jane and Sean effusively at the appropriate moments on the food she hadn't eaten. So when she made her next remark, in the same sort of tone most people used to discuss the weather, it took a moment to sink in.

"Any guesses as to who did this? Murdered Richard, I mean."

Jane, ever the calm voice of reason, was the first to recover. "But, Mrs. Furlong, it must have been an accident. Nobody killed him."

Mrs. Furlong let out a crystal peal of laughter. "Jane, darling, that's so sweet of you to try to pretend, but that's clearly not the case. Apparently the police think so as well, or they surely would be long gone by now."

Even Jane lacked a ready answer for this.

Mrs. Furlong continued, her voice maintaining the same gracious tone amidst everyone else's stunned silence. "What's striking is the number of motives among us.

"Why, you girls—I know you're all like sisters to Emma. And you've all done your best to be polite and hide your feelings, but it's obvious that you detested the man. Matthew's mother was my dearest friend—she had been since we were children, and there was hardly anything I wouldn't do for her. Of course, Matthew's father was an absolute angel, but I wonder how I would have felt if she'd been about to throw her life away by marrying a man like Richard. I wonder if I would have taken matters into my own hands? If I would have had the courage to do so?"

"Mrs. Furlong—" I began to protest, but she cut me off.

"Then there's Peter, here. Were you aware of Richard's new will, darling?"

Peter met her gaze with a frank, open expression. "I wasn't aware of any will, old or new."

"How odd." She smiled slightly. "You didn't realize that you were the primary beneficiary of the old will? Of course, Richard's assets were hardly as substantial as one would hope, but they were still nothing to make light of. The new will, of course, would leave everything to Emma. It's probably contestable now, since the marriage wasn't consummated."

"Mrs. Furlong," said Peter, "I'm afraid I knew nothing about any will."

"Of course you didn't, darling. I didn't mean to offend you—I'm just trying to analyze the situation objectively.

"Let's also not forget Matthew, here. He's been in love with Emma since she was a baby, practically." Matthew opened his mouth to speak, a strange, hard look in his eyes, but she hushed him with a quick hand gesture. "You've always been so sweet to her. You taught her how to swim and how to sail the little sunfish we used to keep up here. And the two of you would make such a nice couple. The very thought of Richard marrying Emma must have made your blood boil.

"And finally, of course, there's Jacob and me. Richard was hardly the son-in-law we would have chosen, what with his rather unattractive background and his questionable business dealings. Jacob was particularly distressed—after all, fathers are always a bit overprotective of their daughters, aren't they? And he's always been a man of action."

She looked around the table, a bright smile lighting up her features.

"There's a certain beauty to it, isn't there?" she mused. "Why, practically everyone here had a reason to want Richard out of the way.

"But I'm neglecting my manners, aren't I? Would anyone

like some coffee? Or dessert? There's an enormous wedding cake just sitting in the pantry. Angel food with meringue and raspberries between the layers. And a heavenly butter-cream frosting. It's from the most exquisite bakery—this little place on East Sixty-Fourth Street in the city. They do the most lovely work, and everything is always delicious. It would be a crime to let it go to waste."

CHAPTER 15

Not surprisingly, we all demurred on the offer of wedding cake. Somewhat disappointed, Mrs. Furlong disappeared upstairs for a postprandial siesta, while we began clearing the table and putting things away in the kitchen. Peter excused himself as well, explaining that he needed to call into his office and take care of some work. I couldn't blame him; anyone would want some time alone to absorb that his hostess had just suggested he might be a murderer and supplied him with a motive in one fell swoop. Nor had Mrs. Furlong's little soliloquy done much to calm my own anxieties.

Matthew went to the library to check in on the police and returned with the now empty plate of sandwiches. Hilary started to ask him if O'Donnell had said anything about her or the fine quality of food preparation, but Matthew silenced her with a rare, stern look. His sense of humor had disappeared about halfway through lunch. With the exception of Hilary, whose high spirits were just about invincible, we were all considerably less cheerful than we'd been an hour before.

"Who do they want to see next?" Luisa asked Matthew.

He shrugged, his expression tired. "How about you? Are you up for it?"

"Not especially, but I may as well get it over with. It's probably more fun than washing dishes."

"I wouldn't be too sure about that," said Matthew.

"You don't know how I feel about dishes," said Luisa, with a half smile. "Besides, just think what all that scrubbing would do to my nails." She squared her shoulders and headed for the door with her usual regal bearing, which always made me think of a queen off to greet her adoring subjects.

The rest of us busied ourselves rinsing plates and glasses and loading the dishwasher. Nobody was very talkative, except, of course, for Hilary, who chattered on, oblivious to the fact that nobody was paying any attention to her. With so many helping out, we were done in a matter of minutes. The afternoon stretched before us, alarmingly empty. It was barely 1:00 p.m. I realized that we'd forgotten to cancel the reservation we'd made at a café in town for the bridesmaids' lunch. Well, I thought with resignation, that was the least of today's problems.

"Now what?" I asked. I felt like I should be doing something to figure out what had happened to Richard, but I wasn't sure what that something would be.

"It's a beautiful day," said Jane. "I was thinking it would be nice to take a swim."

"In the lake, I'm assuming?" asked Hilary. "I have a feeling the pool's off-limits for now."

"Ugh, Hil," I said.

"The lake sounds good to me," said Jane. I agreed, thinking that it might give me time to collect my thoughts until I could figure out a better plan of action.

Matthew begged off, saying that he had to attend to the police, and Sean said he'd stay behind to talk to them after they were done with Luisa. Matthew asked Jane not to stay out too long, noting that she still had her own police interview to go through. "I'll bring Peter in after Luisa and Sean are done, but after that I expect you'll be up. The police spoke to the Furlongs this morning, and Rachel, Hilary and I have spoken to them already, too. I thought I'd try to save Emma until last, and I should probably keep an eye on her while her mother's resting."

"That's probably wise," said Hilary. "I think Lily needs some time to recover from her liquid lunch."

He sighed. "Has Jacob come back to the house?" he asked. "Has anyone seen him?"

"I don't think so," I answered. "Should we try to track him down?"

"No. I'll go get him if the police want to see him again."

Back in Emma's room, I took off the old locket of my grandmother's that I always wore and placed it on the dresser. I quickly exchanged my sundress for my bathing suit, an emerald green one-piece, and wrapped a Thai silk sarong around my hips. I hadn't actually had time to hit the beaches when I'd been in Thailand a few years ago on a deal, of course. I'd been shut up in conference rooms during the day and busy rerunning numbers in my hotel room at night. But I'd had just enough time to purchase some lovely beachwear in the duty-free at the Bangkok airport before my flight home.

I was almost out the door when I remembered that I'd forgotten sunblock. I stepped into the bathroom and began rummaging through Emma's medicine cabinet. We both shared an astonishing inability to tan, hers derived from her pure stream of Anglo-Saxon blood and mine the product of a childhood spent in a land where if you blinked you could easily miss summer. The contents of the medicine cabinet made me laugh. Where other people kept their aspirin and mouthwash, Emma stored a set of watercolors and an array of paintbrushes. I found a bottle of lotion claiming unparalleled sun protection power lurking behind some linseed oil and a mortar and pestle. I pulled it out and applied it liberally to the exposed parts of my body before rewrapping myself in the sarong.

I went back down the stairs and headed out through the kitchen door. I retraced the steps we'd taken the previous night out to the dock, delighting in the feel of the summer sun on my bare shoulders. My flip-flops slapped gently against the soles of my feet, and the path was covered with a thick carpet of loose pine needles. What with the sunshine, blue skies and chirping birds, it really was an idyllic day. I couldn't help but be glad that I wasn't spending it watching Emma make the biggest mistake she possibly could.

I left my flip-flops and the sarong on an old upturned canoe that rested on the grass and stepped onto the narrow strip of beach that edged the water. The sun had warmed the sand, and the heat felt welcoming to my bare feet. The lake stretched out before me, a gentle breeze stirring some mild ripples along its surface. In the distance I could see a few lonely sailboats dotting the horizon.

Jane was already standing waist high in the water, a navy-blue maillot hugging her lean frame and broad swimmer's shoulders. Not only had she been a world-class sailor in college, she'd also been one of the stars of the diving team, single-handedly compensating for the utter lack of athleticism among her friends. "Come on in," she called. "The water's great."

I knew that she was lying. No matter how I chose to enter the water, I would find it shockingly cold. It was one thing to dabble your toes as I had the previous evening; total immersion was a different matter altogether. Even in August the lake retained an Arctic tinge. I gingerly poked a foot in and then jumped back. "What are you talking about? It's like ice!"

"That's just at the edge," she told me, flipping onto her back and fluttering her legs. "It's balmy out here. Like a bathtub." One that had been filled with barely melted snow. I gave her a dubious look.

"Come on," she cried again. "Don't be a wuss."

"I'm proud of being a wuss. It suits me."

"You should just dive right in. Otherwise you'll be there forever."

She was right, I knew. No amount of mental preparation could prepare me for the iciness that awaited, and the longer I waited the less likely I was to brave it. There was only one way to handle it. Before I could change my mind, I strode out onto the dock, and with a running start, dove in headfirst.

"Aaacckkk!" I howled, as soon as my mouth reached the surface. "Jane, you rat, it's freezing." My teeth began to chatter. Surely water this cold should be ice, I thought. Perhaps lake water was special and didn't actually freeze when its temperature went below thirty-two degrees Fahrenheit? I knew I should have paid more attention in my high school chemistry class.

Jane laughed. "Well now that you're in, I'll race you to the raft." She took off with long, even strokes. I didn't bother to try to race her; competition's no fun when you don't stand even a chance of winning, and Jane was probably in training for a megatriathlon or some such thing. I followed with a lazy sidestroke.

The raft was anchored roughly a hundred yards from shore, a set of wooden planks that floated atop empty barrels. By the time I'd hoisted myself up the ladder, Jane had already stretched out on her back. "Slowpoke," she said.

"Show-off," I answered, stretching out beside her. The sun-baked surface of the raft radiated warmth, and the gentle rocking motion was soothing. "Aah," I sighed. "This is more like it."

"Mmm," Jane murmured her agreement.

"Oh, bugs," I said.

"What's wrong?"

"I was supposed to get a fax from my office, and I forgot to check the machine."

"Relax," she said. "Wall Street's not going to implode if you take an hour off."

"I know, I know."

"Besides, weren't you supposed to be putting in fewer hours now that you're a vice president?"

"Yes," I admitted, "but it doesn't seem to be working out as planned. The head of my department keeps throwing deals at me."

"Is that a good thing?"

"I suppose so. I mean, it's helping me to reestablish credibility after that mess last year," I said, referring to the deal Richard had screwed up.

"Well, not to be too coldhearted or anything, but it looks like Richard finally got his payback for that," said Jane in her no-nonsense way.

"True," I acknowledged. "But it would have been far better if the deal had never gotten so messed up in the first place. It's like I'm on a probation of sorts right now, and I have to prove myself all over again."

"Do you think you're going to stick it out?" she asked.

"At the firm, you mean?" She nodded. "Yes," I said, without hesitation. "I'm too close to making partner to give up now. Once I get elected, my hours really will get better, and I'd hate to think that all the years of drudgery I've put in so far would come to nothing. Plus, the money at that point will be pretty spectacular."

"That's nothing to sneeze at. I just hope you don't neglect your love life in the meantime." Her voice took on a teasing edge. "You know, spend too much time worrying about your work, when exciting, seemingly eligible men are around."

"You're a subtle one, aren't you?"

"I try," she said modestly. "It's just that I think Peter's really great. Sean thinks so, too."

"He is," I agreed. "Definitely a cut above the guys I've been meeting in New York." Not that I really met anyone in New York—I was always at the office or in meetings or traveling on business. My romantic life of late had been limited to occasional blind dates, all of which had been fruitless except for the comic stories they yielded. Like the guy who brought his own utensils, plate and glassware to dinner and then lectured me on the fat content of every bite I ate. He'd nearly fainted when I ordered crème brûlée for dessert.

I changed the subject. "What's going on with you and Sean?" I asked.

"Not much. The biggest news is that I'm going to be teaching trig this year along with algebra, so I've been busy prepping. Unfortunately, it's hard to wing it when it comes to sines and cosines. And nothing much changes with Sean—just the usual valves and pipes." Jane taught math at a private school in Boston, and Sean's family owned a small industrial concern that supplied municipalities with pipes, fire hydrants and other pieces of equipment. It wasn't glamorous, but it provided a healthy living for the large and close-knit Hallard clan.

We chatted a bit more about the Hallards and their insatiable appetite for grandchildren before lapsing into a comfortable silence, each busy with our own thoughts. I hadn't gotten much rest the previous night, and a wave of tiredness swept over me. I struggled to stay awake, reminding myself that I was supposed to be developing an action plan, but the bright sun and gentle motion of the raft soon lulled me to sleep.

When I woke, I saw Hilary wading in the water near the shore with Peter. I used this opportunity to discreetly check out his body, which up to now had been hidden by relatively baggy clothing, and I was delighted to see that his torso was long and lean but nicely muscled. He was also wearing a pair of completely reasonable swim trunks that would never be a source of embarrassment to anyone who was with him. Swim trunks, perhaps even more than shoes, were an excellent indicator of what else might lurk in a man's wardrobe. I shuddered as I recalled a Winslow, Brown summer picnic at which my date, who up until that point had seemed perfect in every way, showed up in a neon-green Speedo.

Then I took in Hilary's string bikini, in a shade that could only be described as shocking pink. However, it was unclear whether the shocking part was due to the color or the striking lack of material. A hot stream of jealousy coursed through my veins. Hilary had always had an easy, flirtatious way about her that was part of her breezy confidence and sensuality. But usually her tastes in men were so wildly different from mine that I'd never felt even remotely threatened. And if my romantic history was checkered, Hilary's was a minefield. She went through men like Kleenex, seizing upon them eagerly when the need arose, then balling them up and discarding them without a second thought.

You didn't need a Ph.D. in psychology to understand her behavior. Although Harvard prided itself on its diversity, my group of friends was relatively homogenous, if not in terms of interests, at least in terms of backgrounds. Emma and Luisa both came from immense family fortunes, and Jane's family was comfortably well-off. My parents had struggled to make

ends meet on their slim academics' salaries, taking out a second mortgage to help send their three children to college,
but we'd never wanted for anything important. And we all
had parents who were still married. My parents' thirty-eight
years of domestic bliss was nearly eclipsed by Jane's parents'
forty years, the tight-knit clan of the Caselanzas, and, at least
so I'd thought until this morning, the golden perfection of
the Furlong family. We had a shared history of secure and
stable childhoods.

But while the majority of Harvard's student body was on
financial aid, Hilary was the only one among us whose parents were completely unable to contribute to her tuition. She
was the only child of a single mother, and her father was nowhere in sight, having deserted her mother when Hilary was
still a toddler. She made jokes about the times she and her
mother had been on welfare and made do with clothes from
Goodwill, but it was clear that these experiences had shaped
her. Her mother blamed her father for their impoverished
state, and her bitterness was not lost on Hilary.

These seeds from her childhood manifested themselves in
her fierce independence and her tendency to view men not
as potential soul mates but as conquests. She derived no small
satisfaction from the act of seducing a man and then tossing
him aside in an explicit assertion of her power. Her early experiences bore themselves out in her choice of profession as
well. As a journalist, she'd flitted from one dangerous place
to another. Her bylines had come from Afghanistan and
Bosnia, Indonesia and Colombia. She seemed to court danger out of spite, eager to show that she was master of any
situation.

"Relax," said Jane, following my gaze. "He's not her type.
And I don't think she's his type, either. She's not interested.
And she knows that you are. You don't have anything to
worry about."

I flashed her a grateful look. It was remarkable the way she could still read my thoughts. "On a rational level, I know you're right. It's just that she's gorgeous, and I'm—well, me."

Jane laughed. "Don't be an idiot, Rach. You're gorgeous, too. And he completely has a thing for you. It's just that Hilary needs continuous affirmation."

"I don't mind affirmation. In fact, I actually sort of like affirmation."

"It's not the same. Sometimes I worry that Hilary doesn't know who she is if she's not getting attention from men. I mean, most of the time she's the one doing the breaking up, but the few times when she's been on the receiving end it's really been a mess. She doesn't handle rejection well."

"Nobody handles rejection well," I argued. "Rejection sucks."

"I know, but with Hil, it's totally out of proportion. When Richard dumped her in Los Angeles—"

"What?" I interrupted. This was too much. How had I missed out on this, along with the prenup and everything else? Within any group of friends, there were clearly some relationships that are deeper than others. After all, Emma had remained my closest friend of all of our roommates, no doubt due to sharing a room freshman year. Still, I was always surprised when I learned that somebody else knew things about one of my friends that I didn't.

"Don't tell me you didn't know about Richard and Hilary?"

"Know what?"

"They dated. When she was in journalism school at USC, after we graduated. You didn't know that?"

I searched my memory. Right after college, I'd been in an entry-level position at Winslow, Brown. If my hours were bad now, they were unspeakable then. The two years I'd spent there before returning to business school were a blur to me, a montage of sleepless nights, too much caffeine, and piles of paper swimming with numbers. Weeks would go by without having the time to have a conversation of any length with my friends or family.

"I think I was sort of AWOL right after college," I confessed when my recollection yielded nothing.

"Well, Hilary dated him for a while when she moved to L.A. They went out for about six months, and then he dumped her, and I assure you, it wasn't pretty."

"And I thought she just hated him for the reasons the rest of us did."

"I'm sure she does. But she also has a reason of her very own."

Great, I thought. Just great. I felt my stomach churn as I made a mental note to add Hilary to the list of people who had an extraspecial grudge against Richard. I rolled onto my side and propped my head up. "This isn't good, Jane." My voice sounded shaky. I hadn't meant to share my various suspicions with anyone until I'd gotten to the bottom of Richard's murder, but Jane was one of the least likely suspects among us, and I needed to unburden myself.

"What do you mean?"

"Look, Richard's dead, and it wasn't an accident. I told you all about Emma arguing with her father. And apparently Emma met Richard last night after everyone else went to sleep." I related what Peter had said about Richard's rendezvous and seeing Emma from his window. "That's bad enough, but then Luisa said…" I trailed off, not sure I had the right to tell Jane about what Luisa had confided.

"That Richard raped her?" asked Jane.

"How do you know?" I asked, shocked. Luisa said she'd never told anyone.

"I guessed. I mean, it never made sense—Sean and I saw them together that night, and I knew how she felt about Richard. And then the way she rushed off the next morning. It's true, though, isn't it?"

I nodded. "And then, finding out about Richard and Hilary...it's just too much. One bad thing keeps piling on top of another, and no matter how much Richard had it coming, I don't want to think that someone I care about was the one responsible."

Jane sighed. "Well, here's something else to add to the pile. You know that Sean and I are staying in the room next to the one that Luisa and Hilary are staying in?"

"Yes?"

"Well, I couldn't sleep much last night. Sean was making an unholy racket with his snoring. And I heard them."

"Heard who?"

"Luisa and Hilary. Not what they said, but I could hear their voices."

"So?" I asked. It wouldn't be the first time Hilary had kept someone up half the night with one of her monologues.

"They left their room. Around three-thirty. And they didn't come back until around four."

CHAPTER 16

From the corner of my eye, I saw Sean and Luisa come out to the end of the dock. "Jane," called Sean, "you're up."

"Okay," she answered. "I'll be right there." She sat up reluctantly, combing her hands through her damp hair. "Yuck. I was sort of hoping they'd forget about me. But I guess it's probably time." She paused and turned to me, taking in my tense expression. "Don't worry. I'm not going to say anything about Luisa and Hilary last night. And relax, Rachel. I'm sure it was all nothing. I know it looks bad, but there's probably a very simple, very innocent explanation for everything. There usually is."

I wished I was as sure, I thought, as I watched her dive cleanly into the water and swim off. It must be nice to have such a confidently benign view of the world.

Sean helped her climb up onto the dock, and Luisa handed her a towel. I saw Hilary steal up behind them, and I knew what she was going to do before Luisa even hit the water. She surfaced spluttering and indignant, a stream of Spanish epithets pouring from her mouth.

"Dammit, Hilary! This bathing suit isn't supposed to get wet."

"Brilliant, a bathing suit that's not supposed to get wet. Where do you find these things?"

"Chanel," said Luisa as if Chanel was the most natural place to shop for swimwear. "You wretch," she added, almost as an afterthought. She began swimming towards the raft with a ladylike breaststroke. Hilary dove in after her, and a moment later Peter followed from the shallows. They all joined me on the raft, spattering drops of icy water as they pulled themselves up the ladder.

"Geez, Rach," said Hilary, poking me in the leg. "You really need to get more sun. You're practically see-through."

"Not all of us can be bronzed goddesses," I said.

"True," she agreed, plopping her nearly six feet of long, tanned self down.

Luisa carefully lowered herself into a sitting position on my opposite side, safely out of Hilary's reach. "Do you think we can convince someone to boat out to bring us back to shore? The water's freezing."

"But at least the cold water keeps the sharks at bay," said Hilary.

"Funny," said Luisa, still peeved. "I don't know how, and I don't know when, but I'm going to get you back, Hilary."

"Okay, I guess there aren't any sharks. But there're probably fish and snakes and eels. And leeches. Definitely leeches. Leeches are good, though. There's nothing like a close encounter with a leech for building character."

"I have more than enough character, thank you. And it's so soon after lunch—what if I get a cramp when I swim back?"

"Don't worry," I said, "I earned a gold medal in lifesaving at Camp Hiawatha."

"See, you'll be fine," said Hilary.

"Camp Hiawatha, my foot," grumbled Luisa. "That hardly inspires confidence."

"Rachel," explained Hilary to Peter, "was the star of Camp Hiawatha. She earned gold medals at the Camp Hiawatha Olympics in just about every single sport."

"I have a feeling there were lots of gold medals given out at Camp Hiawatha," said Luisa.

"They were big on building self-esteem," I agreed. "Sometimes you got a medal just for participating."

Peter chuckled and sat down facing me. Beads of water glistened on his arms and legs.

"So, how do you guys think we can get O'Donnell to take a break and come swimming?" asked Hilary. "I would really like to show him my bikini."

"What there is of it," said Luisa.

"It seems to have shrunk since I bought it," said Hilary happily.

"Well, let's just hope it doesn't shrink anymore. You'll get arrested for indecent exposure," Luisa replied.

"Do you think O'Donnell would do the arresting?"

"For your sake, Hil, I definitely hope so," I said. She giggled and rolled over onto her stomach, propping her head up on her hands.

"So, Peter," she said, a mischievous glint in her eye, "why don't you tell us a bit about yourself?" I groaned inwardly. For a writer, Hilary didn't place much value in segues, and I had a pretty good idea what was behind her abrupt change in topics. Peter was about to be interviewed for the position of my boyfriend, whether he was ready or not.

"Sure," he answered. "What do you want to know?" Poor man. He had no idea what was coming.

"Well, tell us about where you grew up, and where you went to school, and what your family's like, and what you do for a living. And if you have any pets." She might as well have asked for copies of his grade school report cards, medical records and tax returns.

"You already know he's from San Francisco," I protested.

"There are millions of people from San Francisco," she retorted.

"Indeed," added Luisa, but I held out little hope that she wasn't going to play an active part in the interrogation.

"Well, that's where I grew up. My family's still out there, too."

"Do you have a large family?" asked Luisa. "Brothers, sisters?"

"Two brothers. I'm the youngest."

"So is Rachel," cried Hilary. "She's the youngest, and she also has two brothers." Thatta girl, I thought. Subtle to a fault.

"What a coincidence," said Peter. I smiled. He was being a good sport.

"And did you go to university in California?" asked Luisa.

"Yep. At Stanford. I did a double major in history and engineering."

"How interesting," said Luisa. "You know, Rachel did a double major, too—economics and English."

"Wow," I said. "Maybe somebody cloned me at birth and Peter and I are actually the same person." They ignored me.

"She was the only one of us to graduate summa," added Hilary. "But she always made it look easy." I shot her a threatening look, which she blithely pretended not to notice. "And how do you like San Francisco?" she continued, unabashed. "Have you ever though about moving to New York? Rachel's very attached to New York."

I couldn't handle it anymore. Another couple of minutes and they probably *would* be requesting bank statements and medical records.

"I'm getting hot," I announced to no one in particular. "I think I'll take a dip." I stood up and dove from the raft into the water. As I flipped onto my back I heard Hilary asking him why he didn't have a girlfriend. At least the water was cold enough to promptly freeze any beginnings of a blush.

I swam away from the raft in the opposite direction from shore. Once I got used to the water, it actually felt refreshing.

I remained in the water until I felt my lips beginning to turn blue and then made my way back to the raft. As I climbed the ladder I heard Hilary discoursing on her most recent assignment in Pakistan. I smiled to myself. Peter had clearly realized that the best way to distract her from interrogating him was to get her going on her favorite subject—herself.

"—nuclear capability," she was saying. "If most Americans only knew the half of it, they'd be terrified."

"How was your swim, Rachel?" asked Luisa. We'd had an earful from Hilary on Pakistan and geopolitics on the drive up from New York the previous day.

"Brisk," I said, lowering myself down next to Peter. Hilary seemed to take that as a cue.

"Well," said Hilary. "I'm going to go in, too. Come on, Luisa. I'll race you back to shore." She jumped to her feet.

I could see Luisa weighing her options. Did she value my friendship enough to voluntarily brave the lake water? Was it worth it, simply to leave me alone for an intimate tête-à-tête with Peter? She slowly rose and inched over toward the edge of the raft, peering at the water suspiciously. "It still looks awfully cold."

She should have known better than to stand so close to the edge, especially when she'd been pushed in once. Hilary grabbed her around the waist and leaped off the raft, pulling Luisa in with her. She let out an even more blistering stream of curses this time, some of which I'd never heard in either Spanish or English. Hilary took off for the shore with long, effortless strokes, a California girl to the core. Luisa swore again and followed.

My laughter joined with Peter's. "Your friends are really..." He searched for the appropriate words.

"Insane?" I asked.

"*Inquisitive* is the word I was looking for."

"How did you bear up?"

"Under the interrogation, you mean? Let's just say that I'd rather be interviewed by the police for the rest of the weekend than face down those two again."

I appreciated his good-natured answer. I surmised from my friends' willingness to leave me alone with him that he'd passed their exam with flying colors.

"I don't know if you could pull that off," I warned. "I think Hilary's already staked her claim to any of O'Donnell's spare time."

"I don't know if he'll have any. They seem pretty intent on the investigation."

"Hilary's always loved a challenge."

"Well, I think she's found one. O'Donnell seemed all business to me." His tone remained pleasant, but I sensed a note of tension.

"Did they give you a hard time?"

"The police? Let's just say that Emma's mother isn't the only person who's curious about the matter of Richard's will. I guess they found copies of both the old and the new one in his room. And they also seem to have discovered that my company's desperate for cash. They seemed pretty hung up on the idea."

"They can't honestly believe that you would have..." my voice trailed off.

"Who knows?" He shrugged. "The irony, of course, is that I don't think Richard had much money to speak of. His mother did a pretty good job of running through his father's estate, and Richard himself was the master of the highly leveraged lifestyle."

"I keep hoping they'll decide the entire thing was an accident and pack it in."

"Richard wasn't the sort to meet with accidental death. Untimely death—certainly. But accidental death? I don't think so." He seemed to be talking to himself as much as to me.

"How—how are you doing?" I asked.

"What do you mean?"

I chose my words carefully. "Well, everyone's so casual. It must seem sort of inappropriate to you since you and Richard were actually close. And it must be hard, to be upset when the rest of us have barely skipped a beat."

He paused before answering. "You know, I told you last night that Richard and I weren't really in touch. To be candid, we haven't been really close since we were teenagers. I felt incredibly awkward when he asked me to be his best man, but I would have felt even worse refusing him. That's not the sort of thing you say no to."

"No," I agreed. "It's not." I had briefly thought about refusing Emma's request to be her maid of honor. It had seemed so dishonest given how I felt about the groom. But her friendship was more important to me than taking a stand, and I'd realized that she was intent on going forward with the wedding, regardless of whatever stand I took.

"Richard didn't seem to have endeared himself to Emma's friends."

"No, I'm afraid he didn't." I liked Peter too much to try to get by with a platitude.

"I guess that all of the qualities that were so much fun when we were kids didn't make him a lot of friends as an adult."

"What do you mean?" I asked, curious as to what Richard had been like as a child. I'd always wondered whether he had been born an utter jerk or evolved into one.

"Oh, stupid things, mostly. He always had a plan up his

sleeve, a scheme of some sort. Not just silly pranks, but ways to get good grades without doing a lick of work, ways to get extra money from his mother, that sort of thing. He was always looking for shortcuts. And he had this incredible ability to pull anything off, because he could talk his way out of any situation. Our teachers loved him. They would fall for all of his lines. And he just sort of skated along on the basis of his charm and his wits."

"That sounds a lot like the Richard I knew," I said, as non-committally as I could.

"It's funny—my parents never liked him much. I think they were relieved when he went away to school and I wasn't spending as much time with him. They thought he was a bad influence." He gave a small laugh, remembering.

"Well, it sounds like he didn't have much of a family life to ground him in any way," I commented, referring to the conversation we'd had in the kitchen before lunch.

"No," agreed Peter. "He didn't." He was quiet for a bit, but then he continued in a firmer tone. "Still, there comes a point when someone has to take responsibility for his own actions—you can't just keep blaming your mother for screwing you up."

I thought about that, silently agreeing with him. I'd never had much patience for Freud or the endless analysis of one's childhood experiences that seemed to constitute so much of psychotherapy. So many people just seemed to use whatever happened in their childhoods as an excuse to keep them from moving forward. I thought about my most recent ex-boy-friend, a guy who spent more time with his therapist than he did with me. I'd heard the story about how his mother had lost him in the park one day on seven different occasions. Surely, thirty years later, he should have been able to get beyond that? And then, of course, there was all of that stuff about penis envy. What a hoax.

"In a way," Peter confessed, "I wasn't surprised when you

told me this morning that Richard was dead. It was as if I somehow always knew he'd come to a bad end. I just wish that there had been a way to make things turn out differently."

"There's nothing you could have done," I said. Reassuring words seemed called for.

He shrugged again. "I know that, on a rational level. Still, I feel like I had some sort of responsibility to him. That I messed up somehow." I knew exactly how he felt. I'd long since realized how fortunate I was to have such a close-knit group of friends. The loyalty we'd pledged to each other was more than idle words or a rush of ephemeral emotion. If anything were to happen to any one of them, I knew I would be asking myself the same questions.

I looked at Peter. His brown eyes were pointed toward shore, but his gaze was unfocused, as if he were deep in thought.

I reached over and put my hand on his arm. "There's nothing you could have done," I said again, this time more forcefully.

He turned to me. "I hope you're right."

"I know I'm right." Our eyes locked for a long moment. I realized that I was holding my breath. His head drew a tiny bit closer and I was painfully conscious of the touch of his skin under my hand.

"Thank you," he said.

I shook off the moment, suddenly scared, and drew back, my heart beating rapidly. "You won't be thanking me when I beat you to shore." I quickly jumped to my feet and dove back into the water, not turning to see if he was behind me.

"Chicken," I said to myself as I raced through the water. "Goose, wimp, wuss. Chicken."

CHAPTER 17

Peter and I tied each other in the race to shore, but as we dried off our conversation felt stilted and awkward, as if we'd come close to a precipice and backed away. He put on his T-shirt and I knotted my sarong tightly around my waist, and we proceeded together up the path to the house. The entire way, I cursed myself for having succumbed to skittishness and let such an exquisite moment pass. Maybe to have let things go any further would have been to take advantage of Peter's tenuous emotional state, but he had seemed willing to be taken advantage of. I sighed. If he hadn't realized what a freak I was before, that fact had to be blatantly obvious now.

We didn't run into anyone as we passed through the kitchen door and headed up the back stairs. We parted ways on the second floor. We both wanted to shower, and Peter said he had some more calls to make for work. His diligence made me remember, somewhat reluctantly, my own responsibilities. I made a mental note to check Mr. Furlong's fax machine for the papers from Stan after I'd showered and changed.

I was halfway to Emma's room and Peter had already mounted the first few stairs to the third floor when he stopped and turned. "Rachel," he called.

"Hmmm?" I answered, retracing my steps.

"Thank you. For what you said out there. You made me feel a lot better." The slight smile on his face was almost shy.

"Of course," I answered, embarrassed. I headed back down the hallway before he could see me beginning to blush all over again.

Emma's door was slightly ajar, and as I approached I heard a male voice within.

"Look, Emma, you know what you have to do." It was Matthew, I realized.

"I can't. You know I can't. How can you even ask me to? You, of all people, should understand."

"Well, maybe I should do it."

"No! Promise me you won't. Matthew, you can't."

I heard him sigh. "I promise. But just for now, Emma."

I reversed a few paces, coughed loudly, and burst through the door with as innocent a smile as I could muster plastered on my face. "Hello," I said brightly.

Emma was sitting on her bed wearing a thick Irish fisherman's sweater, much like the one she'd given me. Her knees were pulled up to her chest as she leaned against the headboard. Matthew was perched on the windowsill.

"Hi, Rach," said Emma.

"How was your swim?" asked Matthew.

"Chilly," I answered.

"In a good way?" asked Emma.

"No, in a cold way. But it was a nice break."

"Speaking of breaks," said Matthew, pushing himself off the sill, "I should get back downstairs and see if the police are done with Jane yet and if they're ready for you, Emma. It'd be good to get your interview over with so that they can leave already. I'll be back in a minute." He slipped through the door, and I shut it after him. Emma remained on her bed, her arms wrapped around her knees, her eyes downcast.

I started to sit down next to her, then remembered that my swimsuit was still wet. I took the place that Matthew had vacated on the windowsill instead. I wanted to confront her with what I'd heard—with all the questions I had—but she hadn't been willing to tell me anything earlier. Still, one way or another, I was determined to get to the bottom of everything. I couldn't help unless I had more information, and I couldn't get any information if Emma kept hoarding her secrets.

"So, how are you feeling?" I asked, easing into conversation.

"Spacey," she said. "I don't know what was in the pill my mother gave me, but I still feel as if I'm in a cocoon of some sort." I watched as she toyed with her engagement ring, a ruby surrounded by diamonds in an antique platinum setting. "I hear I missed quite a scene at lunch today," she continued. "My mother sounds to have been in rare form. Grandmother Schuyler would be scandalized. I don't think she'd approve much of a hostess suggesting that her guests are murderers."

I guessed that Matthew had recounted the lunchtime conversation for Emma. "Your mother was—well, I think she's had an upsetting day," I said, as delicately as I could. It's one thing for someone to mock her own mother, however affectionately. It's an entirely different thing for somebody else to concur, much less to point out that she'd consumed an entire bottle of wine unaided, no matter how much pressure the poor woman was under.

Emma gave a soft laugh. "Very tactful, my dear."

"Thank you. Grandma Benjamin didn't speak much English, but what she did say was always extremely polite. I try to do her memory proud."

"I bet they would have liked each other."

"Who? Our grandmothers?" I tried to picture it. Arianna Schuyler had been an icon of style in her time, with blood so blue it was practically royal. Grandma Benjamin, on the other hand, had been a Russian Jewish émigré. But she had been formidable in her own way. "You're probably right," I said, after I'd thought it over. "Although, I have a hard time imagining them gossiping over lunch at La Côte Basque."

"And what fabulous gossip today's events would be." She chuckled. "Poor Richard. He'll end up getting more press by dying than he could have ever hoped for alive." Her voice didn't indicate even the slightest bit of grief or anguish.

"You must be…" I hesitated, searching for the right words. She interrupted before I could find them.

"Relieved?"

"Emma! That's not what I was going to say."

"It's all right, Rachel. I am. Relieved. I mean, I'm sorry it all had to turn out this way, but I can't say I'm sorry that I'm not ever going to be Mrs. Richard Mallory."

This was the opening I'd been looking for and I seized it. "If you felt that way, Em, then what was this all about? Why were you marrying him? Please, Emma. If you tell me, then maybe I can help in some way."

She sighed. "Look, I told you before. I can't tell you. Even if I could, it's too complicated even to begin to explain. And, given the circumstances, it's probably not wise. People would think that I did the evil deed myself." I realized with a vague shock that I was glad to hear her say that. On some level, I had been scared to find out that she had, in fact, been guilty in some way of Richard's death. Her words, while cynical, seemed to point to her innocence. I fought the urge to ask her directly about the late-night rendezvous Peter had mentioned.

"Will you at least tell me what you think happened?" I asked instead. She replied with equal bluntness.

"I think somebody put something in his drink that knocked him out, and then, when he was unconscious, pushed him into the pool. I mean, even if you weren't very strong you could probably push him or roll him over the side into the water."

It chilled me anew to think that she'd already thought this through. Especially when, as far as I knew, she'd been the last person to see Richard alive.

"Don't get me wrong," she continued, as if she were reading my mind. "I didn't do it. I was ready to go through with the whole wedding, no matter how horrifying it would have been." She gave a small shudder.

"But even more horrifying," she went on, "is that here I am, surrounded by the people I love most, and somebody had the guts to do what I never could have. And whoever it was did it for me."

"Em, you must realize you're not responsible for this. For Richard being dead."

She shrugged. "Unfortunately, the fact of the matter is that, on one level or another, I am. If I'd been smart enough to stay away from him in the first place and to see through all the initial romance and excitement of it, he would have never gotten close to us and none of this ever would have happened. I wouldn't have had to put anybody through all of this."

I thought about the romance and excitement. Emma had always had a weakness for men who were aggressively social and ambitious, men who were interested in her for all the wrong reasons. On some level, I guessed that she was trying to live up to what she felt her parents expected—that her own life be as high-profile and glamorous as their own. But, even if the initial attraction had been there early on and could be easily understood, I was still confused about why she'd continued the relationship once she'd gotten a clear sense of what Richard was all about.

The frustration of not knowing was making me crazy. It was all too cryptic for me. I dealt with numbers and facts, earnings releases and stock prices. The nuances of human emotion—well, if I had that figured out, surely I would have a more fulfilling love life at the very least. Emma's stated desire not to tell me what had been behind the entire fiasco only rendered me insatiably curious. I'd held my tongue for so long, and now I'd had the barest glimpse of the surface of the truth. Surely I had a right to know, after everything that had transpired, what it was that Richard had held over her to force her into a union of which she so clearly wanted no part.

I gazed out the window, trying to figure out how I could get Emma to open up. It was after four, and although it would stay light out until well past eight, the sun was beginning its slow descent, casting a golden sheen on the lake and gilding the tops of the pine trees that fringed the shoreline. It would have been a beautiful wedding, at least aesthetically, if it had been actually taking place. I imagined us all here in Emma's room, helping to zip up each other's dresses and going through the requisite oohing and aahing over Emma's gown from Vera Wang.

Emma seemed to be thinking along the same lines. "You know, the funny thing is, I would have preferred a really small wedding. Just family and close friends and a string quartet playing Mozart and Vivaldi. Up here, of course, just minus a few hundred guests. No three-ring circus with tents and bands and caterers galore. Just us." Emma looked past me, through the window and out toward the lake as if she were picturing the scene she'd described.

"I sort of always thought that's the way it would be, too," I answered. I didn't say that I'd also always thought that it would be Matthew waiting for her at the end of the aisle.

"And instead, here I am, a widow, before I've even been

married." She giggled. "Do you think I have to return all the gifts?"

"I don't know. Surely there's a chapter in Emily Post that tells you how to handle such a situation?"

"Yikes. I don't think even Emily ever contemplated a chain of events quite like this."

"Interesting. There's probably a real market opportunity here."

"Etiquette for unthinkable events?"

"Exactly," I said. "Maybe we should put together a book proposal. I have some connections in the publishing industry. I could make a few calls and hook us up with a deal."

"We'd be on the bestseller list in no time."

"Not to mention the talk show circuit. Too bad Oprah cancelled her book club. Maybe she'll resurrect it, just for us."

"I think she usually stuck to fiction, but who knows? Maybe she'd take a look."

"Hmmm. I wonder what I should wear?"

"For our appearance on *Oprah*?"

"Yes."

"I'm thinking casual but chic."

"That's probably a good call. There'll probably be a lot of ancillary revenue opportunities, too. Product endorsements, American Express ads, the works. Remind me to send in my resignation to Winslow, Brown on Monday."

Emma laughed. "What about dismantling the establishment from within? How are you going to do that if you're no longer an employee?"

"Good point. Do you think we could maybe work on the book in our spare time?"

"Like you have any. I'm surprised they let you out for an entire weekend."

"Drat," I said, thinking again about Stan's fax.

"What?"

"There's something I need to take care of for work. It seems to keep slipping my mind."

"Maybe your mind's trying to tell you something. After all, there's no such thing as an accident."

I started to laugh at her words but stopped before I'd started. If only the police didn't feel the same way. Emma must have been thinking the same thing, because she was suddenly silent. Her fingers went back to their nervous fiddling with her ring, and she pressed her lips together in a tight line. I knew her well enough to recognize that she was trying not to cry.

"Okay, Emma. What the hell is going on?" I asked, throwing tact and subtlety to the wind for yet another try. "I heard you two just now. What do you have to do? What was Matthew talking about?"

"Oh, Rachel, it was nothing," she protested. "Really." But she kept her gaze resolutely fixed on her hands.

"Come on, Em. You're a rotten liar. I know that's not true. There's something important you're not telling me about you and Richard. You know, I heard you last night, too."

"What do you mean?"

"You and your father. Arguing on the porch at the club. He was practically begging you not to go through with the wedding."

"You heard that?" She finally raised her eyes to meet mine.

"Yes. It was an accident. I didn't mean to eavesdrop."

"I know you didn't. You wouldn't do that."

"Come on, Em. Tell me, already. There must be something I can do to help."

"I can't tell you, Rachel. I told you that before, and I mean it. You just have to trust me on this." She managed to sound both sad and exasperated at the same time.

"I do trust you. I know that you'd never do anything to hurt anyone."

"No. I never do, do I?"

Emma looked away and ran a hand through her hair. "I should probably go downstairs. The police must be ready for me by now." She slid down from the bed and crossed to the closet, pulling out a pair of sandals. I watched in silence as she slipped them on and headed for the door.

"Emma, wait. Maybe you shouldn't do this alone."

She stopped and turned back to face me. "What do you mean?"

"Maybe you should have a lawyer with you or something," I suggested gently.

"Good Lord, Rachel! How many times do I have to tell you? I didn't do it."

"I know you didn't. That's not what I meant. It's just that it might be best to have someone there to protect you, to help you—"

"Enough, already! Jesus, first Matthew and now you. When will you realize that I'm not an idiot, and I'm not a child? I can take care of myself, dammit." She stormed out of the room, slamming the door behind her.

CHAPTER 18

I'd never seen Emma so angry and I felt terrible—ineffectual and obtuse. All of my probing and prying had accomplished nothing except to bring out a temper in Emma I'd never known existed, much less seen aimed at me. This was the only time in all of the years we'd known each other that she'd even yelled at me. Something was desperately wrong in her life, and not only wouldn't she tell me, she thought I was condescending to her.

I felt foolish, too. I'd spent much of the day playing amateur detective, trying to piece together the events of the previous night, assuming that if I could get to an answer, I could manage the situation. But I hadn't been managing anything except a gross display of hubris—I'd just been fabricating scenarios that implicated my closest friends in Richard's death. I was a fool, and I wasn't a very good friend, either, projecting my idle suspicions everywhere I looked based on conversations I hadn't been meant to hear.

I hoped again that Jane was right—perhaps there was a

very simple, very innocent explanation for everything. Regardless, I should probably stop meddling, before I pissed off anyone else for no reason with my blundering arrogance.

Dejected, I stepped into the shower to rinse off the lake water, checking for any sign of a tan line as I toweled myself off. No such luck. There was a patch of pink on my right ankle where I'd missed a spot with the sunblock. It went nicely with the bruise that had spread like a rainbow across my instep, a colorful blotch that was black in the center and rimmed with a purplish-navy-blue that faded into greens and yellows at its outer edges. The good news was that I wasn't going to have to squeeze either of my feet into satin pumps that had been dyed seafoam-green to match my bridesmaid's gown. Instead, I put on my sundress and sandals again and combed my wet hair, leaving it loose to dry. I fastened my grandmother's locket around my neck and slipped a cardigan over my shoulders.

I left Emma's room and went to Jacob's study. I was a lousy friend and a rotten detective, but I was pretty good at my job, and, unless I wanted to screw that up, too, the time had come to stop procrastinating and work on Stan's new deal. I checked the fax but the pages in the output tray were smudged and unreadable, completely in keeping with everything else that was happening that day. I threw them in the trash and opened up the machine, removed the toner cartridge, and gave it a good shake before replacing it. Then I picked up the receiver and dialed OS again.

When Cora answered, I explained that the fax hadn't come through clearly the first time around, and she agreed to resend it. That done, I glanced around the room, looking for something to keep my mind from trains of thought that might further offend any of my friends. I crossed over to the bookshelves and scanned the titles. Mr. Furlong's taste ran to history and biography, but I found something more interesting tucked discreetly into a lower shelf. It was an oversize tome with glossy photographs, designed to grace coffee tables and proclaim to guests that the house in which it sat was an erudite and cultured one. For the Furlongs to display it in such a way would have been tacky, at best—it was a complete retrospective of Jacob Furlong's work.

I took the book and settled onto the sofa, idly flipping the stiff pages. I didn't know much about art, particularly not about abstract art, but many of the paintings were achingly beautiful. When Lily came into the room, I was so deeply immersed that I gave a start.

"Rachel, darling. So sorry—I didn't realize anyone was in here."

"I'm just waiting for a fax to come through from the office," I explained. "Is there anything I can help you with?"

"Oh, no, thank you. I just realized that I'd scheduled a cleaning crew to come on Monday, and there really won't be any need for it. I couldn't find their phone number, but Jacob has a phone book in here." She opened a desk drawer, removed a Yellow Pages, and began leafing through it. "Oh, dear. I left my reading glasses in the other room and the print is so small—would you mind looking it up for me?"

"Not at all," I said, joining her at the desk. She gave me the name of the service, and I found the listing and printed the number on a scrap of paper.

When I turned to hand it to her, Lily had bent to examine the title of the book I'd left on the sofa. "Ah, Jacob's retrospective," she said. "They put that out after the big show at the Museum of Modern Art last year."

"It's very impressive. I saw the show, too."

"Yes, it was a lovely exhibit. MOMA's always been very good to Jacob." She changed the subject. "And how are you, Rachel? Things have been so hectic that we haven't had a chance to catch up." She moved the book aside and perched on the sofa, readying herself for a good girlish chat. Apparently the discussion we'd had at lunch didn't count. It was a relief to see her so relaxed, so normal, after her earlier behavior.

"There isn't much to tell," I confessed. "My life is really dull."

"That's because you work too hard, dear. Emma's always talking about how they have you there until all hours. You must be terribly important."

I laughed. "If you only knew. I don't even qualify as a cog in the wheel."

"You're too self-deprecating, darling. You're a brilliant young woman—they're lucky to have you."

"I wish they felt the same way."

"And are there any young men or have you just been hiding yourself away in your office?"

"Nobody worth mentioning."

"It's odd, isn't it? New York is such a big city, but it can be hard to meet people."

"Meeting people is easy. It's meeting people I like that's difficult. How did you and Mr. Furlong meet?" I asked, eager to move the conversation away from my love life, or, more accurately, my lack thereof. The words were no sooner out of my mouth than it occurred to me that her relationship with Jacob was probably not the best topic to bring up right now, but it was too late to take them back.

She laughed again. "Oh, darling, that was so long ago. You can't really want to bore yourself with old stories."

"No, I'd love to know." I couldn't figure out a way to back-pedal without sounding awkward.

"Well, let's see. It was at a party down in the Village. The hostess was one of those Smith girls with intellectual pretensions, always trying to mix it up with the art world. A friend of a friend of Matthew's mother, actually. I felt very risqué, going all the way downtown. Matthew's mother prac-

tically had to drag me there. It was a good thing she did—
Jacob was at the party. And the rest, I guess, is history." Her
smile seemed a bit sad.

"Speaking of history, it was fascinating to see how his
work has evolved over time." I was eager for a segue, no matter how clumsy.

The smile faded, and she was silent for a moment, looking from me to the retrospective beside her. "Yes, well, he's
had a long career." She traced the image on the cover of the
book with a long, tapered finger.

The fax machine rang once then began to hum. "That
must be for you, Rachel," said Lily, rising to her feet.

"Unfortunately," I said. I returned to the fax machine to
check the page it was spitting out. This time there were no
smudges, but the print was too faded to be read. The toner
probably needed to be replaced, I realized.

"Mrs. Furlong, I'm sorry to bother you about this, but do
you know if there's more toner for the fax machine anywhere? I think it's just about out."

"Toner? Oh, I don't know. I've never understood how
that thing works. You should probably ask Jacob. He's in
charge of everything mechanical around here. He'll be able
to help you."

"Okay, I'll do that. Thank you."

"Of course, darling," she answered distractedly. She was replacing the book on the shelf when I left.

I went downstairs, passing the closed door of the library.
Emma was still inside with the police, and I tried not to worry
that they seemed to be spending more time with her than
they had with anyone else. I repeated Jane's words to myself
like a mantra—there was a very simple, very innocent explanation for everything—as I made my way across the lawns
and along the path to Jacob's studio in the old stables.

The door to the ramshackle building was ajar, and I could hear music playing within. Beethoven, I recognized. Not the Ninth Symphony, the *Ode to Joy,* but the melancholy, deliberate strains of the Seventh. I hesitated; I had little experience in interrupting geniuses at work, much less ones whose daughters had just told me they were adulterers. I stopped at the threshold and peered in.

Little had been done to renovate the interior, but the stalls now held stacks of canvases instead of horses, and the floor was so spattered with paint that it looked as if Jackson Pollock had been there. A rumpled daybed showed evidence of having been slept in, and judging by the stack of books next to it, this was indeed where Emma's father spent his nights. The aroma of turpentine and linseed oil infused the air along with a faint tinge of pipe smoke. Jacob himself was not standing at his easel but sitting in an armchair, hunched forward with his elbows on his knees. His eyes were gazing sightlessly at a spot on the wall. He looked up when I gave the open door a tentative knock, his startled expression quickly replaced by his usual avuncular smile. "Rachel? Come in, my dear. Do they need me back at the house?"

"Oh, no, at least, not that I know of. I'm sorry to intrude like this—it's just that my office is trying to send me a fax and the machine is out of toner. Mrs. Furlong said you would know where I could find some more."

"Toner? Sure. In fact, I think I have some in here, somewhere. Hang on a sec and I'll take a look for it." He rose from the armchair and crossed to a row of cabinets. The stiffness with which he knelt to rummage through a low shelf showed his age. It was hard to imagine him with Nina, who was only a few years older than me. Jacob was still a handsome man, but he was also eligible for Social Security. Emma must have been mistaken, I thought. But she had sounded so sure, and there was no reason to make up something like that.

"Here it is," he said, holding a box aloft and shutting the cabinet door. "Do you know how to change the cartridge?" He handed me the box.

"Yes, thanks." Winslow, Brown may have had an enormous support staff, but I'd fought more than my fair share of late-night battles with copiers, printers and sundry other office machinery.

"So, everything's under control back at the house?"

"I think so. Emma's in with the police right now, and they've talked to everyone else." It felt wrong to have to be telling him this; surely he should have been up there himself rather than having Matthew act as the surrogate man of the house.

"Emma's talking to them? Damn, I thought I told Matthew to come get me when…" I shifted uncomfortably as his voice trailed off. He ran a hand through his hair, disheveling it yet more. "Well, I'll walk back to the house with you."

I waited while he shut down the stereo, and then we proceeded toward the house together, pine needles crunching under our feet. The sun cast long shadows across the path, and there was the beginning of a chill in the air. I was glad I had my cardigan.

"So, Rachel, it's been quite a day, hasn't it?" he said, more of a statement than a question.

"Not exactly what I'd expected," I admitted.

"Nor I."

"How's Emma doing? Is she hanging in there?"

It wasn't my place to point out that if he'd been up at the house he would have been able to ascertain this for himself, firsthand. "She seems to be," I replied. "Mrs. Furlong and Matthew have been keeping a pretty close watch over her."

"Poor girl."

"Yes."

"But there's more strength in her than people realize."

"Yes, there really is," I agreed. Not that I'd given her any credit for it, I thought glumly.

"She must be exhausted, too," he continued. "You all were up late last night, on top of everything else, weren't you?" The inelegant way he asked this made me feel that he was fishing for something, but I wasn't sure what.

"Actually, I think Emma's one of the only people who got a good night's sleep. She went to bed right after the dinner."

"She did?"

"Sure. I came in around two and she was sound asleep."

"She was?" He sounded relieved.

"Yes," I confirmed.

But I was busy thinking that I didn't like that tone in his voice one bit. It was as if he'd just laid some important concern to rest.

As if he'd suspected his own daughter.

A very simple, very innocent explanation, I chanted to myself. But no amount of chanting could banish the sick sensation from the pit of my stomach.

CHAPTER 19

Emma was still sequestered in the library with the detectives when we arrived back at the house. Jacob took up a position outside the library door to wait for his daughter to emerge, and I headed upstairs to the fax machine.

I quickly replaced the toner with the fresh cartridge and called in to OS yet again. Cora had been replaced by the evening supervisor, who agreed to dig up the fax and resend it. She sounded harried and cautioned that she had a couple of rush orders to deal with so it might take a while for her to get to it. I told her that was fine, hung up the phone, and went downstairs. My own late night, early morning and midday cocktail hour was beginning to take its toll, and I was in dire need of some more caffeine.

I took a can of Diet Coke from the refrigerator in the kitchen and stepped onto the porch, hoping for some quiet time to figure out the very simple, very innocent explanation for why Jacob had suspected his own daughter and to remind myself of all of the other reasons that there was a very simple, very innocent explanation for Richard's death.

I started to turn back when I saw Hilary sitting on the wide old-fashioned bench swing that overlooked the lake. Her nose was buried in a thick book, but I'd known Hilary long enough to recognize that the odds of finding quiet time with her around were about as slim as the odds of winning the lottery. But the spring on the screen door foiled my retreat, drawing the door shut with a small bang. Hilary turned at the noise.

"Hey, Rach," she called, motioning me over. I went to sit beside her, the swing rocking with my weight. I flipped open the can of soda and took a sip.

"What're you reading?" I asked. She showed me the title, something dry-sounding about oil, Islam, and politics in the Middle East.

"Prepping for my next assignment," she explained. "I pitched a series of articles about fundamentalism in Egypt, and there are a couple of magazines that have expressed an interest."

"That's great. And there's lots of indoor plumbing in Egypt, isn't there?"

"More than most of the places I go."

"That's not a very high bar," I commented.

"So, have you heard any news?" she asked, gesturing in the vague direction of inside, and, presumably, the library where the detectives were ensconced.

"No. You?"

"No. I brought some iced tea in to the police a little while ago, when they were between interviews, but they weren't very talkative. I'm beginning to think that O'Donnell must be gay."

"You know, Hil, it's possible that he's just busy doing his job. I'd imagine that most police detectives aren't very flirtatious when they're conducting an investigation."

"True, but do most of the people police interview for a murder case look like me?"

There didn't seem to be a good answer to that. I shrugged and took another sip of my soda instead.

"What's wrong, Rach?" asked Hilary. "You seem a bit cranky."

"I'm just stressed. We are in the middle of a murder investigation," I reminded her.

"Maybe you should take something. I've got some Xanax upstairs. It's great for anxiety."

"What're you doing with Xanax?" I asked, alarmed. Hilary was a handful all on her own; Hilary on drugs was too much to contemplate.

"Oh, I've got a whole arsenal of stuff in my bag. You can get pretty much anything over the counter in Asia, so I stock up. Xanax, Halcion, Ambien. Nothing too serious. Just the sorts of things that help me sleep on red-eyes or deal with jet lag." It occurred to me that if I hadn't been so intent on convincing myself that there was a very simple, very innocent explanation for everything I might have found it disturbing to discover yet another person besides Matthew with the means to knock Richard out.

"I think I'll be all right," I said, demurring on the Xanax.

"Okay. But let me know if you change your mind."

"I'll beep you. All drug dealers have beepers, right?"

"Funny."

"I try." I nursed my soda, and Hilary fell into an uncharacteristic silence. It lasted for a good thirty seconds, probably a record for her.

"Rach?" she said, with a rare tentativeness.

"Hmm?"

"There's something you should probably know." Her words reminded me with a jolt that Luisa had said something remarkably similar before Matthew had interrupted her. That combined with Jane's account of Hilary and Luisa's nocturnal activities made me loath to hear what was on Hilary's mind. I had a feeling that anything she might say would do little to contribute to finding a very simple, very innocent explanation.

"What?" I asked, my heart beginning to beat faster. I took a bracing swig of my Diet Coke.

"Here's the thing—" began Hilary.

"Do I want to hear this?" I interrupted.

"I don't know. And what I'm struggling with is if anyone wants to hear this. Or if anyone *should* hear this. But Luisa and I discussed it and we've chosen you as the guinea pig."

"Lucky me."

"Be quiet already and just listen," she demanded. "We want to know what you think. Luisa tried before but she said she didn't get the chance, and we agreed that the next one who got you alone would try again. You're the analytical thinker in the group. Jane's too eager to believe that everything was all an accident, and when you hear what I have to say you'll understand that we couldn't talk to Emma about it."

"So just tell me already." Like the icy lake water, the best way to get this over with was probably to plunge right in.

"Well, after we came in from the dock last night, Luisa and I went up to our room and were talking for a while about how horrifying the entire situation was. You know, about how Richard was such a pig and how incredibly unhappy Emma seemed. And eventually we decided to come back down. It was around four or so. We were just going to go into Richard's room and give him a bit of a talking-to. We felt like we owed it to Emma." She paused, as if she were reluctant to say what happened next. This was peculiar. Hilary hardly ever paused for breath when she was telling a story in which she played a leading role.

"And…?" I asked, impatient. "Then what?"

"Well, we found him sprawled out on a lounge chair next to the pool. We thought he'd just fallen asleep, and we tried to wake him up. It took us a few minutes to realize he wasn't breathing." She gazed before her, as if she were reliving the scene in her head, and shivered. "It was really creepy."

It may have been creepy, but it was nice to hear that she and Luisa didn't seem to be the reason Richard wasn't breathing, especially now that I knew about Hilary's arsenal of dubiously obtained prescription drugs. "And…?" I prompted again.

"It was also worrying, for another reason. You see, when we came downstairs, we heard someone coming in from outside, and we ducked into the library so we wouldn't be seen. We only caught a glimpse, reflected in a mirror in the hallway, so it was hard to be sure who it was, exactly."

"Who did you think it was?" I asked with a sinking sensation. I had a bad feeling about what she was going to say next.

"We're pretty sure it was Emma," she continued. "So there we were. We'd just seen Emma on her way in from the pool. Then we found Richard dead, and there were two empty glasses beside him. It looked really, really suspicious. We couldn't be sure of what had happened, and we knew that Emma would never have done anything to him, but it still didn't look good for her. So we thought we'd try to make it appear as if Richard had had an accident of some sort. We picked him up and slid him into the pool. We were very careful to wipe away any fingerprints we may have left. Then we took the glasses into the kitchen, put them in the dishwasher, and ran it. On the superscrub function. And then we went back upstairs and waited until somebody found him."

"Geez," I said. "You could have warned me. I nearly had a heart attack when I saw him."

"It never occurred to us that you would be up at the crack

of dawn. There's no precedent whatsoever for such behavior on your part. You usually sleep until noon on weekends. And I guess you managed to sleep though Emma leaving your room and coming back in, too."

I thought about this. I really was a deep sleeper; Emma *had* managed to sneak out without waking me. And it fit with what Peter had told me.

"Maybe Emma thought he'd just passed out and went back to bed."

"Maybe. But do you really think that's likely?"

"Are you suggesting that Emma killed him?" I asked, an accusing note in my voice.

"Look, Rach. I know that Emma wouldn't hurt a fly, much less a cockroach like Richard. But how can you explain it?"

"I don't know. But Emma couldn't have done it. Come on, Hil. We've been friends with Emma for half our lives, practically. Can you really imagine her killing someone so cold-bloodedly?"

"Is cold-bloodedly a word?"

"Hilary," I replied, in my most threatening tone of voice.

"Okay, okay. I don't want to think Emma did it. But, for chrissakes, explain to me who did."

"God, Hil. I don't know." I was trying to sort through the logistics in my head. Peter said he saw Emma with Richard at the pool around three. And Hilary and Luisa had seen her around four. What could have happened in that one-hour window of time?

"So. Now what?" Hilary asked.

"What do you mean?"

"Luisa and I decided that we shouldn't tell anyone about this. But we wanted a second opinion. And, as I said, you're the guinea pig."

"Thanks."

"Anytime."

I thought for a moment, looking out at the still waters of the lake. "I don't think you should tell anyone else."

"Really?" Hilary sounded relieved. "We didn't think so, either. But it's reassuring to hear it from someone else."

Reassured was the last thing I felt, but I laid out my reasoning anyhow. "You and Luisa destroyed whatever evidence there might have been that would have proven who *did* kill Richard by cleaning everything up. You probably got rid of any fingerprints, and you washed the glasses. It's a good news-bad news scenario. On the one hand, you made it hard to tie Emma to any crime. On the other hand, you also made it difficult to tie anyone else to it, to exonerate Emma by getting at who really killed him."

"So what will happen? If the police can't tie anyone to it?"

"I don't know. Won't they just have to chalk it up as an accident?"

"Sounds good to me."

It sounded good to me, too. But I still wanted to know what had happened during that mysterious, unexplained hour when Emma was alone with Richard.

Somehow, that very simple, very innocent explanation seemed to be getting more and more elusive.

CHAPTER 20

Dinner that evening was about as pleasant as lunch had been. After Emma finished with the police, she met Lily's suggestion of another sedative with an acquiescent nod and let Matthew and her parents lead her up the stairs to bed.

I couldn't see how Emma's time with the police could have been anything but excruciating. O'Donnell seemed too thorough to cross her off the list of suspects simply out of courtesy. Between fighting off lines of questioning that called into doubt her own innocence and trying to protect the family and friends of whose innocence she was unsure, Emma, who was not an extrovert under the best of circumstances, must have been tested to the utmost. A deep, drug-induced sleep was probably a treat for her at this point. I, for one, would have been delighted to excuse myself from dinner and hop immediately into bed.

Alas. I knew enough about being a houseguest to recognize that dinner was a mandatory event. O'Donnell and Paterson left for the night, but at their request, we were all staying on—in fact, we were all staying until we were given notice that we were free to go. The situation created a bit of a Catch-22, given that we all wanted to seem cooperative. To protest would suggest having something to hide. Nor could any of us claim we had anything else to do—we'd all planned to be here through the weekend for the wedding and the Sunday morning brunch.

Jane and Sean once again took the lead on the culinary front, whipping up a gourmet feast of chicken marsala and asparagus risotto with their usual effortless grace in the kitchen. However, the quality of the cooking, the nice way Peter held my chair for me as we sat down, and even the fine Italian wines Mr. Furlong brought up from the wine cellar couldn't begin to mitigate the tension and gloom that hung over the table like an uninvited guest. Mr. and Mrs. Furlong positioned themselves at opposite ends of the table and did their best to imitate how genial, well-mannered parents would behave when hosting a dinner for their daughter's circle of friends, but few of us were feeling particularly talkative.

Fortunately, Hilary was capable of talking at great length with minimal support from her dining companions. She had taken advantage of the downtime that afternoon to sneak in a nap and had materialized at dinner thoroughly refreshed, radiating so much energy that it made me tired just to look at her. She danced from one topic to another, drawing on her extensive travels as a journalist, delighting in unraveling for her captive audience the Byzantine political intrigues of countries I'd never even seen on a map. The only participation required from the rest of us was an occasional murmur of wonder or assent.

Probably only a few people at the table caught the sharp edge in Mrs. Furlong's voice when she commented that Hilary traveled even more than Matthew's sister. "How is

Nina?" she asked Matthew. "It seems as if she's always gal-livanting about from one exotic locale to the next. What a fascinating job your sister has, but it does seem to make for a difficult schedule. We were so sad that she couldn't be here this weekend, although I guess, given the way things turned out, it's just as well." I snuck a peek at Mr. Furlong's face to see how he reacted to the mention of Nina's name. But his expression betrayed nothing as Matthew updated everyone on Nina's trip overseas to cover the designer shows in Florence.

I wondered again if Emma was right about her father's af-fair; if he truly was involved with Nina, he had one of the best poker faces I'd encountered, even in my years of nego-tiating with some of the wiliest, most poker-faced deal mak-ers on Wall Street. But Emma wasn't one to jump to conclusions, and she'd seemed very sure of what she'd told me.

Hilary neatly regained control of the conversation after this divergence, steering it away from Nina and back to her-self. I found my mind wandering as she held forth. I was hav-ing that strange feeling again, as if we were trapped in an Agatha Christie novel gone wrong. I was confident that Emma was innocent, and I was trying to hold firm to my re-solve to stop meddling, but the way every new piece of in-formation seemed only to strengthen a case against Emma made it hard to sit silently by while events ran their course. I kept trying to take comfort in the knowledge that all of the things I knew—that Emma was so unhappy at the prospect of marrying Richard, that she'd been alone with him around the time he must have died—the police didn't.

The convenient thing about Hilary's monologue was that it gave me the opportunity to collect my thoughts, to think through what could have happened in a structured, analyti-cal manner. I still didn't know what I would do if I got to an answer, but anything had to be better than being both anxious and clueless. One by one, I considered the options—or, more accurately, the potential suspects.

Of course, the first, most obvious person to address wasn't at the table but safely tucked away in one of the twin beds in her bedroom. From what Emma had said to me that afternoon, and from what I'd witnessed of her relationship with Richard, she had agreed to marry him under some form of duress. I couldn't even begin to think of what he must have held over her; Emma, unlike most people I knew, led a remarkably blameless life. I briefly considered the idea that she might be pregnant, but then discarded it just as quickly. Beyond the fact that her birth control pills were sitting out in plain view on the counter next to her bathroom sink, she'd had several glasses of champagne the previous evening. And in this day and age, pregnancy wasn't enough of a reason to marry someone, particularly if you were independently wealthy and had a strong emotional support network of family and friends.

Regardless of how Richard had coerced Emma into their engagement, it was becoming increasingly clear that she had been desperately unhappy about it. So I guessed that was motive right there. And, according to Peter, she'd had opportunity. She, of all people, easily could have snuck something strong into Richard's drink when she met him out by the pool. But on the amorality and sheer guts front, Emma just didn't stack up. I'd once seen her trap a fly in a jar and set it free outside rather than simply swat it with a magazine, like a normal person would do. That was hardly the act of a person who could murder her fiancé in cold blood.

Across the table from me sat Matthew, another high-potential suspect. His motive was abundantly clear. As for opportunity, Matthew was a doctor—he probably had easy access to something that could have been used to knock Richard out. And, staying in the pool house with Richard, he probably had the opportunity to act once Emma had returned to bed. But, once again, I just couldn't picture it. Matthew had dedicated his life to healing others, not to harming them. He'd shunned offers to join prestigious Park Avenue surgical practices in order to devote himself to a free clinic in one of the worst neighborhoods in South Boston. I was confident that I had more potential for evil in my little finger than Matthew had in his entire body. Besides, he of all people would realize that the medical examiner would be able to trace any drugs or poisons found in Richard's bloodstream.

I turned my gaze to the head of the table, where Mr. Furlong sat. His relief at my reassurances that Emma had been asleep the previous evening might have been relief that he didn't have to worry that she'd witnessed any treachery on his part rather than suspicions about what she may have done. Since he was staying in his studio last night, it would have been easy for him to move about without fear of being seen by someone in the house. The argument he'd had with Emma last night, the one Peter and I had overheard, left no doubt that he, too, was intensely opposed to the imminent marriage. He was also a fiercely protective father. Still, lots of fathers were unhappy about their daughters' choice of husbands, but that didn't mean they killed the groom before the wedding could take place. And I couldn't help but think that if Mr. Furlong was going to kill someone, he'd do it in a far more violent and direct manner than poison. He probably wouldn't even use a weapon but rely on his bare hands and ferocious will.

Mrs. Furlong sat opposite her husband at the foot of the table. I wondered what she had really thought of Richard. Before today, I had never heard her express anything but enthusiasm about Richard and the wedding. Except for her momentary lapse at lunch, she was usually so unfailingly polite that it was impossible to know what was really going on in her head. While her delicate exterior belied extraordinarily strong resolve, as well as a great deal of inner turmoil, surely her rigid sense of decorum would rebel against anything as inappropriate as doing in her daughter's fiancé the night before the wedding? It would be the ultimate social faux pas, not to mention the way it had created a logistical nightmare, what with all of the plans we'd had to cancel that morning, the gifts to be returned, and the wedding announcement to be pulled from the *New York Times* at the very last minute.

Next to me sat Peter, who was eating with a gusto that I found very appealing. I was confident that Peter had no motive to kill Richard. Why, he'd clearly been just as shocked to learn about Richard's will as any of us. So what if Peter's company needed money? Richard could hardly have had enough to make a difference, especially if Peter needed to get his hands on it quickly. I guessed he'd had the opportunity, although he would have had to wait until after Emma and Richard's rendezvous, which would have involved a lot of lurking around in an unfamiliar household without being seen. Besides, what kind of person would travel three thousand miles across the country to kill off his oldest friend? Peter was far too cute to be capable of such deceit. I crossed him off the list of suspects.

That left only my four roommates and Sean, an equally unpleasant set of potential candidates. Sure, we had made a pact many years ago, had joked about "wasting" a guy if he proved unsuitable. But like the pact we'd made to give up caffeine, it wasn't actually practical. And when I considered my friends, I couldn't believe that any of them had really seen fit to act on that long-ago promise.

What Hilary had told me out on the porch explained the noises Jane had heard coming from the room she and Luisa shared as well as their lack of surprise this morning. Still, Hilary also hated Richard, not only on Emma's behalf but because he'd had the gall to break up with her, something that undoubtedly had made her blood boil. But if Hilary killed every man with whom she'd had a failed romantic encounter, there would have been a long and gory trail of bodies in her wake. While she was usually the one doing the breaking up, she was confident enough to take the occasional rejection in stride. Murder in a fit of passion, I could almost picture, but the way this had been carried out didn't mesh with anything I knew about Hilary's style or character.

Luisa, of course, had the best reason of any of us to hate Richard. There would have been a lovely sort of poetic justice, as she herself noted, to turning the tables, putting something in his drink and doing him harm, just as he had done to her. But more than a decade had passed since he had, by her own admission, raped her. And even if revenge was a dish best served cold, Luisa's mantra of laissez faire when it came to the affairs of others would have prevented her from intruding on what was now Emma's business.

I recognized that Hilary's and Luisa's account of finding Richard already dead could have been a cover story on their part, but I doubted this was the case. And while I knew that Jane and Sean hated Richard as much as the rest of us, murder, no matter how you sliced it, was not playing fair. Jane and Sean, with their athlete's code of honor, were all about fair play.

Finally, there was me. It would be unfair not to turn my analytics inward. I had as much of a motive as anyone at the table, after all, between the professional harm Richard had done me and my friendship with Emma. And poison would have been right up my alley, given my inability to stomach any form of blood and guts. I'd once even passed out watching a particularly gruesome episode of *ER*. And that was just ketchup.

One of my favorite Agatha Christie's had always been *The*

Murder of Roger Ackroyd, in which the narrator ultimately revealed himself as the killer. I was the first to confess that I was deeply ambitious, and the embarrassment Richard had caused me in my professional life was great. And I would do just about anything for Emma, who was the closest thing to family I had, with the exception of my actual family. I might have a killer instinct at work, but could I have a killer instinct in any other part of my life?

I laughed to myself. If Agatha Christie were writing today, would she replace Miss Marple, Hercule Poirot, and Terrence and Tuppence with an overworked, admittedly avaricious investment banker? Many of the contemporary mysteries and thrillers I picked up in airports to sustain me through my business travels had female heroines, but they were usually FBI agents, private detectives or at least district attorneys. But Yuppies? I doubted that there was much of a market for MBAs turned amateur sleuths.

Besides, I didn't even know how to knit.

CHAPTER 21

Dinner finally ended a little after nine, with the gathered company once again declining Mrs. Furlong's strangely insistent urgings that we all try some wedding cake. It looked like all of that angel food and buttercream frosting was going to go to waste, and I, for one, usually reluctant to pass up anything involving disproportionate quantities of sugar and cream, was perfectly happy to let this opportunity pass me by. Mrs. Furlong sighed with regret then brightened up. "There's always lunch tomorrow," she said.

The "children," such as we were, with an average age among us of thirty-two, assured the Furlongs that we would take care of the cleanup. They agreed without protest and left the dinner dishes to us. Mrs. Furlong admitted to a slight headache before excusing herself and retiring to her room. Given the way she'd been hitting the bottle, I was surprised that her headache was only slight. Directly after his wife disappeared up the stairs, Mr. Furlong bid us good-night and returned to his studio as if this were the usual course of events. I wondered what kind of work he could possibly be getting done with everything that had transpired. I guessed nothing stood in the way of genius, but his powers of concentration were remarkable. Or perhaps he was actually spending long hours on the phone with Nina, whispering sweet nothings across the Atlantic.

We cleared the table and made quick work of rinsing and stacking the dishes in the dishwasher. The rest of the evening stretched before us, and while I was tired, I was also increasingly aware that my time with Peter was limited. My analytics at dinner had left me somewhat reassured—if I, with a thorough understanding of the cast of characters and the events of the previous evening, could not figure out who was responsible for Richard's death, the police would be at an even greater loss. Surely they'd be forced to give up their investigation and chalk the entire incident up as an accident, or at least an unexplained mystery? Inevitably, I hoped, they would give us all permission to leave at some point tomorrow, and while it was nice to be feeling less anxious about one of my friends being found out as a murderer, I now had time to worry about my romantic interests. Once we were free to go, Peter would return to California and I to New York, back to my empty apartment, my overflowing briefcase, and the never-ending stream of voice mails from Stan. To let any potential romance slip through my fingers, even if the object of desire did live on the opposite end of the continent, would be nothing short of a tragedy. I would be a fool to go to bed early, regardless of how tired I was.

"So, now what?" asked Hilary, as Jane flipped the switch to run the dishwasher. "It's really too bad that we can't go into town and check out the nightlife. There must be at least one great dive bar nearby, with a pool table and really cheesy jukebox. I wonder how O'Donnell spends his free time up here?"

"You really do have a one-track mind," observed Sean. He

seemed surprised, after all the years he'd known her, by Hilary's tremendous ability to latch onto an objective and pursue it, refusing to yield to either obstacles or distractions.

"It's important to stay focused," responded Hilary flashing him a smile. Perhaps I should take her advice, I thought. I wondered how she'd handle the Peter situation if she were in my shoes.

"Why don't we go into the living room and light a fire?" I suggested. "We could toast marshmallows or play Scrabble or something." Probably not how Hilary would have handled it, but at least I'd presented an option that didn't entail everyone going immediately to sleep.

Luisa laughed. "Parlor games? Oh dear. What have we come to?"

"I think that sounds nice and normal, which should be a refreshing change," said Jane, neatly folding a dish towel and placing it on the counter by the sink. "Besides, I'm too wound up to go to bed right away."

"Okay," said Hilary. "But no charades. I hate charades. And no Pictionary. Lord, but that's a stupid game. And no chess. It's too slow. And no…" she headed toward the living room, trailing a list of the games she wouldn't play behind her.

Matthew begged off and went to check on Emma, but the rest of us filed into the living room, where Sean skillfully built a fire in the old stone fireplace. I opened the wooden armoire that housed various board games, some dating from the 1950s: original editions of Chinese Checkers, Parcheesi, Dominos, and Life. Hilary squealed with delight when she unearthed the battered boxes for Candy Land and Chutes and Ladders, but these were rejected unanimously by everyone else. After some debate, we also rejected Scrabble as being too difficult to play with so many people.

"How about Monopoly?" asked Peter innocently. "I've always liked Monopoly."

Jane groaned. "That's because you've never played it with Rachel."

"What's that supposed to mean?" I asked indignantly.

"Are you a sore loser?" asked Peter.

"Of course not," I said. "I never lose at Monopoly."

"She's more like a sore winner," explained Luisa. "She rejoices in beating others mercilessly and then rubbing their faces in their defeat. And it's not just Monopoly. Anything that involves dice or money or numbers turns her into a demon. There was one spring break when we had to ban Rachel from all of our card games because she was such a shark."

"Hypercompetitive bitch would be a more accurate description," said Hilary. They'd clearly exhausted their abilities to talk me up that afternoon on the raft.

"Well, in that case, maybe Rachel and I should be on the same team," said Peter. Ah. A kindred spirit.

"Unless, of course, you're all too chicken to play," I added.

"Oh God, here we go," said Jane, resigned. We paired off, Peter and I against Jane and Sean and Hilary and Luisa, and set the board up on the coffee table. I loved Monopoly with a passion that probably bordered on unhealthy. It was so much easier to make piles of paper money than it was to make piles of real money, and much more fun than dealing with Stan and his ilk. During the next ninety minutes, Peter proved that he could play Monopoly just as well as he could dance, which, in my book, was an even more desirable trait. Our strategies were perfectly aligned, and we acted as a seamless commando unit. Boldly, we stormed the board, buying up every property we landed on and mortgaging them all to the hilt so that we could buy yet more, then using our rents to build houses and hotels.

"This sucks," said Hilary, after she and Luisa landed on a hotel-studded Park Place for the second time. I chortled with glee as they handed over the rest of their cash and two railroads to make payment. Jane and Sean hit it, too, on their next trip around the board, and it wiped them out. Hilary and Luisa lasted one more turn before turning over the rest of their properties.

Peter and I were happily counting our winnings when the losing teams announced, in unison, that they were going to bed.

"Winners get to clean up," said Jane, gesturing to the debris of the game and the scattered coffee cups and glasses from after-dinner drinks.

"Are you sure you don't want to play again?" Peter asked. "It's not even midnight." We were both energized by our stunning victory.

"I'd rather poke my eyes out with a stick," said Hilary with a pout.

"Now who's being a sore loser?" I asked.

"Good night, all," said Sean with finality, steering Jane toward the door.

"Be good, you two," called Hilary over her shoulder, unable to leave without at least one embarrassing parting shot. Luisa smiled tiredly and followed them out.

"Some people just flee from a challenge," I said to Peter.

"Well, it must be disheartening to be so completely blitz-krieged. Maybe we can stir up a rematch in the morning once they've had time to recover." He started sorting the multi-colored bills and placing them back in their slots while I began gathering up the property cards.

"With those cowards? I doubt it." I handed him the property cards and turned to rounding up the green plastic houses and the red plastic hotels. My hands felt clumsy as I fumbled with the small pieces, and I realized that my heart was starting to pound.

A moment of reckoning was drawing near. If one of us

was going to make a move, the time was as ripe as it was going to get. And, except for the lingering memory of Richard's body in the pool, I couldn't have asked for a more romantic moment. The fire had burned down to dying embers, emitting a warm, orange glow that burnished the room with soft light. We were seated next to each other on the overstuffed sofa, and my arm still tingled from where it had brushed Peter's as we'd moved our miniature top hat around the board.

Peter reached for the bag of houses and hotels, and I passed it to him. He took it in one hand and tossed it in the box while with the other hand he took gentle hold of my wrist. I froze, astonished by the overwhelming effect this simple action had. Trying not to blush, I slowly looked up at him.

"Hi," he said softly. His dark gaze fastened on mine.

"Hi," I answered back, unsure what else to say. His look was unexpectedly serious, and I felt a pang of alarm at the gravity of his expression. It suggested that he was about to deliver some very bad news. My heart began to pound yet faster.

"I know that this is—er, well, inappropriate, given the circumstances, and I have no idea what you're thinking," he began, while I fought the urge to jump up and flee before he could tell me why he wasn't interested in me. I willed myself to stay calm.

"It's just that I've been wanting to kiss you ever since I first laid eyes on you last night."

I almost fainted with relief. And disbelief. "Really?"

"Really." He nodded, his expression still serious.

"Me, too," I admitted. I let my eyes linger on the smooth curve of his lips.

"Really?" He seemed surprised. Which was surprising, given the degree to which I'd done little but blush and giggle in his presence since we met.

"Really," I confirmed, trying neither to blush nor giggle and for once succeeding.

"Good." His eyes were still focused on mine.

I summoned up my courage. "So, are you going to?"

"Going to what?"

"Kiss me?"

He laughed and ran his free hand through my hair, tracing the line of my cheek with his index finger. "Well, since you put it like that." He leaned forward and touched his lips to mine.

And I melted.

It had been a long while since I'd made out on a sofa with somebody's mother sleeping upstairs. I made a mental note not to wait so long until the next time. Kissing Peter felt like coming home in a way that actually coming home didn't even begin to replicate.

We must have spent the better part of an hour tangled up in each other's arms. He was, hands down, the best kisser I'd ever encountered. And while my list of encounters was dwarfed by Hilary's, a decade and a half of dating had added up.

"You're an excellent kisser," I told him when we came up for air. I was trying to remember what size the bed was in his room on the third floor and wondering how I could gracefully get us both into it without coming across like a complete slut.

"As are you," he answered with a grin. I was lounging against a needlepointed throw cushion, my legs twisted up in his. He propped himself up on one arm and looked down at me, leaving his other arm nicely wrapped around the curve of my hip.

"What's this?" he asked, reaching up to touch the locket I wore around my neck.

"It was my grandmother's," I explained. "My father's mother. Look." I opened it up to show him the tiny old-fashioned pictures, my grandmother on one side and my grandfather on the other. "I never knew them—they died before I was born. But my father was an only child, and my brothers would look funny wearing it, so it came to me." I didn't tell him that sometimes I studied their faces and wondered if one day my own granddaughter would wear this locket, with the pictures of my grandparents replaced by ones of me and my husband.

"Nice," he said. He gave me a deep, searching look, and then bent his head to kiss me some more. But he stopped before his lips reached mine and picked his head back up.

"Rachel, there's something I really should tell you." His voice suddenly held a somber note. My heart skidded to a stop. I knew he was too good to be true. I waited for the other, very heavy shoe to drop.

"Is this the part where you tell me about your wife and three children back in San Francisco?" I asked, striving to sound lighthearted. With my luck, there were probably four children and an adorable Wheaton terrier named Rags or Bailey or something equally adorable.

He chuckled. "No, no wife. Never married. No kids. Nothing like that. I promise. I'm even straight." As if I needed reassurance on *that* front.

"Hmmm. Then you need to tell me about your fatal disease, which also happens to be contagious?"

"Nope. Last time I checked, I was in pretty good health. A few gray hairs, but that seems to be the extent of it."

"Okay, then," I said, struggling up to a sitting position. "I think I know what it is. You still live with your mother."

"You have a very active imagination."

"You clearly have never sampled the dating scene in New York."

"That bad, huh?"

"Don't get me started."

"Seriously, there is something you should know." I found myself holding my breath, waiting for the words that would destroy any future we might have had together. Oh well, I tried to console myself, at least we'd had one nice hour of heavy necking before it all came crashing to a halt. I began pasting Peter's picture into the mental scrapbook that housed the faces and memories of love affairs past.

"Go on," I said. "The suspense is really more than I can bear." I steeled myself for what was undoubtedly going to be a deal-breaking confession.

"It's just that—" He paused, searching for words. To my astonishment, I realized that he was beginning to blush. Perhaps *I* was the one with a contagious disease. "It's been a long time since I met someone I really, really liked. And, I know this is completely premature and not the best of timing and everything and we couldn't live farther away from each other without moving to entirely different hemispheres. I guess what I'm trying to say is that I don't know quite how to say this."

If he didn't say whatever it was soon, I was going to have to kill him.

Fortunately, he finally blurted it out. "It's just that I think I'm falling in love with you. Ever since we met last night, and then this morning, and then again when we were out on the raft. You're so beautiful and smart and funny. And every time I'm with you, I feel like everything's falling into place. Like you're the missing piece."

I looked away, speechless and overwhelmed, trying to absorb his words. He couldn't have said anything better, not even if I'd written the lines myself.

"I'm freaking you out, aren't I?" he asked, trying to read my thoughts.

"No," I said slowly. "No," I said again, meeting his gaze. "It's just that you are too good to be true."

"It is true. Everything I said. I swear it."

"Then will you kiss me some more?"

"I'm completely at your service."

"Good answer."

It was less than two hours later that I discovered he was a murderer.

CHAPTER 22

A creaking noise out in the hallway startled us out of another prolonged session of kissing.

"What was that?" I asked.

"Anyone there?" called Peter. There was nothing but silence in the hallway. "Probably just the house settling. It must be at least a century old," he said. "And everyone's been asleep for ages."

"I don't know how they can sleep." It was funny how declarations of love and truly superb kissing could wash away exhaustion. It must have been one in the morning, but I felt well rested, even energized.

"Me, neither. Hey—I have a brilliant idea. Any interest in a midnight swim?"

The prospect was so romantic that I completely forgot just how icy the lake water had been in broad daylight. "That sounds wonderful."

We hurried upstairs to change into swimsuits. Emma didn't wake as I slipped in and out of her room. I met Peter in the kitchen, and we let ourselves out the door and headed toward the lake. He grasped my hand in his as he led us down the moonlit path.

"It's so quiet," I said.

"Peaceful," he agreed as we arrived at the beach. His white T-shirt glowed in the moonlight as he took it off and tossed it on the overturned canoe. I left my sarong and the towels I'd grabbed next to it and started to join him at the water's edge before I remembered my locket. I hastily undid the clasp and left it alongside our discarded clothes; I would feel terrible if I lost it in the lake.

"I don't think wading in is going to work," said Peter after sticking a toe in the shallows. "Too cold. Come on."

He took my hand again and we walked out to the end of the dock. We stared at the icy water.

"Okay. Last one in is a rotten egg."

"More like first one in is a frozen egg?" I responded.

"Why don't we do this together?" he suggested. "On the count of three." I agreed, and still holding hands, we jumped into the dark water. Not surprisingly, it was even colder than it had been that afternoon. But somehow, being there with Peter, I didn't mind.

After lots of splashing around interspersed with kissing— which was even more impressive given the extra challenge of having to tread water at the same time—we made our way back to the shore. My teeth were chattering as we toweled ourselves off, and he wrapped me in a bear hug, stilling my trembling lips with his warm ones.

"How do you do that?" I asked.

"Do what?"

"Keep your lips so warm?"

"The fire of passion, obviously. Come on—I should get you inside before hypothermia sets in."

We hurried up the path. "Now I have a brilliant idea," I said.
"What?"
"Hot chocolate."
"Do you even know how to make it?"
"No, but you probably do, don't you?"
He chuckled. "I might be able to figure it out." We let ourselves back in through the kitchen door. By the single light left on over the sink, we scrounged up the necessary ingredients and equipment.

I perched myself on the counter next to the stove as he poured some milk into a saucepan and lit a flame under it. I watched him stirring in cocoa powder and sugar.

"How interesting," I said. "I always thought you just added water to one of those little packets and put it in the microwave for a few minutes. I never realized it was so complex."

"It's much better this way. Authentic. No preservatives or partially hydrogenated anything."

"Preservatives and partially hydrogenated things are two of the major food groups, along with caffeine and alcohol. Besides, it seems like a lot more work to make it from scratch. And the packets sometimes have mini marshmallows in them."

"Sorry, no mini marshmallows. Can you find something to drink out of?"

"Sure." I slipped off the counter and found a couple of earthenware mugs in a cabinet. He divided the steaming liquid between them and deposited the saucepan in the sink.

"This is so nice," he said, when we were seated at the kitchen table, sipping the cocoa. "I've been so stressed from work, and then everything with Richard—well, I suddenly feel so relaxed."

"Is work that stressful?" I asked.

"Yeah. You know how it is with a startup. It's a constant race—all you want to do is build the business, get the products to market, but you spend most of your time trying to scrounge up financing."

"I know. I'm actually supposed to start work on a take-over. My boss, the 'drunken preppie' I was on the phone with this morning, just told me about it. Some young tech company's about to default on a loan and the vultures are circling."

"The economic climate's done in a lot of startups. It's definitely a good time to be a vulture."

"Apparently, our client prefers to be called Smitty. And I prefer to be called a financial advisor."

"I'll remember that," he said.

"Thank you."

"You've stopped shivering."

"The magic of cocoa. You're an excellent cook."

"But a complete dunce at napkin folding. Good thing you're here. We make a great team."

I giggled. "You have a cocoa mustache."

"I do?"

I nodded and wiped his upper lip with my finger. He put his hand on the back of my neck and pulled my head towards his. His mouth tasted deliciously of chocolate when he kissed me.

A few minutes later he deposited me at Emma's door. Drowsiness had kicked in, and I hadn't protested when he suggested that it would be wise for us to get some sleep. After one last lingering kiss, we parted ways.

Emma was still peacefully asleep, her breathing deep and regular. I quickly brushed my teeth and combed the knots out of my damp hair before slipping into some embroidered satin pajamas Hilary had bought me in Hong Kong. I slid under the fluffy duvet of the other twin bed with a sigh of pleasure.

I was in that nebulous state of almost-sleep, cocooned in the down comforter, when I remembered my locket. My hand went to my throat and it wasn't there.

"Drat," I whispered. I must have left it at the lake. I couldn't imagine that it would go anywhere before daylight, but it made me nervous to know it was out there. I could picture it catching the eye of a nocturnal bird, who would spirit it away to decorate its faraway nest. With a sigh, I threw back the covers and got out of bed.

I grabbed my flip-flops and tiptoed out of the room. I hurried down the carpeted stairs; the creak of a loose board seemed to ricochet in the silence of the sleeping house. I felt my way through the darkened rooms into the kitchen, pausing to jam my feet into the flip-flops. The hinges whined as I opened the door, and I was careful to shut it behind me so it wouldn't slam.

The moon had disappeared behind a cloud, and it was difficult to pick out the path to the lake without its light. I hurried along as best I could, cursing when I stubbed my big toe on a tree root. The still night had seemed so tranquil and welcoming when I'd been with Peter; now it seemed threatening, as if danger skulked among the pines that lined the path. A gust of wind stirred the branches and rippled through my loose pajamas. I thought longingly of the smooth sheets and cozy blankets on my bed in Emma's room.

I finally reached the beach, but not before stubbing my other big toe on another tree root and narrowly avoiding a wipeout when I tripped over a strategically placed rock. At least Peter wasn't along to witness my display of grace and coordination.

I could barely make out the dim outlines of the canoe in the murky light. I bent and ran my hand along its hull, searching for the locket, but all I got was a nasty splinter in my index finger. Fortunately, it was big enough and long enough that I could extract it by gently pulling on the end.

With more caution, I returned to my search. I gingerly felt up and down the hull of the canoe but to no avail. I took a few steps back, hoping that I'd catch a glimmer of gold but saw nothing but shadows.

A rustling in the trees distracted me. I jumped. The dark had me more scared than I wanted to admit, even to myself. "Hello?" I called. My voice sounded thin and hesitant.

There was no answer, but there was more rustling. I saw a shape move, and a shiver of fear jolted up my spine. I grabbed one of the loose oars next to the canoe, thinking I could use it as a makeshift weapon against whatever evil might lurk in the undergrowth.

Then, a lone deer leaped soundlessly from the thicket and onto the narrow beach. It paid no attention to me but padded gracefully up the shore a bit and began lapping at the water.

Bambi. I'd been afraid of Bambi. I let out the breath I'd been holding and almost laughed aloud.

I dropped the oar and returned to the mission at hand, first circling the canoe and then kneeling alongside it. Swearing softly, I started sifting through the sand, wondering what I was going to do if I couldn't find the necklace. Perhaps Mr. Furlong had one of those handheld metal detectors I'd seen advertised on late-night television, trumpeted as a surefire way to turn up buried treasure. I doubted it; Jacob and Lily didn't have much of a need for supplementary income.

After several minutes of fruitless sifting, I leaned back on my heels and brushed the sand from my hands. There was no way I was going to find anything in the dark, and I was probably making matters worse. I should stop before the locket was completely hidden by a pile of sand. I'd come back in the morning, when I could see. I'd bring a strainer or a colander or something, and I'd draft my friends into helping me.

I got to my feet, taking one last look at the deer, wondering if it was a male or female. This one didn't have antlers, but I couldn't remember which gender got the antlers. It looked delicate, with cute little white spots and big dark eyes, but I decided it was a boy. I took small steps in his direction, trying not to panic him. If I was going to be trapped in nature for a weekend, it would be nice to at least be able to pet a deer. Too bad I hadn't thought to bring a salt shaker so that I could fashion an impromptu salt lick.

He looked up from the water as I approached but didn't move. "Here, Bambi," I said softly, holding out my hand, palm down, the way I'd been told you were supposed to do with strange dogs. Bambi stepped forward, his nose twitching. I was within a couple of feet, nearly close enough to touch, screwing up my nerves to give him a little stroke between the ears, when he suddenly jerked his head toward the trees. Quick as lightning, he vaulted away into the underbrush.

So much for communing with wildlife. I turned to make my way back to the house.

I saw a glint of white from the corner of my eye, but I didn't have time to figure out what it was. I heard a whoosh in the air above me, then a crack as something made contact with my head. The dark night erupted into color, and I felt myself crumple to the sand.

CHAPTER 23

The next thing I knew, there were strange lips on mine, blowing air into my lungs. I coughed, feeling water pouring out of my mouth. "Ugh," I said, starting to sit up but somehow unable to lift my head, which felt as heavy and as capable of clear thought as a bowling ball. "Ooh," I groaned. I never realized I could feel so hungover without actually being dead. And I wasn't even hungover.

"Rachel? Can you hear me?" The faces in front of me swam into blurry focus.

"Jane? Sean? What are you doing? Where am I?"

"Jesus, Rach, what happened?" Given their greater experience with and appreciation of country life, they'd thought to bring a flashlight with them, and by its light I could make out the look of concern on Sean's face as he helped me into a sitting position. I looked around. We were on the beach, and not too much time could have passed, because it was still quite dark.

"I don't know," I answered slowly, confused. "I'd come

down to get my locket. Peter and I went for a midnight swim, and I left it here by accident. But I couldn't find it, and then Bambi ran away." God, my head hurt.

"Bambi?" asked Jane.

"The deer."

She turned to Sean. "Do you think she could have a concussion?"

"Look, Rach, Jane and I found you passed out here on the beach. We both woke up in the middle of the night and couldn't get back to sleep, so we came down for a midnight swim. We found you lying here, facedown. Your head was in the water."

"If we hadn't come when we did you could have drowned," said Jane. Her usual calm was gone. "Sean knows CPR, thank goodness." None of us would have guessed that CPR would turn out to be such a valuable skill this weekend.

I reached a tentative hand up to my aching head. A bump was rising from the crown, which I had a feeling would go all too well with the one on my instep, my two stubbed toes, and the puncture from the splinter in my finger. Too bad being a klutz wasn't the sort of thing people looked for on a résumé.

"I think maybe I fell and hit my head on something," I said sheepishly.

"On what? There's nothing around you," Jane pointed out, using the beam of the flashlight to scope out the sand and the water.

"I don't know. A rock or something?" I tried to remember, but my head hurt too much. "You know how clumsy I am. If there's something to trip on or slip on or hit my head on I always manage to find it."

"Come on," said Sean. "We should get you back inside." I let them hoist me up. My legs felt shaky, and I saw silver spots before my eyes for a moment, but my vision soon cleared. They flanked me, each keeping a firm grasp on one of my arms, as we trudged up the path. With the aid of the flashlight, I managed to avoid doing any further damage to myself on the way to the house.

Back in the kitchen, they deposited me on a chair. Sean began examining the back of my head, and I heard Jane rummaging in the pantry. "There's definitely a lump," Sean announced.

"Ouch—there's no need to poke it," I said. Jane returned with a glass of brandy and handed it to me with the sort of look that implied I should shut up and drink it. I took a big sip, coughing with its fiery warmth.

"We should get Matthew," said Jane.

"No," I cried. "I'm fine." I felt foolish enough; I didn't want to rouse Matthew in the middle of the night and have to explain my latest exercise in gracelessness. I was already bracing for extensive retelling of the story I'd been stupid enough to tell my friends in college, about how my childhood ballet teacher diplomatically suggested that perhaps I should try modern dance instead. "Ouch," I said again, as Sean placed something cold on the back of my head.

"Here," he said. "I wrapped some ice in a towel. Hold it in place, okay?" I did as he told me. They both pulled up chairs and sat facing me.

"So, tell us everything," said Jane.

"I told you already," I protested.

"Tell us again," said Sean.

"Look. I went swimming—"

"With Peter?" asked Jane.

"Yes," I confirmed. "And when I got into bed I realized I'd left my locket down at the beach. And I didn't want anything to happen to it. So I went to look for it."

"Alone?"

"Uh-huh. But I couldn't find it in the dark. And then I

saw a deer. He'd come to get a drink of water. He was really cute. And he almost let me pet him. But then he freaked out and ran back into the woods."

"Then what?"

"I don't know," I confessed. "Next thing I knew you guys were there."

"Why didn't Peter come back to the lake with you?" asked Sean.

"He was already in bed. It didn't make sense to wake him." I saw a look pass between them that I didn't like.

"Look, Rach, Peter seems like a good guy and all, but you need to be careful," said Jane.

I bristled. "What do you mean?"

She glanced at Sean. They had their version of good cop-bad cop down to an art form, although in this case it was more like good cop-good cop. "She didn't mean anything, really," he said. "But we know that somebody killed Richard, and we don't know who. Peter seems cool and everything, but he's still an unknown quantity."

"He's known to me," I said hotly, taking a swig of the brandy.

"Let's look at this another way," Jane said. "Sean and I come along and find you passed out, facedown in the water. You think you tripped and fell on something, but the bump is on the back of your head. Beyond the fact that we didn't see what exactly you tripped on, or what exactly you could have hit your head on, why were you lying on your front and not on your back? That doesn't make sense when the bump is on the back of your head."

"Since when did you start writing for *CSI*? What are you trying to say?" I felt defensive, and I wasn't sure why.

"Someone could have hit you with something," said Sean gently.

"Why would anybody do that? You're being ridiculous."

"Maybe," he answered. "But it's a possibility. Do you know something? Something that somebody doesn't want you to know? You've got to remember, there is a murderer loose in the house."

"Oh, come on," I said, exasperated. "This is absurd. You know what a spaz I am. I've managed to do all sorts of damage to myself before without any help."

"Okay, okay," said Jane. "But, when it's light out, we're going to go back down to the beach and look around."

"Fine," I grumbled. "While you're at it, you can help me find my locket."

"And you're going to tell the police about this in the morning," she added, in the voice she usually reserved for recalcitrant students who'd failed to do their homework.

"All right. Geez. I never knew you were such a tyrant."

Sean grinned. "How do you think she got me to marry her?"

"Oh, please. You begged me to marry you. I only agreed because I felt sorry for you."

I wasn't in the mood for any cute happy-couple banter. "Well, thanks for helping me out back there." I didn't want to be ungracious; they had saved my life, I guessed.

"Our pleasure. Now, are you sure you don't want us to get Matthew to take a look at you?"

"No. I feel fine. Really."

"We should make her walk a straight line or something," said Jane.

"Or close her eyes and touch her fingers to her nose."

"I can't do that under normal circumstances," I reminded them.

"Well, then, let's get you to bed," said Sean.

I felt too wound up to sleep, but I doubted I'd be able to withstand further bullying. I polished off the rest of the brandy and pushed my chair away from the table. "Okay."

"Just do us a favor, Rach."

"Hmm?" I asked, emptying the towel of melting ice into the sink.

"When we get you back to your room, go to bed and stay there until morning, all right?" Jane had on her I-will-brook-no-nonsense-from-anyone face.

"And no more roaming around the house alone in the dark," contributed Sean.

"Or roaming around outside in the dark," Jane added.

"Jawohl, mein Führers. No roaming around anywhere in the dark. Anything else?"

She sighed. "Just be a little bit careful, Rachel. Is that too much to ask?"

"No," I grumbled. "I promise, I'll be a little angel."

"You always are." She smiled.

"Make way for me and my halo," I said.

They followed me up the stairs.

CHAPTER 24

Just because I'd been told to go to sleep didn't make it easy. My nice swim with Peter and the hot cocoa had left me cozy and relaxed, but my second nocturnal trip to the beach and its aftermath had left me with the strung-out, frazzled feeling I got after I'd pulled an all-nighter—exhausted but unable to sit still. In Emma's room, I fished some Advil from my bag and washed it down with a glass of water from the bathroom tap. I envied Emma the sedative she'd taken; if I knew where to find some I'd be tempted to take one myself. Another night with minimal sleep was the last thing I needed.

My pajamas were all sandy, so I exchanged them for an oversize T-shirt and got back into bed, where I tried to recapture the warm drowsy feelings I'd had before I'd gone to retrieve the locket. But my body throbbed at every extremity, and my mind was racing. Jane and Sean were being alarmist, I knew, but I still found their warnings discomfiting. I hadn't liked their concerns about Peter, or that look that had passed between the two of them. I'd finally found someone I really liked, and he even seemed to like me back, and my friends were busy trying to find things to make me doubt him.

I was trying to figure out how I could arrange to do more business in San Francisco when I remembered, yet again, the fax that had been sent to me from my office. Whatever it was, it was sure to be sufficiently tedious to knock any whirling romantic thoughts out of my head and put me right to sleep. Surely Jane's and Sean's admonition not to roam around in the dark couldn't apply to a simple trip down the hallway to Jacob's study. I slid out from under the covers, grabbed Emma's bathrobe from the hook on the bathroom door, and let myself soundlessly out of the room. I made my way down the unlit hallway to Mr. Furlong's study, fumbling about in the dark before I located the switch on the wall that turned on the desk lamp. A stack of papers had gathered in the fax machine's output tray, and I picked them up and settled myself onto the leather sofa to take a look.

But I just couldn't concentrate on work. My head pounded, and when I tried to begin reading, the words on the top page swam together, rearranging themselves in the shape of Peter's face. I was either losing my mind or desperately in need of glasses. I stood up again and went over to the phone on the desk to check my voice mail, but lost momentum before I'd even picked up the receiver. If I couldn't read the fax, I was in even worse shape for processing any interminable messages from Stan, et al.

I perched on the edge of the desk and let my gaze roam around the room. Again, the two paintings on the opposite wall caught my attention. I walked over to study them more closely.

The more recent one was definitely the more striking, even to my untrained eye: a cacophony of brilliant colors that gave a first impression of boundless passion and energy.

But when you looked more closely, there was a meditative quality to it, a sense of peace and harmony, as if the most exuberant Jasper Johns or Rauschenberg had mated with a Rothko to produce this canvas. In the lower right corner was Jacob Furlong's distinctive signature, just his initials in bold script. And the date, May 30, 1972. A week after the day Emma was born. Without even knowing what had inspired the artist it was a tremendously moving work. When you realized that it was an homage to his newborn daughter, it held all the more power.

I turned my attention to the older painting, a much smaller piece that was different in just about every way. This one also appeared to be abstract, but upon closer examination it revealed itself to be a portrait of a woman. The palette here was subdued, the strokes careful and almost hesitant. Altogether, it was an unimpressive work, although I, of course, was hardly an art critic. Still, the magnificent talent of Jacob Furlong was barely visible in this painting.

Well, I told myself, if anyone judged me by the way I looked at financial statements my first year at Winslow, Brown, I doubted that they would have been very impressed, either. And if they could witness my complete inability to focus on my work, they would have been even less impressed. With a sigh, I settled myself back down on the sofa to look at the fax, willing myself to pay attention.

I'd read the first page twice before I realized that it wasn't even part of the documents I had been sent, but rather the scanned copy of a page from an outgoing document that somebody else had sent from Mr. Furlong's fax machine. It wasn't until I'd read if for the fourth time that the words began to make sense. I dropped the page like a hot potato. Then I picked it up and scurried over to the fax machine, where I deposited it with shaking fingers into the output tray, quickly, as if it might bite.

My heart began to beat unreasonably fast. I wasn't sure what upset me most—that the words I'd read completely incriminated Peter or the fact that I'd read them, which pretty much reduced the odds of us having a successful relationship to nil. Attractive, interesting, nice-smelling men confessing their love to me were in short supply, but even the sparse pickings made me loath to settle on a murderer as the father of my children.

Because what I'd read implied that, all claims of ignorance to the contrary, Peter was thoroughly aware of Richard's will and was counting on the money he'd receive to keep his business going.

> Good news [it read]. *I've just received word that I will be able to access an additional source of capital. While I won't have the money in hand immediately, the guarantee should be sufficient security for the bank to extend our line of credit as necessary to stave off any takeover attempts.*

I paced the room, trying to figure out how this could mean anything but that Peter was planning to use his inheritance from Richard to unleash desperately needed financing for his company. But no matter how I rearranged the facts, the outcome smelled rotten. Very, very rotten. It was true, I guessed, that nothing good ever came of eavesdropping or reading anyone else's correspondence uninvited.

I sat back down on the sofa and tried to collect myself. The fax didn't necessarily prove anything, argued the part of me that was thoroughly smitten with Peter. Perhaps he had received news about some other source of cash—who knew what could have happened? All roads didn't point to Richard's estate. Peter himself had said that it was unlikely to be large enough to be meaningful, anyhow. Although, a small voice reminded me, Peter would have said such a thing to throw off suspicion. The duplicity of it was breathtaking—and nauseating.

Concentrate, I told myself fiercely. You read something you weren't supposed to, and now you're jumping to conclusions. Quite shocking, unappealing conclusions. Behave yourself like the cool, rational professional you're supposed to be. I sat up straight and turned my attention to my own documents, the ones that I'd been supposed to read.

If I was hoping that Stan's fax would provide a distraction, I was wrong. That was clear before I even got to the second page. While I'd heard that there were billions of humans, all over the world, of multiple races and religions and professions, carrying on their own lives in ways that in no way overlapped with mine, it was truly amazing how everything in my personal existence kept circling back to a small group of people. It seemed an absurd coincidence, not to mention disastrously unfair, that Smitty Hamilton's takeover target was a small software firm in San Francisco, run by one Peter Forrest.

I didn't even start going through the mental motions of trying to convince myself that the Peter Forrest in question wasn't the same Peter Forrest with whom I'd recently completed an extended session of passionate kissing. Further reading confirmed to me just how vulnerable his company was and how tenuous his own position in it. Apparently Peter's company had a major bank loan outstanding on which it was expected to default in the upcoming month. Hamilton Tech had already made overtures to the bank, which was more than eager to sell the note to Smitty Hamilton. And once Peter defaulted, the bank had every right to sell, which would turn control of the company over to Hamilton Tech.

If I had any loyalty toward Peter, which, I reminded myself sternly, I most definitely did not, I would have felt sympathy for his predicament. His company had been well financed at inception, but the implosion of the NASDAQ and the resulting fallout among the venture capital community had dried up most sources of capital for young technology companies. That Peter had managed to keep the company going was a testament to his management skills, and that vultures like Smitty Hamilton were swooping above was a testament to the value of the technology he'd created, a way of compressing and speeding the transmission of data across the Internet. If the company was worthless, nobody would be interested in an acquisition—particularly an unfriendly takeover. And I couldn't imagine that Peter was eager to become a Hamilton Tech employee. Or worse, to be ousted by new management from the company he'd built.

But everything made too much sense. The way Peter claimed to have slept through all the commotion that morning when I'd discovered the body and the police had arrived. Surely it would have been nearly impossible to sleep though that, earplugs notwithstanding? Then I realized that as far as I knew, he was also the last person to see Richard alive. Of course, he had told me that Richard and Emma had a secret assignation after Peter came in to bed, but that was clearly just part of his alibi. How dare he, I thought, try to cast suspicion for his heinous crime onto Emma? This last thought was the most infuriating, whipping me into a real frenzy of indignation.

I don't know how long I sat there, trying to process this sudden influx of data and its ramifications. If I had any sense of either personal or professional responsibility, I should have been figuring out how to tip off the police to what I knew or at least trying to figure out how I could help Hamilton Tech take over Peter's company and jettison its bloodyhanded, homicidal CEO. But instead I just sat there cursing my own lack of judgment.

I'd gone on my first date at the tender age of fifteen,

and fifteen years later I was still utterly incapable of assessing the character of a man with any degree of accuracy. You would think that all those years of practice would have taught me a few things, but an hour ago I'd been swooning over a murderer. If anything, I was losing ground. After all, a murderer completely trumped any of my past experiences. And there were a number of doozies that were hard to surpass, beginning with Chris the sociopath. I'd managed to cover all the various male neuroses in my time, from the breathtakingly arrogant hedge fund manager who'd explained to me, in all sincerity, that he had a "brilliant financial mind" to my friends' personal favorite, the guy who only showed up when not expected, resulting in his none too affectionate nickname of Non-Linear-Time-Boy.

"You can't sleep, either?" asked a friendly voice. I stifled a shriek. I'd been deep in thought, and the sudden interruption set my heart racing once again. Really, Peter's habit of sneaking up on me was entirely losing its charm. And sneakiness was very much in keeping with a murderous character.

"You—" I gasped, every bit not the calm, collected amateur sleuth. "You startled me." My voice held an accusation. Surely the best defense was a good offense.

"I'm so sorry," Peter said. "I seem to keep sneaking up on you. I'll have to work on that," he continued. His voice held a note of apology.

"Yes," I agreed, none too hospitably. He was back in his outfit from that morning, a T-shirt and pajama bottoms. This time, however, he seemed far less adorable. Actually, that wasn't true. On every level but the immediately conscious one, he looked every bit as adorable and even more so, if such a thing were possible. I cursed my depressing lack of resolve.

"Me, neither. I just kept tossing and turning. It's been quite a day."

"Mmm," I answered noncommittally, trying to figure out my next move.

He gave me a quizzical look, clearly put off by my cool tone. "So I came down to check on a fax I'd sent earlier to make sure it went though."

"It did," I replied. "The confirmation page is in the output tray. I came in to get a fax that my office sent, and I saw it." You disingenuous swine, I added silently.

"Good," he said, and collected the piece of paper from the fax machine. "While it's definitely fun running your own business, it's hard ever to stop working. But I guess you must keep pretty hectic hours as well in your line of work." He paused, as if he realized how inane this awkward attempt at conversation sounded.

"Yes."

"So, since neither of us can sleep, maybe we should go upstairs or something? There are a bunch of videos in the den." He smiled at me eagerly. Clearly the implications of my neutral tone and nonforthcoming replies weren't sinking in. Just a short time ago I would have leaped shamelessly at the invitation. Now, not only was I not in the mood for another romantic interlude, it occurred to me that I probably should be scared.

I tried to act casual. "Actually, I was reading through my own stuff from work, and it's succeeded in making me very sleepy. I think I'm just going to go to bed now."

He looked exactly like a puppy that had just been reprimanded. "Are you sure?"

I faked a yawn. "No, I'm exhausted. I really should get to bed."

His face fell. "All right. But, you don't need any beauty sleep—I can definitely attest to that." Snake oil from a snake. In most circumstances, flattery, however cheesy, would have won me over, but not tonight.

I stood up and gathered my papers. "I'll see you in the morning," I said.

"Okay. Sleep well." He caught me by the waist and leaned in to kiss me, and I was too shocked to pull away in time. I was even more shocked by the warm spark that I felt when his lips brushed mine.

"Good night," I said, trying to sound firm, removing myself from his grasp.

"Good night. Sleep well." His face was the picture of dejected confusion. But the ability to dissemble convincingly was a critical one if you hoped to get away with murder.

As quickly as I could without breaking into a sprint, I headed back to Emma's room and shut the door behind me, quietly turning the lock from the inside.

CHAPTER 25

I sat down on the bed, pulled my knees up to my chest and wrapped my arms around them, leaning back against the headboard. I needed to still my spinning thoughts and formulate a plan. Emma hadn't stirred, and her breathing was deep and even. I, on the other hand, was in earnest need of a tranquilizer. I wanted to take all of the facts I'd collected and throw them up in the air, in the vain hope that they'd rearrange themselves differently when they fell back to earth. Or at least just magically disappear and leave us all in peace.

This was entirely Richard's fault, I thought grumpily. I was glad that he was dead rather than alive and married to Emma. But the fallout from his death was truly unfortunate. The next time one of my best friends was about to marry someone as vile as Richard, I sincerely hoped that the bridegroom could arrange to meet with premature death by unequivocally accidental or natural causes. It was just like Richard to leave such a mess in his wake. I wondered if the experts had a multistep formula that mapped the grieving process for people who weren't actually grieving. I just kept finding myself right back at anger, and it was starting to get tedious.

After much cursing of Richard and fate, of Peter and his duplicity, and of my heart-stoppingly bad judgment when it came to the character of attractive men, I managed to get a tenuous grip on my diminished faculties of reason. A plan, I reminded myself. I had to stop wallowing in self-pity and come up with a plan.

There was really only one course of action, I realized. I had to get in touch with O'Donnell and tell him what I knew so that he could come and arrest Peter. I would tell him everything—about how Peter's company was about to default on its loan, about Hamilton Tech waiting to swoop in, and about the fax I'd seen, which proved beyond a doubt that Peter was going to use his inheritance from Richard to keep his company solvent and independent.

Did it, though? Did it prove everything beyond a doubt? I tried to shush this thought as soon as it crept into my feeble head. It had clearly been sent from some primal corner of my brain, the corner that concerned itself with trivial matters like my biological clock and fears of ending up a lonely, bitter, prune-faced spinster.

Still, there was a missing piece, something I couldn't reconcile. Peter may have made up his story about seeing Emma and Richard together from his window, but Hilary had confirmed that Emma had been up and about the previous night as well. She must have found Richard dead when she came down, I surmised. Perhaps she'd thought he was merely deeply asleep, passed out, and unable to wake him, returned to bed. That she hadn't mentioned this to me when she found out he was actually dead could be easily explained: she was concerned that she might implicate someone if she told anyone.

The aged house creaked around me, the usual noises a centuries-old structure makes as it settled into its foundation. But in my hyperalert state, every sound reverberated like a gunshot. I was so busy giving myself a stern lecture about not being such a nervous twit that when I first heard the quiet footsteps I convinced myself that they were merely the normal nocturnal noises the house made. But then they came closer to the door of Emma's room, and my heart started to pound. This entire weekend was turning into an aerobic workout.

I sat up straighter as the footsteps stopped. I could almost hear the breathing of whoever stood on the opposite side of the door. The moonlight glinted off the doorknob as it slowly began to turn. I tried to let out an ear-piercing shriek, but regardless of all the good practice I'd been getting of late, nothing came out. I reminded myself that I'd locked the door securely, but that thought did little to calm me.

The doorknob continued slowly to turn. And then, just as quickly as it had started, it stopped. The footsteps proceeded back down the hallway, as quietly as they'd come. I said a silent prayer of relief.

A moment later, I heard muffled voices. At this point I was tempted to wedge a chair under the doorknob as extra protection and burrow under the covers until daylight came. Instead, I took a deep breath and crept out of bed. I tiptoed to the door, putting my ear against its cool surface, but the wood was too thick to let much sound come through. Steeling myself, I reached out for the doorknob, and as silently as I could manage with trembling hands, unbolted the lock and cracked the door open.

I peered into the hallway, cautiously extending my head out in the direction from which the voices came. A small lamp shed a pool of light at the top of the stairwell, faintly illuminating the profiles of Peter and Mrs. Furlong. Mrs. Furlong was in her bathrobe, her hair hanging loose down her back, and Peter was still in his pajama bottoms and T-shirt, a manila folder clasped to his chest.

"I'm so sorry," Peter was saying. "I didn't mean to startle you." Aha—so I wasn't the only person he kept sneaking up on!

"Oh, of course not, darling," Mrs. Furlong assured him. "I just didn't expect to see anyone else up at this hour. I couldn't sleep, so I was thinking I'd go in and check on Emma, and then I remembered that Rachel's in there, too, and I didn't want to wake her. And I'm sure Rachel would have let me know if Emma wasn't all right." Did that mean it was Mrs. Furlong who'd been poised outside the door of our room? What a ninny I was to be scared by my best friend's mother, innocently coming in to check on her daughter. I really did not have the appropriate temperament to get caught in the middle of a crime scene.

"And what about you, dear? You couldn't sleep, either?" she asked.

"No, I guess not. I thought that since I was awake anyhow, I might as well try to get some work done. But I think I've managed to tire myself out. I was just headed back to bed."

I heard Peter offer to make her some tea or warm some milk for her, but she politely demurred. Which was just as well, because if she'd accepted, I'd have had to go downstairs with them to protect her from Peter's nefarious ways. It would be too much to wake up in the morning to find Mrs. Furlong floating facedown in the pool. Not that Peter had any motive to do away with her, but one couldn't be too careful when there was a homicidal maniac on the loose. I watched as Lily made her way back down the hallway to her room, and I waited to hear her door latch behind her. Peter trudged back up the stairs to his room on the third floor.

I wondered what the papers were in his hand. More negotiations, perhaps, based on his newly acquired, ill-begotten gains? Well, I would straighten all of that out as soon as I had a chance to speak to the police.

Once again, I quietly shut the door to Emma's room and locked it from the inside. Emma was still dead to the world. Poor choice of words, I remarked to myself.

I tried the door, just to make sure that the lock had caught. Then I retrieved my cell phone from the dresser, where I'd left it plugged in to a wall outlet to charge its batteries. I pressed the power switch, and its small screen glowed green as it awakened with a soft chirp. Its cool weight was comforting, and I gripped it like a weapon with both hands. I watched anxiously as it searched for a signal, relieved when the date and time flickered onto the screen.

With a shaking finger, I punched in 911. But a lingering doubt kept me from pressing send. If Peter was the murderer, a very important question remained unanswered. Why had Emma agreed to marry Richard? What had he held over her? And was it possible that whatever it was had no connection whatsoever to why he'd ended up dead less than twenty-four hours ago?

Stop it, I told myself. On some level, I was still pathetically searching for a solution that would absolve Peter and preserve him as the wonderful, sweet, attractive man I'd thought him to be, the one who was such a good kisser and had so recently professed his growing love for me.

But the doubt remained, no matter how vehemently I reprimanded myself. After several more minutes of convoluted thought, I made a deal with myself. I would sleep on it for a few hours. I was exhausted and unable to think straight. In the bright light of day, these nagging thoughts would recede, and Peter's guilt would be obvious. Surely there was no imminent danger. Peter had no reason to do away with anyone else during the next few hours. I would call O'Donnell at dawn.

I put the cell phone down on the nightstand and slid beneath the covers, almost serene now that I'd arrived at a reasonable course of action. It was nearly four; I'd force myself to sleep for a while, awake clearheaded and determined, and turn Peter in to the police.

Most people would have been unable to sleep under a similar set of circumstances, but in my line of work you quickly learned to snatch a few hours of slumber wherever and whenever you can, and my body had finally passed through nervous exhaustion to arrive at just plain exhaustion. The twin bed with its fluffy duvet was far more comfortable than the upright seat of an airplane or the cramped space under my desk at the office.

I was in that zone between consciousness and unconsciousness when I heard another noise. I bolted upright, in the proverbial cold sweat.

The doorknob was turning, and the sound I'd heard was the tiny click as it caught against the lock. I heard the click again as whoever it was tried once more. There was a moment of silence, and then the sound of footsteps, heavier this time, retreating back down the hallway. I rubbed my eyes to make sure I wasn't dreaming. But I was awake, and terrified.

There was one person Peter most definitely had reason to harm, I realized belatedly. If he'd guessed that I read his fax and put two and two together—he could hardly rest if he discovered that I was on to him. For all I knew, he was up in his room right now, trying to figure out how to pick the lock on Emma's door or lure me from her room so that he could silence me forever.

Then came the clincher. I was running my hands through my hair in mental anguish when my fingers touched on something long and thin and unyielding. I disentangled it and looked at it in the dim light. It was a splinter, with a bit of peeling paint on it. Like the peeling paint on the old canoe, and on the decrepit oars that were stowed alongside it.

The images came flooding back. The deer, darting into the woods. The flash of white. And the current of air as something rushed toward me, then the thwack of something making contact with my head.

Jane and Sean had been right. I hadn't tripped or slipped. Somebody had hit me, deliberately, probably with one of the same antique oars that I'd briefly considered as a weapon, then left me unconscious, with my face down in the water.

There was only one person who could have done it, who had probably realized that I didn't have my locket when we came in from the lake. After all, he had his hand around my neck when he kissed me. And he knew that I wouldn't go to sleep without it.

But why? What would make Peter attack me? Did he think I knew about how he was going to use his inheritance from Richard?

Of course he did, I realized. He must have guessed—before I even put it together—that I was working on the takeover of his company. I'd mentioned that I was working on the takeover of a startup. Perhaps he even saw Stan's fax before I did, and heard me leave Emma's room and go down to the beach, and followed me, and—

I grabbed a straight-backed chair from against the wall and wedged it under the doorknob. Then I hurriedly snatched the phone from the nightstand and ducked into the bathroom, shutting the door to muffle my voice should Peter return to lurk outside of Emma's room.

I redialed 911 and pressed Send.

CHAPTER 26

One would think that it would be easy to track down the lead detective on a homicide investigation, even if it was the middle of the night and even if we were in the middle of nowhere. The emergency operator connected me with the police station in town, but nobody picked up the phone there until it had rung more than ten times and I was beginning to despair of anyone answering.

Just when I was about to give up, I heard a surprised hello at the other end. This was quickly followed by a tremendous clatter that sounded like a chair had been overturned. I winced as the receiver on the other end hit the floor with an ear-splitting boom. A grunt and a groan followed.

"Durn it," said a crotchety voice into the receiver. "Gosh durn it, that hurt."

"Hello," I said. "Is anybody there?"

"I'm here, I'm here." I heard shuffling noises, as if the over-turned chair were being set straight.

"Is this the police?" I asked, confused.

"Of course it's the police. Who'd you think it was? Don't you even know who you're calling? Lordy. What do you want already?" The aged-sounding man on the other end made no effort to hide his annoyance.

"I'm trying to reach Detective O'Donnell," I said. "Is he there? May I speak to him, please?"

"Why should he be here? It's the middle of the night, for Pete's sake. What's the problem, missy?" Then, under his breath he muttered, "Danged summer people."

"I need to speak to him. About a case he's working on?"

That got his attention. "A case? A case, you say? Is this about that murder up at the Furlongs' place?" His voice perked up.

"It is," I confirmed. "I have some important information I need to give him."

"Well, then, why didn't you say so? I'll connect you to Charlie's home number."

"Charlie?" I asked. "Who's Charlie?"

"Detective O'Donnell. What are you—some kind of half-wit?" The old geezer didn't give me a chance to reply before putting me on hold. I waited impatiently on the other end as strains of Muzak poured forth over the line, a watered-down version of Madonna singing "La Isla Bonita." Just another surreal element in what was becoming a long list of surreal items.

The music broke off suddenly, replaced by a string of geezer-type epithets ("Durned new-fangled phones. Now how in heck are you supposed to transfer the blasted thing?") and then the welcome sound of a number being dialed and the tones that let me know it was ringing.

An answering machine picked up, with O'Donnell's distinctive voice on the tape. "I'm not in," he intoned and began instructing me to leave a message. Hilary would be happy to know that there was no woman's voice on the machine, nor any reference to a "we." O'Donnell himself, however, interrupted before I could take that thought any further. "O'Donnell, here," he said sleepily. The tape shut off.

"Detective O'Donnell. This is Rachel Benjamin. You interviewed me today—I mean, yesterday—at the Furlongs' house."

"Yes, Ms. Benjamin. How can I help you?" He quickly shifted from sleepy to alert.

"I know who did it," I said. "I know who killed Richard Mallory." It was liberating to be out with it after all of my mental hemming and hawing.

I expected some excitement on his end, maybe even a cry of "Eureka!" but O'Donnell stayed calm. "Why don't you tell me what you've found out that's led you to this conclusion," he invited. I could hear the sound of a cigarette being lit and him taking a deep drag.

In as cool and logical a manner as I could manage under the circumstances, I told him everything. I pointed out that Peter was almost definitely the last person to see Richard alive. His story about seeing Emma from his bedroom window was a red herring, designed to divert suspicion. And I explained to him all about Peter's company and the loan it was about to default on and the takeover threat from Hamilton Tech. And then I revealed the clincher—the fax I'd read that showed that Peter was planning on using his inheritance from Richard to shore up his company.

O'Donnell was mostly silent while I poured out the details in a low voice, breaking in only a couple of times to ask a question or to clarify a point.

"Is that it?" he asked, when I concluded my narrative.

"Yes. That's everything. So, are you going to come and arrest him?" I asked, trying not to betray my anxiety. "I think it's sort of dangerous to have him in the house. He's probably figured out that I'm on to him. I mean, I've locked myself in my room right now, but I'm getting a bit nervous." I didn't tell him about Peter attacking me, or about Hilary and Luisa seeing Emma in the small morning hours; I saw no reason to muddy the story with things that would likely cause him to doubt my sanity. Nor did I tell him about the turning doorknob and the quiet footsteps. I still wasn't entirely sure that I hadn't dreamed up that part.

"All right. It sounds like some further discussions with Mr. Forrest are in order. Paterson and I will come by and pick him up."

"Now? You'll come now?" My voice quavered in an embarrassingly girlish manner. I was more than the bit nervous I'd owned up to.

"We'll come now," he affirmed. "You just sit tight."

I made sure he knew the gate code and then pushed the end button on the phone. Relief washed over me. Surely I'd done the right thing?

Amazingly, Emma continued to sleep. I toyed again with the idea of waking her up, but if all of my jumping around and whispering on the phone hadn't woken her, I was reluctant to physically shake her. I would have to ask Mrs. Furlong what kind of tranquilizers she'd given Emma. I could use one on my next red-eye flight.

The minutes crawled by. Predawn light was slowly turning the sky from black to gray. I stepped to the window, which overlooked the gravel driveway and the circle in front of the house. My fear and anxiety continued to mount, and after ten minutes had passed by my watch I couldn't take it anymore. I needed a reassuring big brother type, the sort of person who would never take advantage of a rare moment of terror to tease me for decades to come about waking him up in the middle of the night.

I removed the chair from where I'd wedged it and placed it back against the wall. I unlocked the door and looked into the hallway, checking both ways to make sure the coast was clear of cold-blooded killers. Then, as quietly as I could, I closed the door behind me and made my way, barefoot, down the back stairs to the kitchen. I let myself out the door and onto the porch and sprinted for the pool house.

Matthew was snoring lightly in his guestroom, but he woke quickly when I pounded on the door. I threw it open while he was still saying "Come in."

"Rachel?" he asked groggily. Then he sat up with alarm. "What's wrong? Is Emma okay?"

"She's fine," I told him. "It's me. I called the police and told them that Peter's the murderer, and now they're coming to get him. But I'm scared," I admitted. "And everyone else is sleeping, and I didn't want to be all alone." I felt like a child, seeking solace during a particularly violent thunderstorm. Only I doubted that a rousing rendition of "My Favorite Things" was going to do much to soothe my emotional state. And Matthew was hardly a substitute for Fräulein Maria.

"Peter?" he asked. He ran his hands through his shaggy hair, disheveling it yet further. "You've got to be kidding."

"I'm not." I blurted out everything I told O'Donnell, far less coolly and logically than I had the first time around. This time I added in the part about being hit over the head with an oar on the beach.

Matthew seemed to follow me. "That's incredible," he said in disbelief. "Absolutely incredible."

"I know," I said. "But it's all true. And I think Peter knows that I know, and I think he may try to come after me again, and I didn't want to stay in the house until the police arrive." My voice shook. "Will you come with me and wait for them?"

"Rachel, you're making a mistake. Trust me. I know."

"I'm not, Matthew. I swear. Please." I was on the verge of tears.

He swung his legs over the side of the bed and pulled on a T-shirt and pants. He followed me out of the pool house and around to the front of the main house. I sank down onto the stone steps while he made me repeat the story again, more slowly this time.

I'd just finished recounting the details when O'Donnell and Paterson pulled up in an old Buick sedan. It seemed anticlimactic. I expected at least a police car, even if there weren't any sirens.

We all exchanged subdued greetings, and then Matthew and I led the detectives into the house. I stopped on the second floor, unwilling to go with them up to Peter's room. Matthew escorted them up the remaining flight to the third floor.

I was leaning against the wall of the second-floor corridor, trying to compose myself and wondering what was taking so long for them to come back downstairs with their prisoner in tow, when Sean and Jane emerged from their room.

"Rach? What is it?" Sean asked.

"For chrissakes—it's impossible to get a decent night's sleep in this house. What's going on?" This was from Hilary, who made her way down the hallway with Luisa trailing behind.

Mrs. Furlong joined us, too. "Now what's happening?" she asked, stifling a yawn.

"It's Peter," I said. "The police and Matthew are upstairs. They're arresting him, I think. Peter. He did it."

"Good Lord," said Jane, a horrified look on her face.

Hilary, at an unprecedented loss for words, simply gaped at me.

Luisa's brow furrowed. "But—but that can't be," she said, her accent thicker than normal, the way it usually was when she'd just woken up. "That doesn't make sense," she said.

Mrs. Furlong was silent, her face white and drawn.

We all turned as footsteps started descending the stairs

from the third floor. O'Donnell and Paterson came first, followed by Peter and then Matthew. They'd given Peter time to get dressed, and I noted with consternation that they hadn't bothered to handcuff him, which seemed grossly negligent, at best. I flattened myself against the wall, glad to have Sean's comforting bulk so nearby.

"We just want to ask you a few more questions," O'Donnell was saying. "There are a couple of things we'd like to clear up."

Peter was nodding. "Whatever I can do to help," he said. But his voice sounded confused, and he hadn't taken the time to brush his hair. He looked sweet and innocent, and for a moment I was besieged by a fresh wave of doubt. His eyes met mine for an instant, their rich chocolate color dark in the murky light. The four men proceeded down the stairs to the first floor.

Jane came over and put her arm around my shoulders. "It will be okay," she said soothingly. "Everything will be okay."

"Of course it will," I said, with far more confidence than I felt. I realized then that I was crying.

CHAPTER 27

Dawn had fully broken by the time I made my way back down the stairs, dressed in an old pair of Levi's and a sweater against the early morning chill. I'd felt more than a little bit cranky as I searched my bag for something fresh to wear. It would have been nice if Peter had planned ahead a bit better. Why couldn't he have arranged to kill Richard in New York? It would have been easier to divert suspicion from himself in a city of eight million people, not to mention a lot more convenient for those of us who were stuck here for the weekend with a limited set of wardrobe options.

It was hard to believe that it had been barely twenty-four hours since I'd come into the kitchen in desperate search of some orange juice with which to address a hangover, filled with dread in anticipation of a wedding that would never take place. Much less that it had been merely six hours since I had started mentally planning my own wedding to Peter, complete with seating charts and color schemes.

I was sleep-deprived and grouchy from the emotional

roller-coaster of the last several hours. Perhaps it was better to have loved and lost than never to have loved at all, but it didn't seem fair that I was only allowed to love for the short time between Peter confessing his love for me and discovering that he was a murderer.

The kitchen was empty, and when I saw the phone on the wall it occurred to me that I should check my voice mail, but I sent that thought packing as soon as it slithered into my conscious mind. I didn't have the stomach right now for more urgent messages from Stan waxing enthusiastic about the Smitty Hamilton deal and detailing the list of tasks he wanted me to get done in advance of our Monday morning meeting. I was too depressed already, although getting the deal done would surely be a lot easier with the CEO of the takeover target locked up behind bars.

There was coffee brewed, but the very thought set my stomach churning, so I took a chilled Diet Coke from the refrigerator and made my way out to the porch. I drew up short when I saw Luisa and Hilary huddled in a pair of wicker chairs, their heads close together. I didn't feel ready for socializing quite yet, but I forced myself to announce my presence with as cheery a "Good morning" as I could muster.

"Hey, Rach, the next time you call in O'Donnell, could you at least give me a little advance warning so I could brush my hair or something before he arrives?" said Hilary by way of greeting.

"Sorry, Hil. I just wasn't thinking."

"Clearly. So, what was it like?" asked Hilary.

My synapses were fried from my sleepless, angst-infused night. I looked at her blankly. "What?" I asked. "What was what like?"

"Sex with a felon, of course," said Hilary.

"Hilary, be good. Rachel had a rough night." Luisa scolded her halfheartedly and then smiled up at me. She was dressed in slim navy pants and a sleeveless white sweater, her hair neatly pulled back into its trademark chignon. Twin spirals of steam and smoke rose from her coffee and her cigarette, respectively. "How are you?" she inquired in a sympathetic tone.

"As well as can be expected," I answered. "And, just for the record, I didn't sleep with him," I added with a pointed glare in Hilary's direction. She crossed her long legs, which were completely bare except where they met her cropped shorts. I sank into an empty chair.

"So what *did* you do?" she asked, uncowed.

"We made out. That's all, Hil."

"Just kissing? That's it?" Hilary made no effort to hide the disappointment in her voice.

"That's it. Sorry."

"What's his problem?" asked Hilary. "Didn't he want to sleep with you?"

"Of course he did," I answered. "We just thought we shouldn't rush into anything. Which was just as well, given how things have turned out."

Hilary didn't buy that. She had no point of reference for not rushing into sex. "Maybe he's gay," she mused.

"If so, he does a masterly imitation of a heterosexual," I replied, only a tiny bit indignant. "Almost as masterly as his imitation of somebody who doesn't go around murdering his oldest friends," I added bitterly.

"Lay off her, Hil," said Jane, who'd come out onto the porch and joined us. She perched on the arm of my chair.

"Yes, Hilary. Lay off," said Luisa.

"No offense meant. I was just curious," said Hilary.

"Right," I said, popping open the can of soda.

"Okay, if I'm not allowed to ask about the sex, am I at least allowed to ask about what made you blow the whistle on Peter?" she continued.

"Yes," asked Jane. "What did you find out, Rach? I'm completely shocked. Peter seemed so nice. I mean, Sean and I were a bit suspicious of what might have happened to you out at the beach, but we never really thought Peter could have done anything like that."

"Like what?" asked Hilary. "What are you talking about?"

I quickly filled her and Luisa in on my head's encounter with a blunt object. Then I told them all about finding the splinter in my hair that had convinced me I'd actually been attacked.

"And you think it was Peter? He hit you with an oar?" Luisa sounded incredulous, but her natural speaking voice was usually laced with skepticism anyhow.

"I guess so. I think he realized that I would find out soon enough that his company was the target of a takeover and that I would put two and two together. He was talking about how hard it was to find cash to keep his company going, and I mentioned that I was working on a takeover of a tech start-up." I told them about finding the faxes as well, the one he'd sent, talking about having secured financing, and the one I'd received about Hamilton Tech's launching a hostile takeover of his company. And then I told them what I hadn't told O'Donnell, about the steps of someone in the hallway and the turning doorknob.

They all had questions, especially Hilary, who was particularly curious about whether or not O'Donnell slept alone. She was pleased to hear about the use of the first-person singular on his answering machine.

"That's outrageous," said Jane after I concluded my tale of sleuthing and woe. "Killing someone for money. I would never have guessed Peter could be capable of such a thing."

"Well, neither did I until I found the evidence."

"That fax sounds like it was pretty damning," said Luisa.

"It was. And then when he tried to break into my room…" My voice trailed off as I stifled a shudder.

"What a treacherous weasel," mused Hilary. This was as close to sympathy as I could expect from her.

"It's so sad," said Jane. "I had high hopes for the two of you. I thought you'd be such a good match."

"At least I figured it out before we were married with three kids, a joint checking account and a mortgage," I said, trying to comfort myself. The cycle time on my relationships was getting shorter and shorter.

"I'm surprised by how he did it, though," said Jane.

"What do you mean?" I asked.

"Well, you'd have to be pretty stupid to think that the police would buy the accident scenario. The authorities were going to find out sooner or later that Richard was drugged or poisoned and then shoved into the pool. Anybody who watches *Law & Order* or reads any sort of crime novels would have to know that they'd do an autopsy and find out that he hadn't just drowned," she pointed out. "I guess I judged Peter all wrong, but he didn't seem like he could be that naive."

"That's not naive," protested Hilary. "I, for example, never watch *Law & Order*. I don't think it's syndicated overseas."

"Nor do I," said Luisa. Her tone was defensive. "We don't get it at home."

"Relax," Jane said. "What's the big deal? It's Peter I'm insulting, not the two of you."

Luisa looked at Hilary. "I thought you told them."

"No, just Rachel. I didn't get a chance to talk to Jane."

"Well, Jane should know, too."

"You're right. Here's the thing," began Hilary.

"Oh, no," interrupted Jane, holding her hands up in front of her as if to ward off evil. "I don't know if I want to hear this." I didn't say anything. I was enjoying seeing Hilary on the hot seat after the ribbing she'd given me.

"Don't be silly, Jane. You know we didn't kill him," said Luisa. "What are you so worried about?"

"I don't know, but it scares me to think about what the two of you could get up to when nobody's watching."

Hilary told Jane the story she'd told me, about how she and Luisa had found Richard dead and pushed him in the pool in a misguided attempt to safeguard Emma.

"So," I said to Jane, "that's one question answered. Peter wasn't stupid enough to try to pass the entire thing off as a drowning. But the two of them were."

"What else should we have done?" demanded Hilary. "We didn't think it was Emma, but it didn't look good. We were just trying to protect her. You'll have to excuse us if we don't spend as much time watching silly TV shows and reading trashy novels as the two of you."

"It seemed like a brilliant idea at the time," added Luisa, somewhat sheepishly.

Then I realized something else. "You also managed to destroy the evidence that would have proved beyond a doubt that Peter did it," I said, referring to the glasses, which had probably had Peter's fingerprints on one and the dregs of Richard's tainted last drink in the other.

"We didn't know that at the time," said Hilary. "And, fortunately, you figured it out anyhow."

"True," I said. At least I could congratulate myself on that front. But an undefined something continued to worry me. It was sort of like the feeling you get that you may have left the iron on, because you can't remember, precisely, turning the iron off. At least, I assumed it was the same sort of feeling. Personally, I didn't own an iron. There seemed to be no point to engaging in such undertakings when there was a perfectly nice dry cleaning establishment on the corner of Seventy-Seventh and Lexington that pressed my clothes beautifully and then delivered them right to my door.

"So, it's all wrapped up now," said Luisa. "With no harm— at least, no serious harm, to Emma. Even though all of the evidence is circumstantial at this point, the police will probably find something more tangible now that they know which direction to look."

"But, poor Rachel," said Jane. "I was so convinced that Peter was Mr. Right."

"Let's just remember about all of the other Mr. Rights," I said, trying to be stoic about the matter. "At least this one was unmasked before I'd used up any hard-earned frequent flyer miles jetting out to San Francisco to visit him."

"But I felt so good about him," continued Jane, her brow furrowed. "He seemed so perfect for you."

"You're not making me feel any better," I countered.

"Perfect is as perfect does," said Hilary.

"That's a completely inane thing to say," said Luisa.

"I guess so," she replied. "I couldn't come up with a good cliché. But stop your fretting, Rach. It will give you wrinkles."

"That's not making me feel any better, either," I said grumpily. "I'm doomed. I'm going to die an old maid."

"Better an old maid than a murderer's accomplice," said Jane.

"That's easy for you to say," I replied sadly.

CHAPTER 28

We sat out on the porch talking for a while, my friends doing their best to soothe my battered heart. They'd had lots of practice over the years, but I was too tired and shell-shocked to feel anything but bleak. Eventually I excused my-self. I might as well go do some work, I told them. I was going to be miserable no matter how I spent my time. It wasn't as if anything could darken my mood further at this point.

I trudged up the stairs to the second floor, retrieved my heavy briefcase from Emma's room and padded down the hallway to Mr. Furlong's study. Resigned, I seated myself be-hind the sturdy walnut desk and began sorting documents and files. Immediately I gave myself a nasty paper cut, draw-ing a thin line of red blood on my index finger. Par for the course, I reflected irritably, just another battle wound to add to the others I'd racked up that weekend.

Usually, burying myself in work was a sure way to make me feel as if I were in control of my life. I was good at what I did, even if I wasn't much good at anything else. Dissecting tangled financial statements, crafting intricate negotiating strategies, structuring complex mergers—all these activities usually gave me a sense of accomplishment and satisfaction. Today, however, I merely felt like a gerbil caught in a Habitrail, scampering through a maze of tunnels and treadmills that I'd traveled before and would travel again and again, with nothing exciting or unexpected to look forward to.

I desperately needed a pep talk, but my well of pep, never the deepest of inner resources, was entirely depleted. Instead, I forced myself to call into the office and clear the voice mails that had accumulated since I'd last checked in. As expected, there were several from Stan, detailing how he thought we should handle our meeting with Smitty Hamilton the next day, along with assorted pithy thoughts on other deals we had underway. I took careful notes before deleting the messages.

The takeover of a privately held company was a far easier task than the takeover of a public company. We wouldn't have to worry about tender offers or proxy fights. And a hostile acquisition of Peter's company looked indeed to be a piece of cake, much as Stan had claimed. Once Peter defaulted on the loan his company had outstanding, all Hamilton Tech had to do was purchase the note to gain control. Given that Smitty Hamilton had already initiated discussions with the bank in question, and given that the bank would be relieved to sell the note rather than trying to liquidate the company to recover its loss, all that was left for Winslow, Brown to do was facilitate the negotiations and help Hamilton Tech secure the best possible price on the deal. That the CEO of the target company was a felon was unlikely to complicate the situation significantly; if anything, it would make our job a lot easier.

I quickly drafted some documents for the meeting, writing in longhand on a legal pad. First, I created an agenda listing the topics we needed to cover. For our own background, we would require a thorough record of the discussions Hamilton Tech had already had. Then we would need to craft a negotiating strategy and a plan for how the acquired company would be integrated into Hamilton Tech's existing corporate structure. We would also have to develop a list of questions to probe in the due diligence phase and set up the actual due diligence process. Next, I took a copy of the template for an engagement letter, the document by which a client officially retained Winslow, Brown and agreed to pay for services rendered. I tailored the wording as appropriate for the transaction, being sure to specify a hefty fee and trying not to think too hard about the fact that I actually had a client, a grown man nonetheless, named Smitty.

I called OS to let Cora know that I'd be faxing the pages in to be typed up by the word processing department, asking her to fax back the finished product so I could check for any mistakes. She assured me that she'd take care of everything right away. I loaded the pages onto the machine and sent them through, remembering as I did that I still hadn't recovered my locket. I resolved to go back to the beach and find it as soon as I received the faxed pages back from Cora.

I had some more busywork to occupy myself—there were other deals underway that I had to review, a performance evaluation that needed to be written for an associate on one of my teams, a presentation that I was expected to put together regarding the department's plan for recruiting new MBAs for the upcoming year—but I didn't have the heart or the concentration for any of those tasks. After several minutes of staring blankly into space, I turned my attention to the bookshelves, looking for something to distract myself while I waited for Cora to fax back the typed-up documents.

None of the titles seemed to be calling out my name, so I found myself returning to the retrospective of Jacob's work that I'd looked at the previous day. I'd curled up on the sofa and was idly turning the shiny pages with their vivid illustrations when I heard the fax hum into motion. I was pleased; I guessed that Cora had kicked my work to the front of the queue. Even so, the speed with which it had been completed was unprecedented. I crossed over to the fax machine and took the pages from the output tray. I grabbed a pen and sat back down on the sofa to read everything over, using the book I'd been leafing through as a hard surface on which to write.

But it was with an eerie sense of déjà vu that I realized that the fax wasn't for me.

I did have a brief pang of guilt; after all, it was reading other people's faxes that had only so recently made such a jumble of my love life. However, another part of me pointed out, it was a blessing I had snooped before—otherwise I'd probably still be snuggling up to a criminal. I was in for a penny already—I might as well be in for a pound, I reasoned. So, with some trepidation, I read on.

The cover sheet was addressed to Peter and on the stationery of a hotel in Katmandu. This had to be a joke, was my first thought. Did they even have hotels in Katmandu? Much less fax machines? Where was Katmandu, anyhow? It seemed like it should be near Timbuktu, or Kalamazoo. According to the address, however, it was in Nepal. Was Peter doing business with the Nepalese Mafia? I wouldn't put it past him, assuming there was such a thing.

I was flipping to the next page when I did a double take. I rubbed my eyes to make sure that my vision was clear. Just in case Katmandu seemed too far-fetched, in the space for the sender's name were two words: Sam Slattery.

Sam Slattery? I nearly said the name aloud in a combination of awe and disbelief. Could it be *the* Sam Slattery? The man who was to technology what Warren Buffett was to investing? The savvy entrepreneur, venture capitalist, and mysterious recluse who made Bill Gates look like a pathetic also-ran? Sam Slattery was a legend, a pillar, a god. Companies he had funded from mere seedlings now made up half the value of the NASDAQ, practically. His touch was better than that of Midas when it came to startups. Whereas most venture capitalists were like lemmings, jumping onto whichever bandwagon was most trendy at any given moment— e-commerce, optical networking or biotech—Slattery was known for ferreting out revolutionary technology companies that delivered real value.

My trembling hands caused the fax to shake as I turned to the second, and only other, page. It was a handwritten note, printed in bold, block letters.

PETER [it read]: SORRY AGAIN THAT YOU HAD SUCH A DEVIL OF A TIME TRACKING ME DOWN. SOMETIMES MY SECRETARY TAKES ME A BIT TOO LITERALLY WHEN I TELL HER THAT I DON'T WANT TO BE DISTURBED. PLUS, I HAVEN'T BEEN EASY TO REACH OF LATE. REMIND ME TO TELL YOU ALL ABOUT THE DALAI LAMA WHEN I GET BACK TO THE STATES.

PER OUR DISCUSSION ON FRIDAY, I'VE MADE AR-RANGEMENTS FOR THE FUNDS TO BE WIRED DIRECTLY TO THE BANK, FIRST THING MONDAY. THAT SHOULD KEEP THE WOLVES FROM THE DOOR FOR A WHILE—AT LEAST UNTIL YOU'RE READY TO IPO.

LET ME KNOW IF YOU NEED ANYTHING ELSE. I'M A BIG FAN, AND A BELIEVER, AND I'M HAPPY TO HELP OUT HOWEVER I CAN.

REGARDS,

SAM

I read it over again. And again. But the words stayed the same, and their implication was only too clear. Peter hadn't been counting on Richard's money to keep his company afloat. He had someone much better lined up, and he'd known that on Friday, way before Richard had been murdered. I let the pages fall to the floor and buried my head in my hands.

A mean little voice inside my head was singing a jubilant chorus of I-told-you-sos. Another voice was singing with joy that Peter was innocent. Yet another was moaning in pain. The three-part medley was a discordant cacophony.

Could Peter ever forgive me? There was no reason he should. What a complete and utter fool I'd been. And what a mess I'd created, the mean little voice chimed in.

Poor Peter had been dragged out of his bed and hauled off to the police station, all because I'd leaped to conclusions. I'd roused O'Donnell and Paterson in the middle of the night to send them chasing after a false lead. I'd told my friends that Peter had attacked me and left me for dead, something he clearly had no reason to do. And the worst of it was that I'd definitely ruined any chance of a successful relationship. He'd hardly be feeling too affectionate toward me when the police brought him back, as they undoubtedly would once they'd heard his explanation. Unless the fax I held was a clever forgery of some sort, which seemed unlikely.

I lifted my head from my hands and groaned aloud. "Good Lord," I cried. "Rachel, you are a moron. A dense, brainless, imbecilic, irrational moron."

"Don't be so hard on yourself. I think you're cute."

This time I couldn't help it. I shrieked, a pathetic, girly shriek. As if I'd seen a mouse, or been pinched in an unseemly place on the crowded Lexington Avenue subway.

I vaulted up from the sofa and whirled around to face Peter. All my embarrassment and self-recriminations were temporarily forgotten. Anybody would be justified in suspecting that a man who insisted on sneaking up on people like this could be a murderer. Self-righteous indignation coursed through my veins.

"Why—why," I spluttered. "Why is it that you can't enter a room like a normal person? Have you ever considered knocking? Or perhaps clearing your throat to announce your presence? I've had it with you! You should be belled! Belled like a cat, so that you can't sneak up on unsuspecting birds!"

Peter didn't even have the grace to look abashed. Instead, he just grinned. "Let me get this straight. I'm a cat and you're a bird? Now, were you thinking Sylvester and Tweety? Because, I certainly have the wrong coloring, and Tweety most definitely was not a redhead."

"You planned this!" I accused him. "You plan it every time. What's with all of your sneaking around? Is it some sort of West Coast mating ritual? Instead of flowers and chocolates, you creep up on unsuspecting females, trying to startle their wits out of them so you can see how they look when panicked?"

"You're very attractive when panicked," he assured me, seating himself on the edge of the desk. "But what's with the paranoia?" Typical male. He looked so confident, so entirely charming, that I wasn't sure if, when I lunged toward him, I wanted to kiss him or slap him.

Fortunately, he answered that question for me. He kissed even better in the morning than he did at night. I was glad I'd taken the time to brush my teeth.

"You're a bit edgy sometimes, aren't you?" he asked, some moments later.

"Only when caught unawares," I replied with what little dignity I could muster, detaching his hands from around my waist.

"So, even though you're not apologizing profusely, I guess

I'll forgive you," said Peter. "I'm sure you'll get around to saying you're sorry at some point."

A hot blush spread across every inch of exposed skin. "Oh, dear," I said.

"It's okay. I know you saw the fax, and I assume that you read it. It's the only explanation as to why you went from hot to cold on me in the space of a couple of hours last night and then called the police. You saw the fax, and you thought I'd killed Richard for his money. If I were you, I would have come to the same conclusion. It would have been nice if you'd given me a chance to explain, or at least waited a few more hours to call the police, of course, so that we could have all gotten a bit more sleep."

I sank down onto the sofa. "Peter—" I began, "I don't know what to say. I'm so sorry. It's just that I didn't know what to think. And, I've made so many mistakes before when it came to men. Even though my gut was telling me that you couldn't be guilty—"

He interrupted me. "It's all right. I completely understand. Besides—won't this make a great story for the grandkids? How grandma thought grandpa was a murderer when they first met?" He sat down beside me and touched my cheek lightly with his hand.

"Let's not worry about the grandkids just yet," I said, as he leaned in to kiss me.

"So," he asked when we came up for air, "even though I've explained everything to the police, why are you so suddenly convinced of my innocence? At least, I'm assuming you're convinced since you're willing to let me touch you."

"Very willing," I confessed, shamefaced.

"But I haven't explained a thing to you. I tried to come tell you everything last night, but your door was locked."

I remembered with a pang the terror I'd felt when I saw

the doorknob turning. "Is that what you were doing? I—I thought you were coming to…" I was too embarrassed to complete my sentence.

He chuckled. "You thought I was coming to do you in? This *really* will make a great story for the grandkids. So, what's made you decide that I'm in the clear?"

"Oh, dear," I said again. "I don't think I should tell you." I was reluctant to own up to reading yet more of his correspondence.

"Hmmm. Let me guess. Are you psychic?" he asked.

"If only," I sighed. "It would sure save everyone a lot of trouble if I were." I felt the blush that had begun to recede renew itself with vigor.

"Come on, Rachel. You can tell me. Maybe we should establish a no secrets policy of some sort."

"But if we do that, we'll miss out on all of the exciting intrigue and passive-aggressive harboring of suspicious thoughts."

"True," he mused. "But we'll have more time to make out if we abandon the exciting intrigue and passive-aggressive harboring of suspicious thoughts. Plus, we won't have to worry about how you're going to sneak me files in cakes when I'm in jail. Which, given what I've heard about your talents in the kitchen, sounds like it would pose a real challenge."

"Good point. If I tell you, do you promise you won't hate me?" I asked.

"How could I hate you?" His voice was incredulous. "I'm falling in love with you."

"Still? Even after everything I did?" He really was too good to be true.

By way of an answer, he kissed me again. A very reassuring kiss that sent my insecurities packing, at least for a little while. They were too firmly instilled in my psyche to go away for good, regardless of how persuasive this particular kiss was.

"Okay, then," I said when he relinquished his grasp. "Here goes." I leaned down and picked up the pages of the fax from Sam Slattery that I'd let drop to the floor. "I read this," I admitted. "I really did think it was something for me at first. Although I did keep reading after I realized it wasn't."

Peter took the pages from my hand and quickly perused them. "Good old Sam," he said with satisfaction. He folded the fax and put it in his pocket. "I'll need to show this to the police, and maybe even get him on the phone with them. They were willing to release me once I'd explained where I planned to get the money to save the company, but they're going to need some proof. And this shows that I'd squared away the matter well in advance of Richard being killed."

"It certainly does," I said. "And Sam Slattery of all people. I'm impressed."

"I'm just relieved he came through. He spends most of the year hiking in exotic places where it's hard to reach him. When our financial situation became dire last month, I tried to get in touch with him to see if he'd put up more money, but he was trekking in Nepal, and I couldn't track him down. He just got back from the wilderness, got all my messages, and volunteered to keep us solvent for the foreseeable future. His pockets are pretty deep, and I was fairly confident he'd give us the money, but it was a relief to actually get him to commit to writing another check. I spent the entire train ride up here from Albany on Friday night negotiating the details."

"I like the sound of this guy," I said. "Deep pockets and globe-trotting are very desirable qualities in a man. Is he single?"

"Yes, but he's also seventy-two and has eight grandchildren. I think you'd be better off sticking with me."

I giggled. "Well, if you insist." We kissed some more. But a lingering thought kept me from being able to concentrate. There was one other thing I had to tell Peter, but I was pretty sure that to tell him went against some sort of professional code I'd sworn to uphold.

"Okay," he said, detaching his lips from mine with jarring suddenness. He hoisted us both up into a sitting position. "What is it?"

"What is what?"

"Suddenly I feel like I'm kissing a blow-up doll. Your body's in the right place, but I don't get the sense that your mind's here at all."

"Do you have a lot of experience kissing blow-up dolls?"

"Something tells me that there's no right answer to that question."

"Okay," I said, throwing professional ethics to the wind. "There's just one other thing I should probably tell you. Especially in light of the no secrets policy."

"Yes?" His expression was both patient and amused.

"Well, did you know that Hamilton Tech is trying to take over your company?"

He was revving up for another kiss, but he froze at my words. "What? How do you know? Was there an article in the *Journal* or something? I thought it was all a big, stealthy, insidious secret?"

The way his eyes had opened wide was adorable, and I couldn't help but laugh. "Remember the fax I was reading last night? The one that was actually for me? It was about a new deal that a partner at Winslow, Brown just snagged. Guess who Smitty Hamilton has engaged to advise him on the acquisition?"

"You're kidding." He looked at me in disbelief. Disbelief was equally adorable.

"I wish. I'm in no mood to launch a takeover."

"Well, that's a coincidence. I'm in no mood to be taken over." He was practically growling. The dangerous current in his voice was nothing short of thrilling.

"So, it looks like our interests are aligned."

"Even if they weren't, I've managed to fix things so that we're safe from the Hamilton Techs of the world for a while. Nor are we in danger of being savaged by the likes of you and your colleagues at Winslow, Brown."

"Savaged, no. Ravaged, however, is still an option."

"I'd be okay with that," he said. "Ravage away." He pulled me on top of him, and our lips met again.

CHAPTER 29

We were still kissing, Peter's hands playing delightfully in my hair, when his fingers accidentally brushed against the blossoming lump on the back of my head.

"Ouch!"

"What? What did I do?"

I realized that he didn't know about the other nocturnal adventure I'd had. "There's a little bump there."

"A little bump?" His fingers gently probed. "That's not a little bump, Rachel. What is it? Is this the part where you tell me about your tumor and that you only have a few weeks left to live?"

"Wow. I'm not the only one with an active imagination."

"Seriously. What happened to you?"

"I had a little accident."

"This doesn't feel like a little accident."

I quickly filled him in, both embarrassed and touched by his concern. It was amazing how much catching up we had to do when we'd only been out of contact for a few hours.

"Well, I can answer one question for you," he said, digging into his pocket.

"My locket! Where did you find it?"

"It was caught on my towel. I was going to give it to you when I came to explain about the fax, but you were too busy calling the cops."

"Why do I have the feeling it's going to be a long time before I live that one down?" I asked, bending my head and lifting up my hair so he could fasten the locket around my neck.

"It's too good to forget. But we can talk about that later."

"Can't wait. What are we going to talk about now?"

"We're going to talk about what happened to you. If I'm hearing you right, somebody hit you over the head and left you there, where you could have drowned?"

"That sounds so melodramatic. Jane and Sean found me. Everything's all right."

"No, it's not. I don't want to get hysterical on you or anything, but it sounds like somebody tried to kill you, Rachel."

"Well, maybe."

"There's no maybe about it. This is really bad. Somebody thought you knew something and tried to take you out. Whoever did it is still loose, and if that person tried once— who's to say she won't try again?"

"What do you mean—*she?*" My voice took on a sharp edge. I had a feeling where he was going with this, and I had another feeling that we were about to have our first fight.

"Don't take this the wrong way," he said gently. "But I can't help but think about how Emma was the last person to see Richard alive."

"As far as you know," I reminded him. I sat up straight and turned my back to him, making no effort to hide the sudden chill in my words. "I don't know what conclusion you're trying to jump to, but I assure you that Emma is completely incapable of murder. And I resent your even trying to imply it. Much less that she'd attack me. She's my best friend."

He took me by the shoulders and spun me around. "I'm not trying to imply anything. I'm just trying to put the facts together."

"Now, you see here, Mr. Forrest," I said in my iciest possible tone. "You don't know Emma. Not the way I know her. And I can tell you right now that Emma would no sooner do such a thing, than—than—" I stuttered.

A sudden image flashed before my eyes. The mortar and pestle in Emma's medicine cabinet. Perfect for mixing paint pigments. Equally perfect for crushing something lethal in a way that it could easily be diluted in a stiff Scotch and soda. And if Peter hadn't lied about seeing Emma, and if Hilary and Luisa had found Richard dead right after Emma left the scene, and I was a deep sleeper—

"Oh, crap." I finished lamely.

"Why the sudden scatological outburst?" Peter inquired.

I was momentarily speechless; the evidence was mounting up against Emma, and the only thing standing between the evidence and the logical conclusion was my loyalty to her. I knew her too well, I repeated to myself. She could never have killed Richard. Much less attack me.

I tried to compose myself. "Look, if you forgive me for reading your faxes and turning you into the police, I'll forgive your odious suggestions about my best friend." My voice held a challenge in it. I'd learned from working in an environment populated by Type A personalities that the best defense was a good offense. And my loyalty to Emma took priority over nurturing this budding romance.

He held his hands up in front of him. "Fine. We'll agree to disagree."

"No," I said stubbornly, "you'll agree that you're completely off base on this one. You barely know Emma, and I do."

"Which is exactly why I can be objective," he pointed out. Men and their cool rationality.

"Not an acceptable answer. Take your accusations back," I demanded.

"Christ," he said.

"Don't you trust me?"

"Of course I trust you."

"Then take it back. I'm not joking. I mean it. This can't be hanging over us. I know it wasn't Emma. I can't prove it, but if you don't believe me, then—then—" I stuttered again, not sure what I was going to threaten.

He threw his hands up with resignation. "Okay, I take it back. If you're sure it wasn't her then I'm convinced."

"Good," I said sternly.

He grinned. "I think we just had our first fight."

"I guess so."

"It was fun. Do we get to make up now?" There was a devilish gleam in his eye. But when we kissed this time, it was hard to enjoy it fully. I was too worried about my friend.

Hilary, coming to summon us downstairs to help prepare brunch, interrupted the making up process.

"Well if it isn't the jailbird himself," she said, as Peter and I broke apart.

He shrugged good-naturedly. "It was just an innocent mix-up. However, I'm officially in the clear."

She gave me a pointed look, taking in my flushed cheeks and rumpled hair. Seemingly reassured, she turned to Peter and smiled. "Good to know."

We followed her down the stairs and into the kitchen, where everyone but the Furlongs had gathered. Peter met the curious looks of my friends with a quick explanation.

"I knew it couldn't be true," said Jane warmly, eager to welcome him back into the fold.

"None of us really believed it," said Sean.

"We're glad to see you back," added Matthew, handing me a mimosa. Nothing more was said of the matter, but I knew that I would be teased mercilessly in the days to come about having turned Peter in to the police.

By this point, we all automatically assumed that Jane and Sean would supervise the preparations, and they began meting out tasks. After Peter's crack about my skills in the kitchen, I was itching to prove that I was not a complete culinary dunce, but when most of the eggshell from the first egg I broke ended up in the bowl, hopelessly entangled with the yolk and the white, Jane banished me to the more mundane task of setting the table. Peter eagerly volunteered to help, and we carried plates and flatware out to the porch. In the spirit of keeping no secrets, I even revealed to him the secret of my napkin-folding trick, which he promised to keep strictly between the two of us.

The smell of frying bacon and pancakes on the griddle must have traveled far, because Mr. Furlong hiked over from his studio shortly before the meal was ready. Mrs. Furlong and Emma came downstairs just in time to take their seats around the old oak table. One look at Emma and all my doubts vanished, if not my concerns. I didn't know who had killed Richard, but I would have staked my own life that it wasn't her. I just wished I knew who was really responsible. Well, I tried to comfort myself, if I couldn't figure it out, with all of the little details and subplots I knew, I didn't see how the police possibly could.

It wasn't quite the lavish postwedding champagne brunch that had been planned, but, for whatever reason, the mood of the assembled group seemed lighthearted—even festive. With the sun shining down and a gentle breeze rustling the trees, the anxiety of the previous evening seemed a distant memory.

Matthew sat next to Emma, piling food onto her plate and insisting that she eat every bite. Mrs. Furlong was playing the gracious hostess, keeping everyone's glasses and plates full. I fell into an easy banter with Mr. Furlong, who had always enjoyed teasing me about my position as a high-powered lady banker (his description, not mine) and pretending to pump me for insider stock tips.

"Come on, Rachel," he urged. "We could make a fortune. All you have to do is give me a tiny little hint and I'll call it in to my broker. Who would ever know? I'll split the proceeds with you, fifty-fifty." He took a big swallow of coffee and grinned at me over the top of his mug.

"But there's not much you can use that money for when you're in jail," I pointed out. "For a government agency, the SEC is remarkably competent when it comes to sniffing out insider trading."

"Is that a no?"

"I don't know. Are you willing to front me the costs for defense lawyers? Not to mention all of the future earnings I'll forfeit from never being able to set foot on Wall Street again? If so, then we might be able to strike a deal."

"Ah. You drive a tough bargain. You look so innocent, so sweet-faced. I didn't realize you were such a shark."

"I'm just a dolphin in shark's clothing. We at Winslow, Brown are dedicated to maximizing shareholder value, and that's all I care about." Peter, sitting next to me, muffled a guffaw, but Mr. Furlong smiled at my sarcastic tone and insisted that I take another blueberry pancake from the steaming platter he was passing.

I was intent on adorning that pancake with a liberal swirl of real maple syrup when I realized that a sudden hush had fallen over the table. O'Donnell and Paterson were climbing the steps to the porch, with stern looks on their faces. I hoped that they hadn't heard us discussing, however facetiously, the ins and outs of insider trading. But somehow I knew that they had other matters in mind.

"Good morning, detectives," said Mrs. Furlong, as if this were a purely social call. "You're just in time for brunch. Would you like some pancakes? Jane made them with fresh blueberries from right here on the property. They're delicious."

O'Donnell responded with a polite shake of his head, while Paterson swallowed, either out of nerves or hunger. O'Donnell cleared his throat, ignoring the way that Hilary smiled up at him, crossing her arms to emphasize the impressive cleavage displayed by her tank top.

"That's very kind, Mrs. Furlong," said O'Donnell. "But I'm afraid we're here on business." He turned to Emma. "Ms. Furlong, we'd like to ask you to come down to the station for further questioning."

Forks clattered to their plates as they were dropped, in unison, by the assorted guests. Emma looked as if she'd just been struck; her face turned a ghostly shade of white. Mr. Furlong pushed his chair away from the table with a loud screech and stood, drawing himself up to his full, rather impressive height.

"What the—" he sputtered. "You are making a grave mistake, Detective."

"I hope not, Mr. Furlong." O'Donnell's tone was measured. I had to admire his ability to stand up to Mr. Furlong without even flinching. "But, based on the evidence we've gathered thus far, this is warranted." I snuck a quick look at Peter. It was only his testimony—that Emma had been the last person to see Richard alive—and the way in which it almost certainly conflicted with Emma's own, which linked her in any way to the crime. Peter looked appropriately distraught, but I still wanted to give him a swift kick to the shin.

"And what evidence would that be?" demanded Mr. Furlong.

"Well, it appears that Ms. Furlong was the last person to see the deceased alive."

"Way to go," I muttered to Peter under my breath. Then I did kick him, hard.

"What?" said Emma. She blinked rapidly.

"What?" echoed a chorus of voices from around the table.

Mr. Furlong recovered quickly. "That's simply not the case," he asserted. "And I know that for a fact.

"Because the fact of the matter is that *I* was the last person to see Richard Mallory alive. And I was also the first person to see him dead. You see, I'm the one who poisoned him."

This was met with gasps all around.

"Dad—" began Emma, but she was shushed by a hard look from her father.

"Yes, I poisoned him," he continued. "With tranquilizers I was prescribed after I had knee surgery last year. I'd be happy to show you the bottle. And you can check with the pharmacy in town—I had the prescription filled there. They should have the records.

"As for motive, I could hardly have that scalawag married to my only child. Sometimes a parent just has to step in. So, if anyone is going to come with you to the station, it will be I." Mr. Furlong spoke calmly, his eyes locked on O'Donnell's.

There was silence as everyone gaped at Mr. Furlong. And at O'Donnell. And then at Mr. Furlong again.

O'Donnell cleared his throat, more decisively this time. "I understand how much you want to protect your daughter, Mr. Furlong, and we do, in fact, have the pharmacy records, and your prescription matches the toxicology report from the victim's bloodstream exactly." The pancakes and bacon in my stomach threatened to make their way back up my esophagus. I swallowed hard, trying not to think about words like *autopsy.*

"There you go," said Mr. Furlong. "Well, then. Let's be on our way." He tossed his napkin on the table.

"Not so fast, sir," said O'Donnell. "We did get the records from the pharmacy, but we also got the phone records of calls coming into and going out of this household. And unless you can explain who other than yourself was receiving and initiating trans-Atlantic calls throughout the night from the private line in your studio during the time the murder was committed, it looks like your alibi is watertight."

Jacob was speechless.

"Mr. Furlong," said O'Donnell, "I repeat, we appreciate how eager you are to spare your daughter any unpleasantness. But we really must take her into town."

Jacob's gaze rested upon his wife, expressionless. You could almost see his mind working, trying to figure out what he could say to clear Emma.

I caught Emma looking from one parent to the other and back again. Her hands gripped the edge of the table so tightly that her knuckles were white. I could sense what was coming before she spoke, and I searched frantically for something to say that could possibly stop her. But my mind, like my legs, seemed to have turned to jelly. I sat in my chair, rooted to the spot and utterly at a loss for words.

Emma's lips took on a determined set, and with small, neat movements she folded her napkin and laid it beside her plate. Her chair made a scraping noise as she pushed it back from the table. She stood, drawing herself up in the same way that her father had a few moments before. When she did it, however, it only served to emphasize her slight size and fragility.

But her tone, when she spoke, was clear and assured.

"You'll have to excuse my father, Detective. He's just trying to help. But I think the time has come to set things straight. You see, I did it. I killed Richard."

CHAPTER 30

What?

Her words rang in my ears, and my mind stopped working. I knew Emma better than anyone, was more confident of her innocence than anyone, but the way she spoke was so completely convincing that even I believed her.

But only for a moment. Then my brain clicked back into gear. It was so obvious: Emma was clearly covering for whoever it was she thought *was* guilty. And given that she was already the police's favorite suspect, surely they would readily accept her confession, even if we all knew it was false. I opened my mouth to speak, to explain to O'Donnell that it couldn't be Emma, but I had no firm evidence at which to point except my faith in my friend. O'Donnell didn't skip a beat and began reading Emma her rights in a level tone.

Matthew stood abruptly and grasped Emma by the shoulder. "What are you doing?" he demanded, his voice low and incredulous.

Jacob interrupted with a roar of anger. "That is complete

poppycock, Emma. I won't stand for it." He turned to the police. "My daughter doesn't know what she's saying. Why, she no more killed that swine than—than—" he sputtered with rage and advanced toward the detectives.

Paterson took a step back, but O'Donnell didn't flinch. He concluded his recitation of the Miranda rights before turning to Jacob. "Mr. Furlong, I understand that this is upsetting, but we need to do our job. Ms. Furlong, if you would come with us?" He phrased this politely, but it was more of a command than a question.

"She's not going anywhere without me," said Jacob, his voice menacing.

"Or me," said Matthew, his voice no less menacing. From him, such a tone was even scarier because it was so out of character.

"Mr. Furlong, Dr. Weir, that really wouldn't be appropriate right now. The best thing you could do would be to track down a good criminal lawyer and have him meet us at the station in town."

"Criminal lawyer?" said Lily, her voice rising with alarm.

"I'll make some calls," interjected Luisa. "My firm's New York office should be able to point us to the best local guy there is. Emma—don't say another word until a lawyer arrives, do you understand? Just sit quiet and try not to worry. I'll have someone there as soon as possible."

Emma nodded calmly and reached up to give Matthew a kiss on the cheek before detaching his arm from her shoulder. I watched, dumbstruck, as she began walking toward the front of the house and the waiting police car, flanked by O'Donnell and Paterson.

"Emma," called her father, running after them. "We'll have a lawyer there as soon as we can. And Luisa's right—don't say another word. Nothing at all." He disappeared around the corner of the house, and we could hear the sound of slamming car doors. He returned a moment later. There was a slump to his broad shoulders. For the first time, he looked old. Haggard rather than distinguished, and just very, very tired.

I turned to look at Mrs. Furlong. She was glaring at her husband. "This is all your fault," she said to him.

So much for a pleasant, relaxed brunch. Luisa rushed into the house in search of a phone. I couldn't imagine that it would be easy to find an ace criminal lawyer up in this remote corner of the Adirondacks, but if anyone could track one down, it was Luisa. Thank goodness one of us had seen fit to get some legal training, although it was really too bad that Luisa had chosen to concentrate on obscure areas of international corporate law rather than defending shy young women whose only crimes were falsely confessing to murders they didn't commit.

"We need to talk," Jacob said to his wife, in a tone that terrified me. I was glad that I wasn't on the receiving end of it.

"Of course," answered Lily, as if he'd offered a stroll in the garden. "Would you children mind cleaning up the dishes? I hate the idea of everything sitting out in this weather— we have a terrible problem with ants if we're not careful." Jacob gave her a look that was as terrifying as the tone of his voice had been, then grasped her firmly by the elbow and shunted her in the direction of the library. Even on the porch, we could hear the force with which he slammed the door to the room.

Hilary, for once, showed some restraint. She didn't say a word about how handsome O'Donnell had looked on this particular morning. "What are we going to do?" she demanded of us all instead.

"I don't know," I said. "But we have to do something."

Nobody disagreed with that. But nobody had any brilliant ideas, either. Silently, we began clearing the remains of the meal. I kept thinking about Emma's bright, expectant expression that long-ago night when we had made our pact. We had failed her completely, and the consequences were far more horrifying than we ever could have imagined. The gravity of the situation made me dizzy; I felt as if I might faint, and this was hardly the time to be playing damsel in distress when there really was another damsel in far more distress.

I began stacking plates, but Jane intervened after one slipped from my hand and crashed into shards on the wide oak boards of the porch. "You know, Rach, if Emma's going to be down at the police station, we should bring her some things. Some clothes, and a toothbrush. Why don't you go take care of that?"

I acquiesced and trudged up the stairs. Tears of frustration and anger welled up in my eyes. Who was Emma protecting? And why had that person just let her do it? Surely we all cared too much about her to let her take the blame for a murder she didn't commit? My thoughts felt blurry and unfocused as I did yet another mental scan through the possible suspects. It wasn't Peter, and it wasn't Emma. It couldn't be Jane or Sean. And Luisa and Hilary had accounted for their movements.

I paused at the top of the stairs. Could it be Matthew? I had dismissed him so easily before, but he did have the motive and the means. And that cryptic argument he and Emma had had the previous afternoon—what was that all about? I would have thought he loved Emma too much to let her confess to his crime, but perhaps he felt betrayed? After all, she'd been going to marry Richard.

I played with this thought halfheartedly, knowing even as I did that it was ludicrous. I tried to remember the exact words of Matthew's and Emma's argument as I took a small satchel from Emma's closet and began searching her drawers for appropriate clothing. I couldn't imagine that they'd actually make her wear one of those ugly prison jumpsuits, so I piled in her Irish fisherman's sweater, a pair of jeans and some flannel pajamas. Underwear would be important. You could never have too much clean underwear, particularly not in jail. I found her lingerie drawer and rummaged through it for something appropriately utilitarian and instead came up with a sheaf of papers. Why would Emma hide papers in her underwear drawer? Everybody knew that was the first place people searched when you had something to hide.

I held the papers in my hand, trying not to look, while I had a quick debate with myself. I knew that it was none of my business, but part of me hoped that maybe I could use the papers to help her—maybe they would yield up some part of the puzzle.

I tried to focus on the top page. My vision was strangely hazy, but I could make out the words—it was a prenuptial agreement between Emma Furlong and Richard Mallory. I was still trying to absorb this when another wave of dizziness overcame me. Peter came in just in time to see me sink to the floor, the papers in my hand.

"Rachel—are you okay?" He rushed to kneel beside me.

"Yes. I just felt a bit dizzy. Anyhow, I don't know if I want to talk to you right now." I was still angry with him. If only he'd kept his mouth shut, the police would have nothing to tie Richard's death to Emma.

"Well, I need to talk to you," he said in a low, urgent voice.

"Why?" I asked. I sounded weak, not angry, the way I'd meant to. "Unless you see a way out of this trap you created for Emma, I don't think we have anything to say to each other."

"Trust me, if I'd known how this would all play out, I would never have said anything to the police about having seen her that night. If I could take it back, I would. You know I would."

"You can't take it back," I said, forlorn. "Poor Emma."

"But I think I may have figured out something else. It came to me at lunch, actually, right before the police showed up."

"What came to you? Oh—" Another wave of dizziness washed over me, and my stomach churned. Peter's face swam before me, but instead of one nice pair of eyes, he suddenly seemed to have six. There was a ringing in my ears.

"Rachel? What is it?"

"I don't feel very well," I admitted, leaning against the dresser.

"You look awful," he said. "Green."

"Thank you. You have six eyes."

"Well, your eyes look weird. Your pupils are enormous." I felt the warm touch of his hand on my forehead. "And you're all clammy. You should lie down."

I could barely move, but he lifted me easily and deposited me gently on one of the twin beds. I groaned as a pain shot through my stomach.

"What is it? What hurts?"

I gestured toward my abdomen. "I don't get it. I felt fine before. Maybe it was something I ate."

"You didn't eat anything that anybody else hadn't eaten. We were all taking food off the same platters. Maybe you're having an allergic reaction?"

"I'm not allergic to anything."

"Nothing?"

"Just bee stings. And live jazz."

"This isn't good. Maybe somebody slipped you something, Rachel. Put something in your drink."

"Don't be silly. I didn't realize you were such a drama queen."

"I'm not being silly. Somebody tried to kill you last night and didn't succeed. This could be another attempt."

He did sort of make sense, even in my nauseated, befuddled state. I tried to answer him but another stabbing pain in my stomach took my breath away.

"That's it. I'm getting Matthew."

"No!"

"You need a doctor."

My teeth were clenched against the pain. "Not Matthew," I gasped. "He's the one who gave me my drink. And I think he's the murderer."

"Okay. Now you're being silly. Do you have any evidence against him? Did you see or hear anything?"

"He gave me the drink," I repeated.

"Besides, I think I know who the murderer really is."

"You think it's Emma."

"No, I don't. Not anymore. And it's not Matthew, either."

The ringing in my ears was getting louder and louder. Peter now had more eyes than I could count and while I could see all five of his mouths moving, I could barely hear him. A cloud of black began sliding across my vision.

"Oh, God. You can't fall asleep." Peter's voice was faint but urgent. "Rachel? Rachel?"

CHAPTER 31

Ali McGraw thought that love meant never having to say you're sorry, but I soon learned she was mistaken. True love was offering to stick your own finger down someone else's throat to make her throw up. Ryan O'Neal would never have had that much imagination.

Fortunately, Peter didn't have to make good on his offer. But he did hold my hair back while I puked a seemingly endless torrent of blueberry pancakes and mimosa. After what felt like an eternity, I was down to dry heaves, and after another eternity the spasms finally stopped. My knees trembled as Peter helped me up from the cool tile floor of the bathroom and over to the sink, where I brushed my teeth and splashed cold water on my face. Yet another charming story for the grandkids.

He guided me back to the bed, and we were embarking on another argument about whether he was going to get Matthew when Luisa came in.

"Did you find a lawyer?" I asked.

She nodded. "The best guy in Albany is on his way. He should be here in a couple of hours. How're you doing at getting Emma's things together?"

"Um, I haven't made much progress." I saw her nostrils give a delicate quiver as she sniffed the stale air of the room.

Hilary strode in. "Where's Emma's bag— Yuck! It reeks in here. What's going on—are you coming down with adult-onset bulimia, Rach?" She crossed to the window and threw it open.

"I was a little sick, just now," I admitted as Jane and Sean came in. "Oh, good. We're having a party. But you all missed getting to see me puke."

"Nothing we haven't seen before," said Sean.

"You were sick?" asked Jane.

"Somebody tried to poison her," interjected Peter. "And she won't let me get Matthew because now she's decided he's the murderer."

"Don't be ridiculous," said Luisa. "Matthew's no more a murderer than I am."

"But he's the one who gave me my drink," I protested.

Sean sat down on the bed next to me and began taking my pulse.

"I think that blow to her head messed her up more than we realized," said Hilary. "Geez, Rach. When did you get so paranoid?"

"Her pulse seems fine, but we really should get Matthew," reported Sean.

"No. We're not getting Matthew. Isn't anyone listening to me?"

"Come on, Rach. Are you really trying to tell us that you think Matthew killed Richard, attacked you and just now tried to poison you? Matthew Weir? Dr. Matthew Weir? The guy we've all known since we were practically children?" Jane sounded exasperated; she was using her rational-person-talk-

ing-to-a-hopeless-at-algebra-student voice, as if I were insisting that the quadratic formula wasn't whatever it actually
was or that *i* was a real number, not an imaginary one.

"Well, no, not when you say it like that," I said, feeling
sheepish. "It's just that we know none of us did it, and I can't
really believe that Emma did it. And Matthew's the one who
gave me my mimosa. That's the only thing that could have
made me sick. Breakfast was family-style, remember? We all
served ourselves from the same platters. Whatever it was had
to be in the mimosa."

"Whatever what was?" asked Matthew, appearing in the
doorway.

"Great," cried Hilary. "You're just in time. Rachel's trying
to explain to us how you tried to poison her this morning.
Oh, and how you tried to kill her last night, too. And let's
not forget about how you killed Richard."

"Christ, is *everyone* in this house insane?" Matthew
sounded even more exasperated than Jane. "And what's this
about Rachel being poisoned?" He crossed over to the bed
where I was perched and began conferring with Sean about
my pulse.

"You gave me the drink. And then I got really sick. And
if it was food poisoning, then everyone else would be sick,
too," I explained, trying not to flinch while Matthew pulled
up on the top of first one eyelid and then the other and
peered into my eyes.

"Wow, your pupils are dilated. I've seen junkies with more
iris than you're showing. Would somebody go get my medical bag? It's in my room in the pool house. I want to give
her some syrup of ipecac and make sure there's nothing left
in her system."

"I'll go," volunteered Sean.

"There's nothing left in my system. Ask Peter."

"I'd be pretty surprised if there was," Peter chipped in.

"It sure smells like she puked her guts out," contributed Hilary, turning to see if she could open the window still wider and fanning the air with her hand.

"Well, we're going to make sure," said Matthew. "I don't think it's food poisoning or a stomach virus or anything like that. Not with the way her eyes look. No, if I had to guess, I would say it's definitely something toxic."

"The same thing that was given to Richard?" asked Luisa.

"It's impossible to know without more information— blood tests, stuff like that. We can take some of her blood here and then send it into town to be tested."

"God, haven't I been through enough already? Now you want my blood? You know how I feel about needles."

"Well, do you know how I feel when you accuse me of being a murderer?" Matthew's reply was unusually sharp.

"Nice bedside manner you've got here, Doc."

"Seriously, Rach. Do you really think I could kill anyone? I mean, it's bad enough that you'd think I could kill Richard, but that you'd think that I'd try to kill you?" He looked at me, his eyes hurt behind his glasses.

"I'm so sorry, Matthew. There's no excuse for it, really. It was just that you seemed to be the only option left. If you didn't do it, that only leaves Emma, and I just couldn't..." I couldn't finish my sentence, and I couldn't look at his sad face any longer. I turned my gaze away. Not only did I feel physically awful, mentally I felt as low and dirty as a sewer rat. I was fighting back tears.

Sean rushed in with the big black doctor's bag, and Matthew busied himself rummaging through it. He pulled out a bottle full of nasty dark stuff, a vial, and a big, extralong and sharp-looking syringe. "Which do you want first? The blood test or the syrup of ipecac?"

I squirmed. "I'm feeling much better, really."

"Blood test it is, then. But don't worry, I've got some lollypops in here and I'll give you one when I'm finished. As long as you're a big girl and don't cry."

"Here. You can squeeze my hand," offered Peter. He was really seeing more than I preferred to reveal at the start of a new relationship.

"Hmmph."

"I can't watch this," said Luisa.

"Me, neither," confessed Jane.

"Let's go get some more coffee," suggested Hilary.

"Good idea," said Sean. "We'll be back in a minute."

"Cowards," I called after their departing backs. "Will you at least bring me a Diet Coke?"

"Sounds like somebody's recovering nicely," I heard Jane say.

Matthew donned a pair of latex gloves, and then pushed up the sleeve of my sweater and tied a piece of latex tightly around my upper arm. I tried not to watch while he uncapped the syringe and told me to make a fist. I felt cool wetness as he swabbed my inner elbow.

"Ouch!"

"I haven't even done anything yet."

"Just practicing," I was starting to say when I felt the jab of the needle. "Oof."

"Okay. Unclench your fist now. This will just take another minute."

"Sadist."

I squeezed Peter's hand and stared fixedly at the assortment of items on Emma's night table—a clock, some battered paperbacks, a framed snapshot of Emma with her mother.

"All done," Matthew said. I felt him taping a bandage over the spot where he'd pricked me.

"Good. That means she can let go of my hand before she breaks any bones," said Peter, trying to disentangle his fingers from my death grip.

"I just figured it out," I announced.

"No use trying to distract me, Rach. You're still getting the syrup of ipecac."

"I'm not trying to distract you. I know who did it."

Matthew sighed.

"It wasn't Emma," I said. A statement, not a question.

"No, of course not," he answered matter-of-factly.

"It was Lily, wasn't it?"

Matthew nodded, and I realized he'd known all along.

CHAPTER 32

It was nice to have an answer, but that didn't mean I was particularly happy with it. Even though I was eager to prove that Emma wasn't a murderer, I wasn't eager to pin the evil deed on her mother, either. Lily wasn't the most sympathetic of women, what with her capricious whims and antiquated snobbery, and I couldn't relate to how her mind worked, but I knew how much Emma loved her. I wondered if Emma realized who, precisely, she'd been covering for when she gave her false confession. I had a feeling that she did. And now I understood the argument Emma and Matthew had had the previous day, and exactly the moral quandary with which she'd been struggling.

I checked my memory for anything that would have given Lily away. Her behavior *had* been somewhat erratic. The display at lunch the previous day had been fairly stunning, and Emma herself had said that her mother seemed to be "losing it," and not for the first time. Perhaps she had more than her husband's affairs on her mind. And she didn't seem to have any qualms about dispensing her husband's prescription-strength tranquilizers to others with a free hand. If half of one was strong enough to knock Emma out for hours on end, surely five or six combined with some Scotch could knock Richard out permanently? Could Lily have given Richard a drink infused with a lethal dose of the same tranquilizers she'd been dispensing to Emma? Could she have watched as he lost consciousness forever? A chill went through me, even as the facts started to fit themselves together.

"I thought so," said Peter, breaking the silence that had fallen after Matthew spoke.

"What do you mean, you thought so? And why didn't you tell me?"

"I tried to, but then I got distracted when you seemed so ill."

"How did you know?" asked Matthew.

"I didn't know for sure," said Peter. "It came to me at lunch, actually, right before the police showed up. When Emma and her mother came down."

"What came to you?" I asked, curious as to how he'd gotten to the answer before I had.

"I did see someone out by the pool with Richard. I swear I did, Rachel. But here's the thing. I think it may have been Mrs. Furlong I saw, not Emma." He continued. "Last night, I ran into her in the hallway. It was dark, and when I first saw her, I thought she was Emma. If there's not much light, and you're far away, and you don't get a good look—it wouldn't be hard to confuse the two of them. They're the same size. They have the same hair, and the same build. It could easily have been her that I saw from the window, and I mistook her for Emma."

"That's what just occurred to me, too," I explained. "I was looking at the picture of the two of them on the table, and it's an easy mistake to make. They do look a lot alike. You saw Lily and thought it was Emma. You're not the only one, either. Luisa and Hilary saw someone coming back from the pool that night. They only saw a reflection in a mirror, and it was dark, but they also thought it was Emma. So Luisa and Hilary can testify that they saw her, too."

"Luisa and Hilary can do what?" asked Hilary. She tossed me a can of soda from the doorway. I did what I usually do when somebody throws something my direction and ducked. Peter neatly caught the can with one hand and set it on the nightstand.

Sean, Jane, and Luisa were behind her carrying steaming coffee mugs, two of which they handed to Matthew and Peter.

"You and Luisa saw the murderer," I said to answer Hilary's question, "on her way back from killing Richard."

"So now you think it was Emma, too?" asked Luisa, horrified. "Rachel—you're out of your mind. First Matthew, now Emma. I thought we'd already agreed that it wasn't Emma."

"We're not talking about Emma," Matthew explained.

"We're talking about Lily. Peter, and then you and Hilary all thought you saw Emma. But you simply mixed her up with her mother."

"Incredible," said Luisa. "Lily?"

"Let me get this straight. You're saying that Lily killed Richard?" said Jane.

"But, why?" asked Sean. "Richard—well, we all know what Richard was, and, while I don't understand why Emma would want to marry him in the first place, I can completely understand why she'd want to kill him. But, Lily was the only one who didn't seem thoroughly traumatized at the prospect of a wedding. Why, she and Richard even seemed to get along."

"Maybe she's just very good at hiding what she's feeling," I said.

"So that's what they teach you in charm school," said Hilary.

"But, what about what happened to you, Rachel?" asked Jane.

"Yes? Are you saying that Lily attacked you, and then, when that didn't work, she tried to poison you?" pressed Luisa.

"She poisoned Richard," I pointed out. "And, now that I think about it, she was the one keeping everyone's glasses full at brunch—including mine."

"And she was up and about last night," Peter added. "I saw her. I should have figured it out, then," he reflected.

"And she was wearing a white bathrobe!" I exclaimed.

"Matthew, are you sure Rachel doesn't have a concussion?" Jane asked. "She's not making sense."

"I saw something from the corner of my eye, last night, right before I was hit. It was a flash of white, and then I thought it was Peter's T-shirt, but it wasn't, it was Lily's bathrobe."

"Here's what I don't get," said Peter. "Why would Lily attack you?"

"Maybe she thought Rachel knew something," said Matthew. "Do you, Rach?"

They all looked at me expectantly.

"Me? I think it's pretty clear that I know nothing. I turned in Peter, then I thought it was Matthew."

"Yes, Rachel's obviously clueless," said Hilary. I flipped a finger in her direction.

"I'm just relieved that it wasn't Emma," confided Jane. "I thought, just for a moment, that she… I don't even want to say it out loud. Sean told me I was crazy to even consider such a thing."

"Of course you were," said Luisa.

"Well, what are we going to do?" asked Jane.

"What can we do?" asked Luisa. "Denounce Emma's

mother to the police as a murderer? Besides, what proof is there? Hilary and I didn't even realize it was Lily we saw and not Emma. And we got rid of whatever evidence the glasses might have provided."

"Crap," said Hilary.

"Mierda," echoed Luisa.

The men looked at them in surprise. I'd forgotten that they hadn't yet heard that part of the story. Luisa filled them in, reddening slightly with embarrassment as she related her and Hilary's adventure in the wee hours of the previous morning. In hindsight, their rash actions were all the more unfortunate.

"So, there may have been evidence that would have cleared Emma, but it's gone now," said Luisa. "If only we'd known what had really happened."

"It was pretty stupid of Lily to leave the glasses there in the first place," grumbled Hilary.

"So, it looks like we're back at the beginning," said Sean. "The police still don't have any reason to think Emma's not guilty. And we can't prove to them she's not."

"I wish there were some way I could take back my testimony," said Peter.

"The good news is that what you told them is still not much to go on," said Luisa. "Talk about circumstantial evidence—it will never hold up in court. And if this lawyer knows what he's doing, and I hope he does, it will never even get that far. He'll rip your testimony—and Emma's false confession, to shreds."

"But does it really work that way?" asked Sean. "If you have a confession, do you need to worry about a lack of evidence?"

"Well, no," Luisa admitted. "Although a good lawyer would be able to mitigate that."

"Jesus. Even if she doesn't end up being convicted of murder, I don't want Emma to have that shadow hanging over her for the rest of her life," said Matthew. "We need to do something. We all know that she didn't do it. And I think we're all convinced that Lily did. Lord knows, her mental state has been pretty fragile the last couple of years and she's had breakdowns in the past. I tried to get Emma to tell me what was going on, why Lily did it, but she wouldn't tell me. Maybe she just couldn't stand the thought of Emma marrying Richard." His usually ruddy cheeks looked gray.

"What a mess," said Jane. "Why doesn't Lily just confess that she did it? I mean, what kind of mother would let her own daughter take the rap for such a thing?" What kind of mother would murder her daughter's fiancé, I wanted to ask, even if he was a nefarious troll? But that didn't seem like a very productive direction in which to take the conversation.

"Maybe Lily was counting on the police not being able to figure it out," I ventured. "She couldn't have imagined that they'd go after Emma instead. And after Jacob's false confession, O'Donnell would probably think that a confession from Lily was just another attempt to protect Emma." We were all silent, thinking. I had the odd feeling that I was missing something. There was a puzzle piece that didn't fit, but I wasn't sure what it was.

"There must be some evidence, somewhere, that would point to Lily and clear Emma," said Jane, who firmly believed that every problem had a solution.

"Wait a second!" said Luisa, excitedly. While the rest of us had been spinning our wheels, she'd been sitting cross-legged on the floor. She had the document I'd found earlier, the prenuptial agreement, open in her hands. She looked up, her eyes wide. "You're never going to believe this."

"I'd believe anything at this point," I said.

"Would you believe that Richard was blackmailing Emma?"

"What?" We couldn't have spoken more in unison if we'd been rehearsing the line all weekend.

"How could anybody blackmail Emma?" cried Hilary. "She's practically a saint."

"I can't tell," said Luisa. "There're a lot of references to Exhibit A and Exhibit B, but the exhibits aren't actually in here. This document says that should Emma not comply with the terms of the agreement or initiate divorce proceedings, Richard automatically gets full control over 'the materials itemized in Exhibits A through L' and can publicize them as he sees fit. There's also language in here giving Richard access to the Furlongs' assets and saying that the Furlongs have to do everything possible to further Richard's business and social interests. Wow—they sure didn't teach us anything like this in law school."

"They didn't even teach us anything like that at business school," I said. "So what are these 'materials'? It sounds like whatever they are would affect not just Emma but her entire family."

"I wish I knew. It would sure answer a lot of questions," answered Luisa.

Matthew was sitting next to me on the bed, and I couldn't help but sneak a look at him. It must have been a relief to understand that Emma had been marrying Richard under duress, and not out of love. And I thought I could see a trace of relief on his face, mixed with anger that Richard could have treated Emma so badly.

He'd sat through all of this, not saying much. Now he spoke up. "This all explains a lot. But it doesn't help Emma. She'll never let her mother take the blame, even if she is responsible. Trust me—I spent hours yesterday trying to convince her to either talk to Lily about it or even to the police, but she wouldn't have any of it. That's why she gave her false confession—she was trying to spare her mother."

"But why didn't Lily say something?"

Matthew shrugged. "Rachel had a point—maybe she

thought the police would think she was trying to protect Emma, just like Jacob tried to do. It's hard to say. And the fact that Lily's not that stable doesn't help. Her version of reality doesn't always mesh with everyone else's."

"It's so unfair," said Hilary, frustrated. "Richard completely had it coming, and now he's going to end up destroying the Furlongs anyhow, one way or another."

"Okay," I said. "We need a plan. And not just any plan. A good one."

"Gee, thank you, Rach," said Hilary. "We would never have figured that out."

"Look, you can be as snide as you want after we've decided what to do."

"It would probably help to know what the blackmail was about," said Jane.

"I have an idea about that," I said. "There's something I need to check out, though, before I know for sure."

"Good," said Matthew. "That's a start. But—and it's hard to say this about my own godmother—it would be even better to find some direct evidence tying Lily to the crime." There was a new forcefulness in his voice. I wished Emma could see it.

"There is no evidence," said Jane, sounding dejected for the first time that day. She didn't add in the "thanks to you" that I would have tacked on, with a nod to Hilary and Luisa.

"There's no evidence," I said instead. "At least, there's not any now."

Peter finished my thought. "But maybe we could make some."

CHAPTER 33

I curled up on the sofa in Jacob's study, the retrospective of his work open in my lap. I knew what I was looking for now, and the book didn't fail me. In fact, I was surprised that others hadn't figured it out before me. Jacob was world famous—more than a few art experts had followed his long career; there must have been dozens of published monographs dissecting each series of his paintings.

I'd heard the stories about how Jacob was instantly recognized as a boy genius, immediately upon setting foot in New York. It seemed unlikely, given the early work hanging on the wall, that the international art world would throw itself at his feet based on paintings like that one. But, when I looked at the retrospective, it was hard not to notice that the paintings that had launched his career were dramatically different from anything that came before or after. I was the last person to claim any knowledge of art, but now that my suspicions had been awakened, it was difficult to believe that he

actually painted the initial works himself that made his reputation. I wondered whom he stole them from.

I worked in a business where you were only as good as
your last deal. Reputation was everything in banking. Reputation and connections. But at least the standards by which
bankers were judged were largely objective—you couldn't
argue with a person's ability to analyze numbers and gener-
ate fees. For the very foundation of an artist's career to come
under public scrutiny—that was an altogether different situation. If it got out that Mr. Furlong had passed off someone else's work as his own, it would no doubt forever blemish
his reputation, regardless of the excellence of the years of
work that had ensued. It would be quite a scandal if it ever
did come to light.

Still, I couldn't believe that Jacob would sell out his own
daughter to avoid a scandal. And the bitter conversation Peter
and I had overheard the night of the rehearsal dinner indi-
cated that he was willing to face exposure. But, I realized,
Emma didn't give her father the choice. He might have been
able to withstand having his reputation torn to shreds, but
Emma was probably worried that her mother wouldn't have
been able to deal with it. With Lily's overdeveloped sense of
what was and what was not appropriate, for her husband to
be revealed publicly as a fraud—Emma probably worried that
her mother would have imploded. So much of who Lily was
and what she was about was how she thought people perceived
her and her family. And a big part of that was her husband
and his accomplishments. She'd taken quite a leap when she
married Jacob. Perhaps she thought people were just waiting
for their marriage to fail, and she wanted to prove them wrong,
to prove that the blue-blooded aristocrat and the dashing artist
created a perfect life from unlikely beginnings. It was bad
enough to have to contend with Jacob's clandestine affairs, but
fraud would have cast a new level of shame on the family.

I shivered with the stark realization that Emma would rather be married to a man she hated than for the world to know that her father was a fake and for her mother to have to deal with the consequences. But part of me felt an over-whelming sense of relief finally to understand why Emma had been willing to go through with the marriage, why she had been so intent on her path, like a prisoner being forced to walk the plank on a pirate ship, knowing that there was no other option.

I wondered how Richard had discovered this secret. It didn't surprise me that Richard, being Richard, didn't just ask for money, like a normal blackmailer. He wanted more than money. He was smart enough and slimy enough that he'd always be able to make his own way. But he didn't have the connections and the prestige that the Furlongs had. He needed their stamp of approval. People gave a lot of lip ser-vice to meritocracy, but fundamentally the right names and the right background and the right connections were still in-credibly important if he wanted to climb to the pinnacle in New York. At the core of the city was still an entrenched Old Guard establishment, and Emma and her family could have given Richard access to that in a way he could never have hoped for otherwise. I wondered if part of it, too, was about how much he just wanted to be part of a family. It was an incredibly warped way to go about it, but Richard was pretty warped.

Lily gave me more credit than I deserved, however. She'd seen me sitting here with this book, and then I'd started ask-ing questions about Jacob's early career and how they'd met. She'd thought I figured it all out long before I did.

"Rachel, darling. Jane told me you were up here. How are you feeling? I heard you were ill." I looked up. Lily was standing in the doorway, her dark gold hair swept neatly into a French twist. In her crisp linen blouse and slacks and her discreet jewelry, she looked every bit the Upper East Side matron.

"Hi, Mrs. Furlong. I'm feeling much better, thank you. Still a bit nauseated."

"Well, I've brought you some ginger ale. That always helps to settle the stomach." She handed me a brimming glass and sat down on the sofa beside me. "Drink up," she encouraged me.

I obediently drained the glass and waited for its contents to begin their work.

"Good," she said. "You'll be better in no time." Somehow I doubted that, but I gave her a small smile and let my heavy eyelids droop. My grip on the book loosened and it started to fall to the floor. Lily caught it. "I'll just put this away."

I didn't have much time, so I launched right in. "Jacob didn't do those first paintings, did he?" I asked. "The ones that launched his career."

Lily slipped the retrospective back into its slot on the bookshelf and turned to face me. "I had a feeling you'd figured that out. No, of course, he didn't. It's fairly obvious when you look closely."

"How did you find out? Did he tell you?"

"No, darling, of course not. When Jacob and I became engaged, my parents hired a private detective to investigate him. They were concerned that he was only interested in my money and status. Gracious. If only I'd listened to them." A distracted look came over her face. She crossed to the desk and took a seat behind it.

"And the detective found out about the fraud?" I prompted. My voice sounded weak.

"It wasn't really fraud, darling. That's such an unattractive word. The paintings were by Jacob Furlong, all right. Just not Jacob Furlong, Jr. Jacob's father did them. Jacob Furlong, Sr. They were too avant-garde for Louisiana in the forties, but they made quite a splash in New York in the sixties. Apparently Jacob's father, when he wasn't busy sharecropping or tenant farming or whatever it was, was quite a painter in his own right. I guess there's a long family tradition of creating art in barns." She straightened the blotter on the desk and began untangling the phone cord.

"How did Richard know?"

"I told him, of course. Richard was quick, but he didn't have much of an eye for detail. He would never have figured it all out on his own. So I gave him a little help."

"But—I don't understand. Why would you tell Richard?" I let my eyelids flutter with exhaustion.

"Well, you knew Richard. He had an appetite for sordid activities that I just didn't share. And somebody had to punish Jacob. I couldn't have him making a fool of me, chasing after women half his age, for all the world to see. And now, to be taking up with the daughter of my best friend—it was just too much. It was much easier to let Richard take care of everything."

I let the opportunity pass to point out just how sordid her activities had been of late. "I'm confused. You encouraged Richard to blackmail your husband?"

She nodded. "My one mistake was that I didn't realize the direction in which Richard would take the information. I assumed he'd simply blackmail Jacob for money and make him miserable and scared. I didn't expect that he'd blackmail us all for Emma's hand in marriage, that he'd try to use us all in every possible way. And I surely didn't realize how attached Emma was to her father and what she would agree to on his behalf. It is unfortunate that Emma takes after him in all the wrong ways. I never expected her to be so stubborn. At least she takes after me in the looks department."

"So…then you had to kill Richard?" I asked. My voice sounded like it was coming from far away.

Lily laughed, a gay tinkling sound. I was reminded of the way Nick Carraway had described Daisy's laugh in *The Great Gatsby.* "I wasn't left with a choice, really. I couldn't let Emma marry that appalling excuse for a man. And how better to get back at Jacob for all of the crap he pulled? Oh, it makes me so angry. He loves showing off his society wife to all of his low-class, trashy art world parvenus. Having it both ways. Being Mr. Artsy but having all of my connections and position."

"I'm sorry, Mrs. Furlong, but I still don't understand. How could murdering Richard get back at Jacob?"

"Why, he was supposed to take the blame. Obviously. I'd nicely set everything up so that all of the evidence would point to him. It was really quite clever, actually." The pride in her voice was tangible. Not that clever, I wanted to point out, since the police arrested Emma instead.

"How? How did you set him up?"

"Well, I arranged to meet Richard out by the pool for a late night tête-à-tête. I sent him a note, pretending it was from Emma. Of course, he was a bit surprised to see me, but I handed him a drink with enough of Jacob's tranquilizers diluted in it to kill a horse, and he drank it down like a good boy. Both that glass and the other glass, the one that I pretended to drink out of, had Jacob's fingerprints all over them. Richard was a little confused that I was wearing gloves, but I explained to him all about what a wonderfully rejuvenating treatment it is to cream your hands and then put on cotton gloves to trap in the moisture. It really does do miracles to soften the skin. Have you ever tried it, darling?" She held up her hands to show me how young they looked.

With a flash of understanding, I realized what the remaining loose end that had been nagging at me was.

The two glasses that Luisa and Hilary had cleaned up. Leaving the glasses by Richard's body, with the evidence they undoubtedly held, was a grave mistake for a murderer to make—and you didn't have to be an avid watcher of *Law & Order* to know that. But Lily hadn't made a mistake by leaving them there—it had been part of her plot to frame her husband instead.

She didn't wait for me to respond or thank her for her grooming tips. "It was actually quite fun, the entire planning of it all. Much more fun than planning a silly old benefit or redoing the apartment. Although, the apartment *is* starting to look so dated and tired. All of that toile in the dining room is so 1997. Maybe I should just sell the apartment and start fresh. There are some lovely properties available on Fifth these days. And it's so much nicer to look out on the park." I couldn't believe what I was hearing. She seemed to have gone completely around the bend. I wondered if there were park views from any of the cells at Sing Sing. Or if Sing Sing was still in operation.

"The park is nice," I agreed.

"Isn't it? Anyhow, it would have all worked like a charm if someone hadn't seen fit to mess with the crime scene. Now, I wonder who did that?" she mused.

"Let me get this straight," I said, my words faint. "You handed Richard the materials with which to blackmail your husband to punish him for his affair with Nina."

"Not just Nina, darling. And not just one affair, either."

"Okay. His affairs. But when Richard used the materials to strong-arm Emma into marrying him, you killed him and tried to set it up so that Jacob would take the blame."

"That's right. Now, I just need to figure out how to get him back on the hook. And how I'm going to get him on the hook for doing this to you, as well. Do you have any ideas? Oh, probably not. You must be feeling quite tired at this point."

"I am a bit sleepy," I admitted.

"You were always such an intelligent girl, weren't you? We'll miss you here next summer. But you just know too much. It's such a pity."

I nodded and let my eyes slowly drift shut.

CHAPTER 34

I opened my eyes just in time to see Hilary step out from behind the drapes, brandishing her tape recorder in one hand. Her endless tales of political intrigue in far-off countries could be dull at times, but for once she and her journalist's bag of tricks came in handy.

Lily's calm reaction seemed to demonstrate just how far gone she was. There was no panic at being caught in the middle of confessing to one crime and trying to commit another. "Why, Hilary, dear. What were you doing back there?" she asked mildly.

"I'm sorry, Mrs. Furlong. I didn't mean to eavesdrop. Well, that's not true. But I only did it to help Emma."

I glanced at the door, where Luisa and Jane were blocking the way out.

"Did you get it all?" Luisa asked.

"I think so," Hilary answered.

"Well done," said Jane.

I leapt up from the sofa, and Lily gave me a confused

look. "Rachel, you shouldn't get up, darling. Why, you should be—"

"Practically dead by now?" I finished her thought for her.

"Well, yes, darling."

"Sorry. Matthew switched the pills in your bottle of sedatives with aspirin. You laced my ginger ale with Bayer. And I do feel much better, thank you." I didn't point out that the aspirin helped mitigate the pain from the lump on my head, the lump that she'd given me. I should have felt triumphant that we'd outwitted her, but I felt devious and slimy. This is for Emma, I reminded myself, but that reminder didn't seem to help.

"Oh, that's good, darling. I mean, that's too bad." The calm expression on her face was giving way to confusion. "I wonder what I should do now?" She began to hum to herself, softly. I didn't recognize the melody.

The men were waiting in the foyer as we escorted Lily downstairs. Matthew had explained everything to Jacob, who gazed at his wife with such pain in his eyes that I had to look away. Matthew didn't look much better. No doubt he was thinking of the promise that Emma had extracted from him the previous day, that he wouldn't say or do anything that would jeopardize her mother and his godmother.

"You've got the tape?" Matthew asked Hilary. She tossed it to him. "Okay, let's get going," he said to Jacob.

The rest of us gathered on the front step and watched as Matthew and Jacob led Lily to the old Volvo. They were going to take her into town and try to clear things up with O'Donnell. She hadn't said a word since we'd left the study. If all went well, the lawyer Luisa had found for Emma could be engaged to help Lily instead.

Peter stood behind me, and I leaned back against his chest,

letting him wrap his arms around me, appreciating their warm comfort.

"What do you think will happen?" asked Hilary. "Will she go to prison?"

"I don't know," said Luisa. "I mean, she's clearly not well. Perhaps an insanity plea of some sort?"

"Poor woman," said Jane.

"Poor Emma," I said. "I don't know if she'll ever forgive us. I can't believe we just entrapped her mother."

"Emma will understand," said Jane.

"Will she?" I asked. "Even worse, how will she be able to forgive Matthew…and her father? It's like we all ganged up against Lily, and by ganging up against her, we were ganging up against Emma."

"It wasn't ganging up," said Luisa. "It was helping her."

"You said it yourself, in your toast at the rehearsal," said Hilary. "Sometimes she's selfless to the point where she actually does harm to herself. And if she doesn't understand now, one day she will."

"We did the right thing. Really we did," said Jane in a firm tone.

She was right, I knew. We'd taken matters into our own hands, true to the spirit, if not the letter of our long-ago pact.

I just wished it didn't feel so empty.

I wish I could say that we all lived happily ever after, but that wouldn't be accurate. Lily had the best criminal defense attorney money could buy, but even he couldn't get her completely off the hook. In a rare turn of legal proceedings, the local DA allowed her to plead guilty by reason of insanity, and she was packed off to a state mental institution that was likely far less cushy than the various euphemistically named spas she'd visited during previous breakdowns.

The plea prevented the ordeal of a jury trial, but there was still an immense amount of publicity surrounding the tangle of events. After a couple of weeks, the tabloids turned to a fresh scandal, but I heard a rumor recently that Alan Dershowitz was planning a book on the topic. I doubted that Lily would be pleased to hear that she was soon to take her seat in history next to O. J. Simpson and the Menendez brothers, although she probably wouldn't mind the von Bulow connection. Somehow, the Furlongs managed to keep the blackmail plot out of the papers, and Jacob's reputation remained intact—or as intact as it could be when his wife was publicly identified as mentally ill and inspired by his philandering to commit murder and frame him for the crime.

Emma remained shell-shocked for a while. She'd loathed Richard, but she still felt tremendously guilty about his death. And accepting that one's own mother, however unstable, had killed one's fiancé required a level of maturity that I most definitely didn't possess. She spent the rest of the summer in her loft in New York, hiding out from the paparazzi who camped out by her door when the murder was still making headlines. I called her daily, sometimes even more, concerned about how she was doing and ashamed by my own part in proving her mother's guilt. She'd accepted all of our apologies with an understanding grace, and for that I was grateful, but I was more anxious about her welfare than anything else. Early on, she sounded sad and dazed. As the weeks passed, however, she started to sound distracted instead. Finally, she agreed to let me come by with a picnic dinner one evening just after Labor Day.

New York City in early September was still all but unbearable. To step outside was to be sunk into a slow-moving smog of humidity and pollution that bounced off the pavements, ricocheted off the buildings, and then slowly wound its way around any life on the streets. I climbed up the four flights of stairs to Emma's top-floor loft to find her covered with paint and surrounded by the debris of an artistic binge—empty paint tubes, soiled brushes, discarded pizza boxes and the like. The trouble she'd been having with her work since Richard appeared on the scene seemed to have disappeared when he did. And the paintings she created in the aftermath of his death were nothing short of extraordinary. She had ventured into abstraction for the first time, and while the comparisons to the best of her father's work were obvious, there was also something distinctively her own displayed on the canvases.

I was searching for a couple of clean glasses to use for the bottle of chilled pinot grigio I'd brought when I noticed that among the clutter on her kitchen table was not one but four different boarding passes for the New York-Boston air shuttle, all bearing different dates and times but all with her name on them. I breathed a sigh of relief. Much as I'd worried that she wouldn't be able to forgive her friends for their actions that weekend, I'd been even more worried that she wouldn't be able to forgive Matthew. I was glad to accept that I'd underestimated her talent for empathy. I handed her a glass of wine and settled comfortably onto the sofa in front of the industrial-strength fan. I was looking forward to hearing how things were progressing.

Luisa returned directly to South America after the fateful weekend ended. According to her e-mails, things with Isobel were good, although the pressure from her family to marry was mounting. Apparently she'd arrived at her parents' house one evening for a family dinner to find three eligible bachelors at the table from whom, her father explained to her during private predinner drinks, she would be expected to choose a mate. Luisa was the youngest and had her father wrapped around her little finger, but I was interested to see how this situation would play itself out.

Hilary, with her usual talent for finding the most dangerous place on the globe, had removed herself to Cairo to work on her article about Islamic fundamentalism and oil. I could only wonder how the veiled women in long black robes would react to the six-foot blonde in spandex.

I spent a weekend with Jane and Sean on the Cape before school started, and I noticed a bottle of prenatal vitamins sitting by the kitchen sink. Jane blushed violently when I asked her about them and admitted that she and Sean had decided to start trying to have a baby. We spent the rest of the weekend carefully monitoring her folic acid intake.

As for me, there wasn't much to tell. Stan took the news about Smitty Hamilton's thwarted takeover surprisingly well. Perhaps because he was excited about my ideas for creating a new corporate finance practice based on emerging technology companies. When the NASDAQ had crashed, most major investment banks had decimated their technology divisions, including Winslow, Brown. Now was the time, I argued, to reengage, when a bunch of tomorrow's Microsofts were still flying under the radar screen and none of the major players were stepping up to meet their needs in the capital markets.

So, now I, too, had begun logging some air miles, albeit New York to San Francisco, and it looked like Winslow, Brown would be taking Peter's company public by year-end. Of course, Peter and I managed to squeeze in some personal time amid all this banking talk. And even if he did tease me every so often about turning him in to the cops, he also did a superb breakfast in bed, which was more than adequate compensation.

New from Wendy Markham,
bestselling author of
Slightly Single and *Slightly Settled*

Mike, Mike & Me

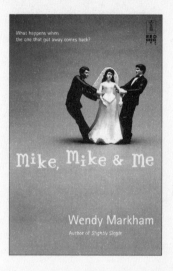

Once upon a time in the 1980s, a girl named
Beau was torn between two Mikes: did she
prefer her high school sweetheart or the sexy
stranger she'd picked up in an airport bar?
One she eventually married, the other she left
behind. But what happens when the Mike
that got away comes back?

**Available wherever
trade paperbacks
are sold.**

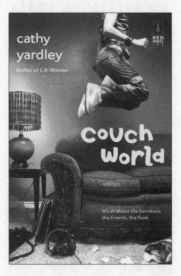

Up and Out

Ariella Papa

Life on the up and up was great for Rebecca Cole,
creator of the new cartoon sensation Esme—fancy
nights out and a trendy new wardrobe. But thanks
to a corporate takeover, Rebecca soon finds herself
on the up and out. Can this food snob find a way
to afford her rent and her penchant for fine dining?

**RED
DRESS
INK**
™

Visit us at www.reddressink.com

RDI12032R-TR